RETURNING SECRETS

Also by Shawn McGuire

WHISPERING PINES Mystery Series

THE WITCHES OF BLACKWOOD GROVE Mystery Series

GEMI KITTREDGE Mystery Series

THE WISH MAKERS Fantasy Series

RETURNING SECRETS

A Whispering Pines Mystery, Book 18

Shawn McGuire

Chapter One

I STEPPED OUT OF THE SHERIFF'S STATION AND INTO THE PINE-scented air. That glorious smell was one of the things I loved most about living in the Northwoods. After this morning's quick, light rain shower, the smell had grown stronger and now encircled me like a comforting hug. Nice.

"Work your magic," I told my trees. "And share a little of it with everyone else around here, please."

Visitors were a requirement for a village that relied on tourism for its survival. We knew that and always welcomed the tourists with enthusiasm. This year, however, the crowds were larger, louder, and more intense than ever before. Which was making the village residents unusually crabby. And the season was only three weeks old. Goddess help us.

As I veered left at the intersection of the station's sidewalk and the Fairy Path, I glanced upward, hoping for a response from the trees. The tops swayed softly, but I couldn't hear their whispers. I swallowed hard then tried to force a yawn to unclog my ears. Something had been going on with them for a couple of weeks. Maybe I had allergies. I should stop at Unity for a checkup.

A few seconds later, a pinecone dropped from above and landed inches in front of me on the wood plank pathway. My West Highland White Terrier, Meeka, who was snuffling around the forest floor instead of walking on the path with me, let out a yelp when another tree bomb caught the tip of her tail.

"Not funny," I told the pines.

An immediate reply came in the form of a loud *caw-caw-caw*. A pair of beautiful black birds were perched high above us. I might not be able to hear my trees, but I sure heard those crows. Were they laughing at us? One of them dropped a third pinecone that nearly landed on Meeka's head, cawed his or her laugh again, and then the two birds flew off in a flapping of wings.

"Knock it off."

"Jayne? Who are you talking to?"

Startled by the voice, I pulled my attention away from the treetops to find hearth witch Reeva Long coming toward me.

"Birds." I pointed skyward. "They're bombing us with pinecones. One landed on Meeka. Just her tail, but still . . ."

"Ah, yes. The pranksters are quite active this morning." Meeka darted over to her, so Reeva bent and gave my K-9 a comforting ear scratch after her traumatic encounter.

"When did this start?" I hadn't heard about crow problems yesterday. "And what do you mean by active? Just dropping pinecones?"

"I noticed them yesterday afternoon."

That explained it. My shift ended at twelve thirty.

Reeva continued, "They're not only dropping pinecones. They're also swooping at people and leaving messes everywhere. I understand it's worst in the commons area."

That's where I was headed. What was I supposed to do about pesky birds?

"How is Rosalyn holding up?" Reeva asked.

"Her hair is frizzy. If you know my sister, you'll recognize that as a sure sign she's in this deep. She's also worn the same outfit for three straight days, and I'm pretty sure she's running purely on caffeine."

Reeva chuckled softly. "I remember being the same way when I opened my catering business. Getting the first event under my belt made a huge difference, as this one will for her."

When Rosalyn lost her job last August, she moped around the house for a couple of weeks, then one day started slowly filling a wall in her bedroom with sticky notes, each one an idea for a possible new career path. Finally, she decided she wanted to open an event planning business. She tested the idea by putting together a birthday party for seven-year-old villagers Peony Flowers and Prim Brittell. It was a huge success. The wedding this weekend was Pine Time Parties' first official event and would, according to my sister, "determine if I'll be a massive success or if I should cut my nails short and be Tripp's dish washer." Rosalyn hated washing dishes. She'd lasted one day as our Pine Time Bed-and-Breakfast kitchen assistant.

"Where are you going?" I asked Reeva, since she was walking away from her shop, Hearth & Cauldron.

"To Pine Time. I want to see how much table space I have to work with and make a plan for how to lay out the buffet. My contract states that changes to the menu can be made up to ten days before the event." She rubbed her hands together gleefully. "We're two days out, so I can start working on the fun part."

Reeva decided at the end of last season that leading cooking classes for tourists who were really only looking for something to do on vacation wasn't as satisfying as she'd hoped it would be. When Rosalyn announced she needed a caterer for her events, Reeva saw it as the perfect time to revive the career she'd loved so much.

"Do me a favor?" I asked as we continued in our

respective directions. "Talk to Rosalyn about self-care. She could really use a shower."

Reeva burst out laughing. "I may be old enough to be your mother, but I will not parent your sister. Have a blessed day, Deputy."

As we did every morning around this time, Meeka and I passed by The Twisty Skein, Hearth & Cauldron, Ivy's Boutique, and finally Skål, the village's newest restaurant, owned and operated by Reeva's boyfriend, Jozef Lykke. Everything seemed to be quiet, in a good way, at those locations. Then we stepped off the Fairy Path and onto the red brick walkway of the village commons. As Reeva had hinted, things were not so quiet here.

Two crew members from village services were sweeping up dirt scattered on the ground around the pointy parts of the Pentacle Garden. At the same time, a team of green witches tended the plants inside the pentacle.

"Heather?" I called out to the woman who normally worked in the village services accounting office. "What's going on? Why are you here?"

The woman in her early thirties with dusky-purple hair looked up and let out a huge sigh. "We were getting ready to head to work this morning when Mr. Powell sent an urgent group message. He said there were issues all around the village that needed to be addressed before the tourists started showing up. Then he assigned us tasks."

"Brittells to the rescue," her husband, Bud, called out sarcastically, a fist raised in the air.

Sweeping up dirt was an urgent task? And why were other people scrubbing the bricks? Then I understood. They were cleaning off bird droppings. Owners of the shops surrounding the garden were scrubbing their porches. Did two crows do all that?

As though in answer, a chorus of caws sounded, drawing

my attention to the treetops. There was a flock of fifteen or twenty feathery black beasties up there. A *murder* of crows. A truly ominous sign in Whispering Pines.

"Is this going on all around the village?" I asked the Brittells.

"That's what Mr. Powell's message indicated," Bud replied.

So that's what Reeva meant by leaving a mess. "What happened to the garden? The crows didn't do that, too, did they?"

"Why do you think scarecrows were created?" Dale Woodthorpe, one of the green witches, called out from his position in the closest pentacle point. "Crows cause enormous damage to crops. I'm finding black feathers amongst the wreckage here, so I can pretty much guarantee the birds did this."

Heather paused sweeping to ask, "Any idea where they came from?"

"You're asking me?" I pointed at myself. "I don't know, the sky?"

"Guess a few showed up yesterday afternoon," Bud offered. "More have joined them."

That's what Reeva had said.

"Something needs to be done," Dale grumbled. "We should be able to save most of these plants, but if it keeps happening, we're going to lose the Pentacle Garden this season."

His tone indicated he expected me to take care of this. What was I supposed to do about birds?

More concerning than the mess was the root cause. During the two years I'd lived here, I'd learned that things like this didn't happen by accident.

"We could try putting up scarecrows," I offered, then tried to ease a little of the tension with a fun fact. "Did you know that children were once used to scare away birds? They would stand out in the fields and throw rocks at them."

"Don't think we want our kids throwing rocks around the commons," Heather replied.

"No," Bud agreed, "but we could let them chase the birds. I know I do all I can to escape when Thistle, Prim, or Hazel come at me."

Heather gave him a withering, unamused look.

"Thanks for being team players," I told them, avoiding the topic of how to deal with the flock.

"Happy to help," Bud said. "It would have taken the regular crew all morning to clean this up."

While the team continued with their tasks, I stood back and eyed the white marble well at the center of the pentacle. We used to call it the Negativity Well because people would throw their worries, secrets, and gripes down to the bottom for the spring water to purify and wash away to wherever the water went.

Last September, the villagers who had lived here since Whispering Pines's inception—we called them the Originals—became sick, and plants in the Pentacle Garden started dying for no discernible reason. After more than fifty years of the practice, Briar Barlow, one of the Originals, reasoned that the water supply swirling beneath us had become toxic, and all that nastiness had leached into the soil.

Briar said, "Whispering Pines, the very land we stand on, is fighting back. We need to fix this. You'll laugh, but I think this is what's wrong with Effie, Cybil, and me. We've been here the longest. It's taking us with it."

We decided the pessimism was slowly killing the Pentacle Garden too. So all the villagers and a few tourists encircled The Well, and High Priestess Reeva led us in a midnight blessing.

Did the blessing work, or did we only succeed in stirring up gloom and making things worse? All the negative stuff had to go somewhere. Was that what was wrong with me and some of the other villagers this past winter? It had felt like more than a seasonal depression thing. Was it now affecting this season's tourists? Should we bless The Well again? Would that help or cause even more problems? I made a mental note to talk with Reeva, Briar, and Morgan about it.

Meeka and I continued our patrol around the commons, staying out of the way of those scrubbing the bricks. I called good morning to Emery as he hosed down The Inn's front walk and waved at Maeve outside Grapes, Grains, and Grub pub. On the other side of Triple G, we took a left and followed a short pathway through a canopy of trees to Biblichor, the village bookstore.

The irritated owner, India Paige, was using a corn broom to sweep dozens and dozens of pinecones off the path and into the woods. The muttering coming from her with each swoosh of the broom made it sound like she was issuing either a blessing or a curse.

"What happened here?" I asked her.

"Those blasted birds. This is easier to clean up than their droppings but equally annoying. Around one o'clock yesterday afternoon, the crows started swooping down from the trees as my patrons tried to get to the store, or they sat on those overhanging branches and dropped pinecones on their heads. Do you know how sharp pinecones are? I had to have someone from Sundry bring me more bandages and begged them to stop at Shoppe Mystique on their way to grab some of Morgan's ointment because I used all of mine. I had to walk people through the canopy using an umbrella. This isn't funny."

Did I laugh? I sure didn't mean to if I did.

India continued, "I offered coupons for free coffees at Ye Olde Bean Grinder to those who got injured. I usually only hand those out as a thank you for purchases of three or more items."

"Tell me people aren't blaming you for this. We can't control what animals do."

"All I know is you better figure out something. Fortunately, Violet only charges us her cost for those coupons, or my profits would have been wiped out yesterday. If this keeps happening, patrons won't bother coming to my store."

"Or the other stores," I concluded. "I understand what you're saying."

She exhaled and let her arms hang at her side. "I'm sorry to take it out on you, Jayne. I'm just so frustrated about this."

"I'll talk with Sheriff Reed. We'll figure something out."

"Talk to River," India called as I walked away. "It's his village; he should be the one handling these kinds of things."

Except River Carr, the billionaire businessman who purchased Whispering Pines from my dad, had people to take care of things like this. When it came to village problems, I was that person. So this problem really was mine to solve, and I had no idea what to do about it. Maybe one of the animal trainers at the circus would have a suggestion?

After completing my loop around the commons, which involved listening to complaints similar to India's from the other shop owners, I went to the beach to check on things at the marina and decompress by staring out at the lake for a few minutes. Then I cut through the woods and over to the two small schools and tiny library on the west side of the village before making my way back to the station.

River had tried numerous times to get me to come back and work full-time at the sheriff's station. I had loved being the sheriff during my first year here. Ridding the village of the nastiness that had taken over was very satisfying. The thing was, I loved my boyfriend more. Tripp running our B&B basically by himself combined with the intense schedule I'd been keeping was hurting our relationship. He and I discussed it, and I told River I would work 7:30 to 12:30 Monday through Saturday during the tourist season—the end of May through October. Tripp agreed that hours beyond that could happen for extraordinary circumstances. The rest of my day was devoted to either Pine Time, Tripp, or doing something for myself.

This meant the station needed a second deputy to help Sheriff Reed. Deputy Jagger was a massive man who had about two percent body fat and could function just fine on three hours of sleep. Less if necessary. I learned *Jagger* was his last name. He wouldn't share his first and wasn't even a little amused when I pointed out I could check our employment records. I decided to not press my luck and left it alone.

Like every day, I ended my patrol at 11:30 to give myself time to reply to emails or tend to station tasks. After typing up my patrol notes, I went to Sheriff Reed's office to discuss the crow problem.

"Birds?" He blinked at me. "It's Litha weekend, and apparently every rowdy good-old-boy and girl within a two-hundred-mile radius has decided this is the place to hang out. The actual celebration isn't until Saturday, *two days* from now, but we've already had complaints about all-night parties at the campground and rental cottages." He covered his face with his hands. "This is going to be a really long season."

Litha, known to most people as the summer solstice or Midsummer, was the longest day of the year. The tradition here was to stay up all night with bonfires and plenty of food and drink to welcome in the Oak King, who reigned over the lighter months. Or did we welcome the Holly King, who reigned over the darker months and took over the day after Litha when the days slowly became shorter? I could never remember which was right. Either way, it had been a rainy spring, but the forecast for this weekend promised plenty of sunshine. Perfect for holding a really long outdoor party. Not so perfect for the law enforcement personnel who would be on duty.

"These birds are causing a significant problem," I pressed.

"Droppings all around the commons. Plants pulled up in the Pentacle Garden."

He looked through his fingers at me. "Are the *droppings* cleaned up and the plants stuck back in the ground?"

"Yes, but the birds are also bombing people with pinecones. They almost got me this morning."

From beneath my chair, Meeka gave a little *ruff.*

"They actually hit Meeka."

"Do you really think this is a law enforcement issue?"

That was a fair question. "No. Probably something for village services."

"Right, so with everything else we have to deal with, I'd put this on Mr. Powell's desk. Not sure why I had to walk *you* through that one."

Because I had a big problem making decisions right now. I felt off, had for months if I was honest, and because I couldn't figure out why, I didn't know how to fix it. Normally, I was a big fan of listening to my gut and trusting my instincts instead of only thinking my way through issues. Or overthinking. Something I'd been doing a lot of lately.

"Mr. Powell is already on it." Although I should let him know it was officially his issue to deal with.

The sheriff swiped his hands together. "Problem solved. Anything else we need to be concerned about?"

"The shop owners were busy cleaning up the bird messes but fine otherwise. I wandered over to the marina, then over to the schools and library to check on the repairs to the Fairy Path. Rourke says they should be done by early next week."

The sheriff nodded and shifted into Martin mode. "How's Rosalyn doing?"

"She's a wreck but in an excited way."

He smiled proudly. "Go on home, then. She could probably use your help."

Except this was her business. Pine Time B&B was only involved to the extent that she held the events on our property.

I wouldn't nitpick right now, however. "Will do, boss. See you tomorrow."

Before he could change his mind and assign me something annoying, like cleaning the station bathroom, which would be payback for the times I made him do it, Meeka and I left the building.

Chapter Two

At home, the first thing I noticed was a big white tent in our yard. Tripp had initially freaked out when Rosalyn told him what she wanted to do.

"Tent flooring?" he objected. "You'll kill the grass."

He had worked hard with the green witches to get our yard looking beautiful using environmentally friendly tactics.

Rosalyn promised to put down the flooring at the last possible moment and to only use as much as was necessary for guest comfort. Fortunately, this wedding was a small family affair with only twelve adults and four kids. It was a good size for her first official event and the test to see if Tripp could deal with the flooring issue since she planned to hold as many of the events as possible outside.

I found my sister in the backyard, where the ceremony would take place. The tent in the front yard was for the reception afterward. She was reviewing papers on the clipboard that I was pretty sure had become permanently attached to her hand. Last I'd seen, most every item had a little checkmark next to it. Many of the checkmarks had diagonal lines drawn through them. Now she was highlighting things.

"What does all that mean?" I asked.

She pulled out one of the three yellow highlighter pens stuck in her messy bun and looked up at me in a daze. "What?"

"The marks." I tapped the list. "What do they mean?"

Turning the board toward me as though doing a presentation, she explained, "A checkmark means the thing was ordered or the person scheduled. The line through the mark indicates the item has been received or the person confirmed they would do what they were hired to do. When I determine that an item is complete and I don't need to worry about it anymore, I highlight it."

Unable to stop myself, I asked, "And what if something happens to the completed thing before the ceremony?"

She jabbed the highlighter at me like she was going to scribble on my face. "That's why I'm using yellow. On event day, I'll do a final check of everything and will highlight it using blue which, combined with the yellow, will turn the line green. Green means go."

How could I argue with that process?

Since I'd left this morning, both the tent and an archway made from pine logs had been erected. The arch stood about ten feet from the shore.

"No big holes," Tripp had demanded regarding the arch, "and nothing permanent. You can pound narrow supports into the ground and bolt those to the arch poles. Better still, use something self-supporting."

The bride's family were farmers from a small town near Fargo, North Dakota. The groom's family ran a dude ranch in the same area. I would think they had enough farm equipment and whatnot in their lives, but the bride wanted a farm-themed wedding. That was why there were hay bales, wagon wheels, lassos, and other items I couldn't identify scattered across my yard. Rosalyn had shown me her vision board, so I knew there would also be rustic crates and various metal containers filled with wildflowers; sunflowers would be prominent as the bride's name was Sunny. Oak barrels placed about randomly would hold some of the arrangements. Still more barrels would stand in as supports beneath a long pine board where Reeva would set out the food. Grapevines would encircle the tent supports and be covered with still more wildflowers. I could hardly wait to see Roz's vision come together.

I was about to ask her when she'd decorate the arch when she pulled a cellphone from the three-pocket apron she had started wearing. The pockets were loaded with pens, highlighters, her phone, a tape measure, a copy of the event agreement, etc.

"I spoke with Reeva earlier," Rosalyn murmured mostly to herself, "but need to check with everyone else about the items they're bringing."

Maeve would provide all beverages except coffee, which Violet would bring. Honey, of course, was making the cake, and Sugar a variety of cookies. Rosalyn knew all that.

"Stop." I put a hand on her arm. "You spoke with them yesterday. These women have been doing this kind of thing for years. Decades in Honey and Sugar's case. Trust your people. Don't micromanage. You've got the best of the best on your team. The last thing you want is to annoy them to the point they won't help you again."

Rosalyn nodded but wouldn't put the phone away.

I looked her in the eye. "Breathe. Save your energy for when the bride gets here."

Her phone rang then. "Oh, it's Kelsey." She clicked answer and walked toward the dock. "Hey, girl."

Kelsey Clarke owned the event planning business Simply Posh. She and her team had planned a wedding here last year. She and Fatima Singh, her event stylist, had become mentors for Rosalyn while she studied the business, took her licensing test, and started planning her first few events. Eventually they'd cut her off and force her to fly solo, but for now they were her solid foundation.

As I watched, Rosalyn lay on the dock with her phone to her ear and the clipboard over her face, blocking out the world. Then I felt a hand at my waist.

"You'd better be my boyfriend."

Standing behind me, Tripp pulled my hair to the side and placed a kiss behind my ear. "Want to get out of here?"

"Yes, please." I spun to face him. "What's the plan today?"

Rosalyn, Tripp, and I had become creatures of habit. Every afternoon at one o'clock, when I got home from the station, he and I went off to do something like paddle around the lake or go on a hike. Sometimes he met me in the village for lunch. Other times we ran errands for the B&B or just went for a drive. As long as we did it together, that was what mattered. At the same time, Rosalyn would grab her laptop and sit in the office, on the front porch, or on the back patio, where she'd be available for guests while she worked on her next Pine Time Parties event. Today the B&B was vacant so she could focus on the wedding.

Tripp held up a waterproof bag. "I made lunch. How does kayaking sound?"

Lunch in a kayak in the middle of Lucy Lake sounded wonderful. "Give me five minutes to change clothes."

By the time I was ready, he had the kayaks in the water with paddles and life jackets sitting on the dock near them. Meeka's tail wagged double time as I secured her jacket around her. She loved going for rides and staring over the side of the boat. Inevitably she'd jump into the water, so her canine PFD was a must.

Tripp put our lunch in the dry well, and we paddled straight out from Pine Time, staying to the left of the buoys put in place to keep people out of the thick weed patch that stubbornly returned every summer. We took our time getting to the far side of the lake, enjoying the sunshine and fresh air.

Once we decided on a good place to float, Tripp used bungee straps to keep the boats together. Then he pulled out our lunch: egg salad sandwiches, baby carrots, and iced tea.

"You treat me so well," I praised and took a big bite of my sandwich. Yummy.

"What did you learn on patrol today?" he asked after I'd eaten half my lunch.

I told him about the crow problem and my concern that The Well blessing didn't work. "You know the villagers are already unhappy. This crow issue is making things worse."

"They're upset about the tourists," he empathized. "That's a hard one. We need them for our livelihoods, but the crowds are getting too large. Rourke, Schmitty, and Gino were complaining about that last Sunday."

He meant at their biweekly poker gathering, where the attendees varied from week to week as did the location. While they played cards, a bunch of us women got together to play any number of card or board games, or just hang out and talk. I loved that we started doing that. Unfortunately, the further we got into the season, the more likely our gatherings would be put on hold until November.

"What else . . ." I mused and then gasped. "Oh! I learned a bit of gossip."

"Gossip?" He leaned toward me. "Do tell."

"Who do we know in the village with the initials VW?"

He let his head drop from side to side as he pondered that. "The only *V* names I know are Vanda Holland and Violet . . . What's Violet's last name?"

I squinted my eyes behind my sunglasses then remembered, "Jardine. They're the only two I could come up with too."

"Spill it, woman. You've got me curious now."

"Well, someone who uses the initials VW has been leaving notices on the community board." I held up my hands to stop the question I knew he was about to ask. We had problems last season with a group called The FF that posted manifesto-like propaganda letters. "We haven't had any Flavia Follower activity since she got hauled away to prison, so it's not them. This appears to mostly be fun gossip column type stuff. Although I suppose some folks might get upset to see details about their personal lives being posted there."

He dipped his paddle into the water. "Don't make me splash you."

I laughed. "Turns out Ruby might be dating someone."

Tripp settled back into his seat. "Ah, that's nice. It's like a plug was pulled out of the dam after her son came back into her life, and now good things keep happening for her."

"The post said they're not ready to reveal anything yet, but it sounds like it might be someone from the village."

He screwed the cover back onto his refillable bottle. "Let it go, Detective."

"I make no promises." As we started paddling again, Meeka swimming between us, I watched a crow fly past before joining a dozen others in the top branches of some nearby trees. They all started cawing loudly.

Tripp saw them too. "Ever seen that many around here before?"

The way he said it made gooseflesh break out on my arms. Like it was a foretelling of doom. "Not that I can remember."

"Huh," he grunted but said no more, and suddenly I got the feeling this wasn't a problem Mr. Powell was going to be able to handle either.

Chapter Three

THE LAST TIME I SAW MY SISTER THIS WORKED UP ABOUT AN event was her thirteenth birthday party. She agonized over whom to invite, what food to serve, whether they should play games or have a spa day—the spa day won—which of the dozen outfits she'd tried on she should wear, what music to play . . . no detail, no matter how tiny, was overlooked. She drove us all nutty, but we had to admit that her obsessing paid off. Her party turned out great and was the talk of the middle school for a week afterward.

"You're lucky," Tripp whispered to me when I came downstairs dressed in my uniform Thursday morning. "You get to escape."

I held my hands out like a scale. "Deal with crows, unhappy villagers, and a bazillion tourists, or listen to Rosalyn mutter incessantly about flower arrangements and appetizers. Yeah, I've got the better deal."

Today in the commons, the village services crew was scrubbing the bricks again, but I was happy to see the crows seemed to have left the Pentacle Garden alone last night.

"We put in some deterrents," Dale explained. "There are now spikes placed throughout the garden and pieces of wool saturated with eucalyptus or peppermint. They hate the smell."

I sniffed the air. "That's what it is. It's really strong."

"Yeah," Dale agreed with a wicked glint in his eye. "The birds tend to attack the garden when there are fewer people around, so we'll put out the wool at night and gather it in the morning."

"That's a lot of work."

"Less work than having to tend pulled-up plants every morning. And it's worth the effort. Like I said yesterday, the plants won't survive being tugged up and replanted more than a time or two."

I left Dale to continue his work and headed off toward the shops. An early morning gathering of witches on the beach between The Inn and Grapes, Grains, and Grub drew my attention.

"Good morning, ladies," I greeted. "I don't usually see you all up and about this early."

"Please don't stereotype us, Deputy O'Shea," Elliana Anders replied with an exhausted tone. "Not all witch gatherings happen at night."

I sighed. Elliana was a great employee for Maeve, but she could be snarly in her personal life. "I'm not stereotyping, Elliana, just making an observation. I patrol the village six mornings a week and can't recall seeing you here in the commons before."

She continued as though I hadn't spoken. "Because Reeva's coven chooses to meet at midnight doesn't mean that's the only time to have a gathering."

"From what I know," I challenged, "Reeva holds primarily full moon gatherings. Hard to do that in the daylight."

"The moon is still there, officer," Thistle Brittell informed.

Oh, boy. I knew an unnecessary battle when faced with one. Fortunately, another witch saved me from the group.

Zinnia Clarke waved me over and when I got to her side,

she said, "I didn't want anything. Just saving you from the Maidens."

"Anything I should be aware of?"

"Elliana seems to be the ringleader, and Thistle is her number two. They feel the traditional ways are too old and the coven should catch up with the times."

"This is the first I've heard about a problem within the coven." Or rather, a current problem. Many of The Flavia Followers were coven members and they caused all sorts of drama. Was this group part of The FF or were they a new bunch of troublemakers?

"I told Elliana it doesn't need to be us versus them. We can have a second coven that practices its own way. Just, you know, *an ye harm none, do what ye will.*"

The only real rule for the Wiccan religion.

Zinnia shook her head dismissively, then gave a sharp inhale, remembering something. "Guess there were a few things for me to tell you about. The Maidens asked me to lead an herb-gathering expedition on Saturday because certain herbs are the most potent when gathered at midnight on Litha. I'm not going to take part in that, but you might want to warn the villagers to watch their gardens."

"Will do. Thanks for the information."

Meeka and I finished a quick patrol of the commons, then wandered over to the rental cottages, and finally back to the station where I noted details and observations in my daily log.

- *More complaints about crows making messes, dropping things on people, and stealing random items from yards.*
- *Guests at the rental cottages were given warnings about quiet hours and reminded that more boisterous Litha celebrations were only allowed in the commons area.*
- *An alarming amount of wood has accumulated on the beach for the Litha bonfire.*

- *The tourists seem significantly rowdier this year than last. This is a potential problem especially if combined with the aforementioned firewood situation.*
- *Zinnia Clarke reported that a group of green witches asked her to lead a midnight herb-gathering expedition on Saturday. Basically, they're planning to steal herbs from villagers' gardens.*

I went to Sheriff Reed's office and waited while he read my log. He said nothing about the crows and thanked me for reminding people about quiet hours.

"I'll do the same at the campground on my way past," I said.

"Good. It's only Thursday. The bonfire won't be lit until right after midnight on Saturday. It's probably fine, but I'll mention it to Jagger. He and I will be patrolling during the celebration." He paused, tapping his pen on his desk blotter, then noted, "Speaking of which, this will probably be more than the two of us can handle alone . . ."

I held my hands up in a stop gesture. "Don't even ask. We've got enough going on at Pine Time this weekend. Call in the volunteers."

Several villagers were always ready and willing to help with matters like this.

The sheriff nodded. "What exactly is going on with herb gathering?"

I told him about my brief encounter with Elliana, and Zinnia's concern that the Maidens might be planning to form their own coven. "To me, this feels a little too much like The FF."

He scowled at that. "All right, I'll send out a village-wide email requesting volunteer help during the celebration. I'll also caution everyone to be on alert for witches in their gardens around midnight. And I'll speak with Elliana." He shook his head and mumbled something about not having time for this. "Is that it? Time for you to head out?"

"The wedding guests are checking in at three." I checked my watch. "This gives Rozzie only two and a half more hours to freak out over every little detail."

"Right. Go deal with the freaking. I'll see you tomorrow."

>[.]<

During the off-season, Tripp and I made tweaks to a few things at Pine Time. Instead of only a wine and cheese gathering on the patio each night, we now gave guests the option of having a tray brought up to their room. Tripp fought that idea because he liked people to socialize. Some of our guests preferred solitude, however, although we noticed they would come down and grab a couple glasses of wine and a plate of food to take upstairs. It was easy enough to assemble a tray while putting together the large platters. Not to mention better customer service. Tripp decided to entice them to come to the gathering by only putting a small carafe of wine and sampling of cheese on their tray along with a note.

There's much more on the patio. Come on down.

That tactic inevitably led to people staying and chatting with other guests. Some even stayed long after the gathering was officially over for the night.

When the bride for this weekend's event told Rosalyn the people in her group weren't really wine and cheese enthusiasts, that they preferred beer and whiskey instead, Rosalyn asked Reeva to arrange a spread for them. Shortly before three o'clock, Reeva arrived with trays of food, cases of beer, and a couple bottles of whiskey. Around quarter after, the wedding party arrived, filling Pine Time's driveway with three full-size pickup trucks, a compact sedan, a luxury sedan, and an SUV modified with a wheelchair lift.

Another part of Tripp's obsession to have Pine Time be on the list of Top Ten Best Bed-and-Breakfasts in Wisconsin involved making the building more accessible. That meant putting in an elevator for those who couldn't manage our stairs. I argued that an elevator would be a lot of money. Instead, Rosalyn could move out of the bedroom on the main floor and into one on the second. His counter argument was, "Why should someone who's staying here with family or friends be separated from them?"

I didn't know how important that would be to a guest but didn't want to make that decision for them. So we installed a cylindrical lift next to the stairway in the foyer. Fortunately, it blended in with the interior much more nicely than I expected it would. When we found out that the bride's father had lost a leg in a farming accident and would be our first guest to need the elevator, I was proud of Tripp for not giving up.

"It's almost like you had a premonition," I had praised.

He gave a humble shrug.

"It's good to have one of us on the main floor anyway," Rosalyn justified, but mostly she really loved the Lakeside room.

We'd also changed our procedure for when multiple people arrived at the same time. While one of us checked in a room, someone else, with the help of Meeka and Janus, the cat who wandered onto our property and refused to leave, chatted with the others and gave them a short history of Pine Time and the village.

Today, I took care of getting the wedding party checked in. The bride had covered the expense of all the rooms and since that was supposed to be a surprise for the others, I only pretended to charge their credit cards.

All of the wedding guests asked about the big tent in the front yard, but Sunny, the bride, had given explicit instructions to not let anyone know about the ceremony. Only she and her mother knew. And the groom, I presumed. It was meant to be a surprise for everyone else, so I dismissively answered that we were hosting an event over the weekend.

"An event?" One of the women grumbled. "How are we supposed to relax and enjoy ourselves with a party going on? How will my girls sleep?"

Five-foot-six, early-thirties, straw-blond hair a couple of inches past her shoulders, flawless complexion. Nell Lockwood had the fit appearance of someone who got in a good workout every day. According to my cheat sheet, she was the bride's sister, married to Bruce, and mother to Eleanor age ten, Talia eight, and Audra six. A note also indicated that she had a few social media pages for the "huge" farmers' market stall she ran so would likely be doing a lot of filming and picture taking.

As I handed her two key cards for The Alcove, I explained the cards would let them in the building if the doors were locked and assured her, "The event shouldn't bother you, and there are plenty of ways for you to relax. We've got kayaks and canoes, lots of hiking trails, and great shopping in the village."

She softened a little at that. "Can I swim in the lake?"

"You sure can." I handed her a map of Whispering Pines along with a sheet of coupons for discounts at the local shops. "There's a public beach on the far side of the village where you can take your girls. The B&B's shoreline is rocky so may not be as much fun for them, but they're still welcome to swim here. If you or they do choose to dive in, be aware that we've got a problem with weeds around the bend to the right, so stay in front of the B&B or go left toward the village."

She frowned disapprovingly at this, as though we should be out there doing something about it. Clearly she'd never tried to pull weeds from a lake.

I finished registering the others—the bride and groom, the parents of the bride and groom, the groom's brother and girlfriend, and the groom's best friend and his girlfriend—and while they got settled in their rooms, I was working on some other B&B tasks when a man appeared in the doorway.

Five-foot-ten, mid to late-twenties, curly blond hair, patchy goatee, broad shoulders.

"Can I help you?" I asked him.

He shoved his hands in his jeans pockets. "Do you have any rooms available?"

"No, sir, I'm sorry. We're fully booked. As is every place else in the village. Whispering Pines is busy in the summer on a normal weekend, but this Saturday we're also celebrating the summer solstice."

"I was afraid of that. It was a last-minute decision, but I came for the ceremony. I'm a good friend of Sunny's and wanted to be here for her day so took a chance that something would be available." He gestured toward our driveway. "I've got a tent and sleeping bag in my truck. Could I pitch it someplace?"

He knew about the wedding? That meant either Sunny or her mom, Mamie, must have told him. "What's your name?"

"Gus." He took off his baseball hat and clutched it in his hands. "Gus Lewis."

"Hang on a minute, Gus."

First I verified with my cheat sheet that we hadn't somehow forgotten him.

Sunny (Swenson) Alexander − bride
Colton Alexander − groom
Clyde Alexander (3) − son
Mamie and Ty Swenson − bride's parents
Nell and Bruce Lockwood − bride's sister and brother-in-law
Eleanor (10), Talia (8), Audra (6) − Lockwood children
Harlan and Victoria Alexander − groom's parents
Tex Alexander and Arizona Heller − groom's brother and Tex's girlfriend
Boone Gonsalves and Dinah Yubero − groom's friend and Boone's girlfriend

Nope, no Gus Lewis on the list. Next I opened up the village reservations site on my laptop. Laurel not only ran The Inn, she also managed the rental cabins on the east side of the village, the campground just up the driveway from Pine Time, and any villager cottages available for rent. To make life easier for law enforcement in the case of a legal issue, she gave us the password to the customer list for all four groups. After Martin accidentally made a change to some guests' reservations, she changed our access to viewing-privilege only, which was all we needed anyway.

I sorted on availabilities and found no vacancies. "Yeah, looks like everything is full. Sorry."

Gus muttered something about staying anyway since he drove all the way from North Dakota and maybe he could find a hotel somewhere.

Even the hotels on "hotel row" as we called the collection just over the village's eastern border were full this weekend. Gus would have to drive a good twenty or thirty miles to find a room, and I had a feeling he'd sleep in his truck before doing that. An idea struck me, and I agonized about offering it to him. Maybe I should put it past Tripp or Rosalyn first. It would only take a minute to hunt one of them down.

No, I was being ridiculous. This wasn't that big of a deal.

Although, if it was the wrong decision and ruined Rozzie's first official event . . . No. I listened to my gut, when it spoke to me, and right now my gut was telling me that letting Gus pitch his tent wouldn't be a problem.

Doubt means don't, a voice whispered in my head.

This wasn't doubt. At some point over the winter, I'd stopped trusting myself and started making decisions by asking someone else what they thought first. This happened for anything. Should I wear a flannel shirt or a sweater? Jeans or leggings? Should I have oatmeal or eggs for breakfast? Should I read a book or go to Twisty and work on a weaving project?

That voice harassed me all winter long, and I was tired of it. I was capable of making my own decisions.

I asked Gus, "You saw the campground on your way past, right?"

"Yes, ma'am." He looked so hopeful. "Are there sites available?"

I stared at the computer screen, and within the span of five seconds, went back and forth with my idea another dozen times. "No, there aren't any sites available, but there is a small field between the campground and the tree line."

He nodded, knowing what I meant.

Deputy Jayne was not happy about this. She envisioned dozens and dozens of people spread out through the field Woodstock-style, destroying the field grass and other habitats. The green witches and Tripp would be very angry at me if that happened.

"If I let you pitch your tent in the field," I continued, "others will do so as well, and I can't have that. The trees are the start of my property. It'll be okay for you to set up your tent inside the tree line, but you'll need to be deep into the woods where no one can see you from the campground or road."

His face brightened with relief. "Yes, ma'am."

"No campfire, not even a little one. No gas burners either. That's far too dangerous. And you need to clean up when you leave. I don't want to see anything more than a depression in the dirt and a few stake holes to secure your tent to the ground."

"Yes, ma'am."

That was why we didn't allow camping anywhere except the campground. People were slobs. Whispering Pines sat on two thousand acres, so many times folks treated it like a state park and set up tents without permission. If we caught them, we kicked them out of town. Mallory, our resident wood nymph, spent her days wandering the acreage searching for *bad fairies*, which was basically someone she didn't like. In this case, when she found people camping illegally, she'd come find me, Jagger, or Martin. Then she'd drag us to where people not only set up their tents and started fires in the middle of an often-dry forest, they inevitably left their trash instead of packing it out. And they usually set aside a spot to serve as a makeshift bathroom and didn't bury their deposits. It was disrespectful and infuriating. And really gross.

"Tell no one," I concluded to Gus. "Seriously. If I find out you told other campers I gave you permission, I'll deny it and kick you out. And write you a ticket for trespassing. I'm also one of the village deputies, so I'm not joking."

His eyes widened for an instant. "I understand. Thank you, ma'am."

"You can use the bathroom and showers at the campground. You'll need quarters for the shower. There's a machine outside the building where you can get some."

He shook my hand, thanking me one last time, and left my office.

I felt something bump against my leg and found Meeka sitting next to my chair, staring up at me. "Don't give me that look. He seems like a nice enough guy."

Meeka sneezed, rubbed her paw over her nose, and trotted off. Leaving me to think about what I'd done.

Rosalyn entered the office next. "All their bags are in their rooms."

She sounded slightly winded. "Did you carry them up? Wasn't Tripp going to take care of the meet and greet?"

"He was, but I have no idea where he went. No big deal, I took care of it."

Where would he go, and why didn't he tell Roz or me? "That's weird. Maybe Reeva needed help putting together the food trays."

Rosalyn gave a heavy exhale, catching her breath. "Come

outside with me. We're about to spring the surprise. Sunny hasn't even told Colton."

I checked the cheat sheet to verify who Colton was. "She didn't tell the groom?"

First Gus hoping for accommodations and now Sunny presuming everyone would be happy about this surprise. This event felt a little off course already.

"It's a vow renewal ceremony," Rosalyn clarified, "not first-time nuptials."

"You didn't tell me that part. A surprise *wedding* seemed like an awfully big leap of faith. This makes more sense. They must really love each other." A little romantic spot in my heart got gushy.

Rosalyn lifted a shoulder in a slow shrug that meant *or maybe not so in love*. My instincts immediately kicked in and cautioned me to be on alert for trouble.

"Their little boy, Clyde," Rosalyn explained, "is three years old. What a cutie. To tamp down any small-town gossip and prevent legal hassles after the baby was born, they had a justice of the peace service when they found out Sunny was expecting. She said she always dreamed of a legit, fancy wedding. Not sure how fancy this will be, but it will be legit. That reminds me, I need to confirm the pastor's arrival time." She sent herself a text, then motioned for me to follow her. "Come on, I want you to be there for the reveal."

Chapter Four

I LOGGED OUT OF THE SYSTEM, PRESSED A BUTTON ON THE keypad to lock the office door behind me, and then followed my sister to the backyard.

Sunny Alexander—*long pale-blond hair, five-foot-five, tanned skin, very pretty*—wore a white sundress and cowgirl boots with sunflowers all over them. She stood next to her mother and seeing them together, the resemblance was obvious. Mamie had the same blond hair as her daughters and healthy appearance of someone who worked outdoors a lot. The other adults had gathered nearby. Well, eight of them had. One of the men followed the three Lockwood girls around the yard and kept them from jumping off the dock. And Colton, the groom, wasn't here.

"Where's Tripp?" I asked Rosalyn while I scanned the area. "Oh, there he is."

He and a man I assumed to be Colton were on the boathouse's sundeck. The bride and groom would be staying in the boathouse apartment. Rosalyn decorated it with flowers, candles, Champagne, chocolates, and other touches to make it feel like a honeymoon suite. Tripp must have helped Colton with their bags.

While we waited for the two of them to join us, the rest of the group analyzed the hay bales set out as seating and the pine log arch covered in grapevines, sunflowers, and wildflowers. They assumed it was for the event I'd told them about. The ruse was secure.

Finally, the two men descended the boathouse stairs. While Colton—*five-foot-ten, clean shaven, medium-brown close-cropped hair, jeans, cowboy hat and boots*—joined the group near the arch, Tripp skirted along the back of the house to stand by Rosalyn and me.

"Why are you holding your hand that way?" I asked him. "Did you hurt it?"

He shook his head, dismissing my concern. "Just a scrape. It's fine."

I pulled his left hand away and saw that his right knuckles were indeed scraped and a little bloody. "What happened?"

"Don't worry about it," he snapped. "I'll clean them up in a minute."

I released his hand, shocked by the unfamiliar tone in his voice.

"Everyone," Sunny began, "I've got a big announcement to make. Colton, honey, come here."

He sauntered over, shaking his head as though knowing he wasn't going to like whatever she was about to say. "What did you do?"

She held an arm out to the arch. "I've got a little surprise for you all."

"What surprise?" Nell asked, phone in hand, camera recording . . . in case something social media-worthy happened? "I thought we were here for a relaxing weekend."

"Everything is planned. None of you have to do anything." Sunny turned to Colton and took his hands in hers. "Baby, we're finally going to have a real wedding."

He stared at her, his mouth gaped open, then violently

yanked his hands free of hers and clenched them into fists at his sides.

"What did you do?" he repeated with a slow snarl.

Beside me, Tripp's whole body tensed, like a cat ready to pounce.

Victoria Alexander, Colton's mother, wasn't any happier about Sunny's announcement than her son was. "You can't just do things like this."

"Why not?" Sunny's smile faded, but she wasn't at all apologetic. Nor did she seem surprised by Victoria's response. "Like I said, none of you have to do anything. You all said you wanted to come here for a weekend vacation."

"And when she says you don't have to do anything," Mamie added, "that includes taking out your credit cards. Sunny is paying for everything."

"She's what?" Colton exploded, his face turning an alarming shade of red. "How much is this—"

"It's not going to cost you anything," Mamie assured him, patting the air with her hands to calm him.

"*You're* paying for this?" he hissed at his mother-in-law. "She walks all over you, you know. When are you going to stop giving her everything she wants?"

"When they were born," Mamie began once Colton's rant had simmered down, "I set up accounts for both Sunny and Nell. I intended the money to be used for future weddings, but they could do whatever they wanted with it. A wedding, college, buy a house, set up a business, travel overseas . . . their choice. It's amazing how ten dollars every month invested wisely over twenty-some years turns into a nice tidy sum. After this weekend, she'll still have enough left to get something for the house or start an account for Clyde."

"You have that much money," Colton now hissed at his wife, "and you're wasting it on this?"

"I'm not wasting it," Sunny insisted. "You know how I always wanted a real wedding. I was looking at Nell's social media one day, and a post for Pine Time Parties came across my feed. I immediately fell in love with the pictures. After looking around their website and learning more about the B&B and Whispering Pines, I knew this was the place. And because we are Rosalyn's first event, she gave us a nice discount. I mean, look at this place. It's perfect."

"You could have at least given me a hint," Nell complained. "I didn't bring anything to wear. The girls have nothing but shorts and swimsuits."

"It doesn't matter." The radiant smile from earlier returned to Sunny's face. "I intended this to be a casual event. Wear whatever you've got. I, obviously, have a dress, and I brought something for Colton."

"You what?" he growled.

"It's not a tux or even a suit. I know you'd hate that. Remember the shirt in the window at the men's shop in Fargo that caught your eye?"

His eyes squinted, then he asked, "The green one with the paisley flower things?" He softened a tad. "You got that for me?"

"I did. You can wear it with your jeans, boots, belt, and hat." She tapped the wide carved-leather belt at his waist and then the brim of his cowboy hat before leaning against him and placing a long kiss on his mouth. "I got a matching one for Clyde."

Their son, the cutest little cowpoke I'd ever seen, peeked out from behind Mamie. Victoria, still hovering near her son with a scowl on her face, held out her hand to the little boy and summoned him away from his other grandma. Mamie's mouth opened slightly as though to object, but she let him go.

Colton's irritation spiked again. "You got him a shirt he'll wear once?"

"He can wear it whenever he wants." Sunny gave her son a loving look.

"Let me get this straight." Harlan Alexander, Colton's

father, wore his gray hair in a military cut and walked with a limp. He shuffled awkwardly to the center of the group and gestured at the arch as well as the hay bales, wagon wheels, and oak barrels set all around. "You brought us six hours east during our busiest time of the year for a wedding that looks pretty much like the ones we host at our ranch? We could have done this there and not had to leave the business."

"Harlan," Sunny began with empathy, "you said you needed time away, and everyone agreed to these days because there isn't an event going on there this weekend. Your sons won't let you down. Josh, Zeke, and your staff are taking care of everything back home." She turned to look at her father. "Yours is, too, Daddy. Please, I know none of you like surprises, but I think you're really going to love this village. Rosalyn arranged a beer and snacks table on the patio behind us, we've got a reservation at the pub in town for dinner tonight, and there are lots of activities to do over the next couple of days. There's hiking, watersports, shopping . . . Pine Time even has a fishing boat we can use. Or you can just hang out on the dock and relax. I've also reserved appointments at the local salon, To Dye For, if anyone wants a little pampering."

I observed the crowd as she spoke. Sunny's dad, Ty, perked when she mentioned fishing, and Harlan appeared to relax a bit at the option too. Victoria's eyebrows raised at the mention of the salon. Colton's best friend, Boone, and Boone's girlfriend, Dinah, stood toward the back of the crowd holding hands and sharing expressions of amusement. Tex, Colton's brother, had a grin on his face that said he was thoroughly enjoying the scene playing out. Tex's partner, Arizona, swatted his shoulder as though to stop him from adding any extra drama. Bruce, Nell's husband, was still busy keeping their daughters from getting too close to the lake so likely missed the whole presentation. And then I spotted Gus peeking around the corner of the house. A deep frown creased his brow. Did Sunny even know he was here? Did I screw up by letting him pitch his tent on the property? Should I tell him I was wrong and he had to leave? But how did he know about this event if she or Mamie hadn't told him? I should probably talk to one of them about him.

Most of the grumbling had died down by this point, so Rosalyn swept in next to Sunny to do a little damage control.

"Everyone, please come help yourselves to drinks and snacks." She nodded at Reeva to uncover the trays of food on a long table draped in layers of sunflower yellow, chocolate brown, and leaf green, the color theme for the ceremony. "You'll want to save plenty of room for dinner, though, because Grapes, Grains, and Grub's menu is fantastic."

"What time is dinner?" Nell asked.

"Six thirty," Rosalyn replied.

"Dinner will take at least an hour," Nell muttered, calculating the timeline, "plus however long it takes to get back here. The girls' bedtime is seven thirty." She shook her head. "You should have talked to me about this, Sunny."

Bruce, now at his wife's side, rubbed a hand over her back while keeping one eye on their girls. "I can leave with them as soon as they're done eating, and you can stay and enjoy the night with your family."

Nell's head tilted side to side as this option settled in. Then she pecked a kiss on her husband's cheek. "You're so good to me."

He kissed her cheek in return. "Happy wife, happy life."

Half the men in the crowd agreed with the quip. The other half groaned in disapproval.

"Don't worry about anything this weekend." Rosalyn made a sweeping gesture with her hands, guiding them to the food table. "That's why I'm here. If I can help, I will. Sunny wanted this to be low-key and laid-back, so no stressing. Enjoy yourselves."

"As for the vow renewal ceremony tomorrow," Sunny

added, "you can come in your pajamas or swimsuit if you want."

This set Nell off again as a bit of hysterical laughter burst out of her. It seemed the thought of a ceremony *that* low-key was too much for her.

"There's a kids' store in the village," Rosalyn offered. "It's listed on your map. They'll surely have something cute for the girls. And there's a boutique if you need something for yourself."

"Oh," Bruce said with a headshake, "that's not neces—"

"Perfect," Nell blurted, silencing her husband. "We'll go in the morning. When is this vow renewal thing?"

"Tomorrow afternoon at three," Sunny said. "That gives you tomorrow morning and all day Saturday to relax and do whatever you want before we head home on Sunday."

"Salon appointments are available between nine and noon," Rosalyn added. "A list of available services is in your room. Let me know what you'd like, and I'll let Massimo, the owner, know when to expect you."

Then, just when I thought tempers had finally settled and everyone had adjusted to Sunny's surprise, the crowd turned toward the patio to dig into the snacks. When they did, all eyes landed on Tripp and me.

Correction. They were looking at Tripp. There was a moment of dead silence as they all seemed to recognize him, weren't sure, and then their expressions turned to glares of anger. As for Sunny, she appeared to be shocked at first, then sparkled like she'd just been awarded the blue ribbon at the state fair.

"You . . . What are you . . . Oh my gosh!" She ran over to Tripp, threw herself into his arms, and gave him a long hug. Too long as far as I was concerned. Colton didn't seem happy about it either. She touched her fingertips to Tripp's face. "Is it really you?"

"It's me." Tripp hugged her awkwardly, keeping his

bloodied knuckles away from her white sundress, then stepped back. "It's been a while, but I recognized everyone immediately." He motioned down at her feet. "Of course, I'd know those boots anywhere."

Everyone looked familiar? Why did they all appear to be so angry at him? And what did he mean by he knew her boots?

What in the name of every goddess imaginable was going on?

Chapter Five

Once Sunny finally released her hold on Tripp and the families were digging in to the appetizer trays Reeva brought, I pulled Tripp inside where no one would hear us.

"What was that all about?" I asked a little aggressively.

"What in particular are you talking about?" He appeared to be half there with me and half somewhere back in time.

"Since when do we greet our guests with hugs?" I hated the note of jealousy in my voice, but that was one serious hug. And what did he mean by he'd know her boots anywhere?

He shrugged. "When I was searching for my mom, I went through North Dakota and met some of them."

Some of them? They all clearly knew him.

"I need to clean up the kitchen." And without another word, he went to do so.

"Oh, here you are." Rosalyn entered through the patio doors. "Come with me. I need help—"

I cleared away my confused thoughts with a deep inhale and then took my frustration out on my sister. "We talked about this. Pine Time Parties is your thing. Tripp and I will take care of the bed-and-breakfast side of things, but we won't help with your events. On top of running a B&B, I also work for the village, remember."

She placed her palms together. "Just this once. Do a walkthrough with me, that's all I want." Her head tilted, and she looked more closely at me. "What's wrong?"

"Oh, I don't know. Maybe the beautiful blond hanging on my boyfriend." Not wanting Tripp to hear me, I pulled her toward the foyer. "Let's go out front."

"Perfect. I wanted your opinion on the tent anyway." Once on the front patio, Rosalyn made a dismissive gesture. "So, regarding the hug, they all met years ago when Tripp—"

"Traveled through North Dakota while looking for his mom. He told me." I scowled. "That's *all* he told me."

Roz leaned back, clasped her hands in front of her, and stared at me. That was her signal that she was going to wait for me to ditch my attitude. I rolled my eyes and sighed.

"First," she began, "the hug happened two minutes ago. He hasn't had time to tell you more. Second, tell me you're not jealous."

"Not full-on want to scratch her eyes out jealous," I replied after taking a moment to analyze my feelings. Morgan would be proud of me for that. "But how would you feel if some woman ran up to Martin and draped herself all over him?"

"Hmm. Fair point, but remember, Sunny is here for a vow renewal ceremony. She's got a bright, bubbly personality and was excited to run into an old acquaintance."

"Not sure *acquaintance* is the right word. Obviously, I don't know any of them, but I'm telling you, there's more to this than Tripp passing through Wherever, North Dakota. He has a history with these people, and by the way they reacted to him, it's not a good one."

And he knew her damn boots. I wasn't sure he could identify my shoes in our closet.

Rosalyn took my hand and pulled me toward the tent. "Wait for the dust to settle, then talk to him."

"Fine." I had B&B paperwork to take care of and emails to reply to. "What did you want my opinion on?"

"The layout. My team is gathering to do the final decorating at six tomorrow morning, and I'd rather not change anything once we start."

The twenty-by-twenty-foot white canvas tent had a steel frame with a pole at each corner and two more on each side. Each pole was currently draped with white gauzy fabric and wrapped with grapevines, which they'd add sunflowers and wildflowers to in the morning. Two wagon wheels wired with lights hung as chandeliers from the center beam. They were also wrapped in grapevines and would be adorned with still more flowers.

"My plan for seating is where I need an opinion." Rosalyn made swooping gestures with her hands as she spoke. "I'm thinking I'll divide the fourteen guests between two larger round tables with Sunny and Colton at a small round table between them." She pointed at the side furthest away from the house. "The buffet table will go there." She indicated the side closest to the driveway. "Cake and cookies there. Dance floor at the other end. And we'll only put down flooring for the dance floor, not all around. We'll do that at the last minute and pick it up when the party is over to limit damage to Tripp's grass."

I did a mental headcount. "That sounds like a great plan. Except there are seventeen guests."

Panicking slightly, she counted the names on her clipboard. "No, sixteen including the bride and groom."

"Plus Gus."

"Who?"

"Gus Lewis. Sunny's friend from . . . wherever they come from in North Dakota."

"Near Fargo," she murmured, her brow creasing as she thought. "The only friends Sunny mentioned were Boone and

Dinah. She figured Boone could settle Colton down if he reacted negatively to the surprise."

Crap. I did screw up. I told her about letting Gus pitch a tent.

She poked my shoulder with her baby-pink manicured nail. "You are too nice. Whoever this guy is, he's not on the guest list." She pondered the problem. "I don't want to risk upsetting Sunny. I could ask Mamie about Mr. Lewis . . . No, Bruce seems like the go-to guy for dealing with family issues. I'll talk to him." She made a note on her to-do list. "Like I said, my crew is coming at six to decorate. Reeva will set up the buffet table early and put the food out once the ceremony starts. Honey is bringing the cake at one o'clock." She gazed around the tent, taking in every square inch, then gave a satisfied nod. "I have a plan."

"You do." I bumped my shoulder against hers. "Sorry I snapped at you about helping."

"No, that's okay. We agreed this is my venture, and I promised to only ask for your help in emergency situations."

"I don't recall agreeing to that."

"But you will because, as we just established, you are a nice person."

I smiled at her. "I'm really proud of you, you know. This was a big undertaking. From the initial idea to studying all those books to convincing Kelsey to mentor you and now this. Good job, sis."

Rosalyn curtsied. "Thank you."

Then I realized I hadn't seen Meeka in a while. She hadn't followed Tripp and me inside. I pointed toward the backyard and asked Rosalyn, "Is Meeka hiding under the food table?"

"Oh dear."

We rushed around to the lake side of the house to find animated conversations going on. Eleanor, Talia, and Audra were chasing Meeka across and around the hay bales as Bruce stood by watching.

"It's okay," Rosalyn murmured to herself. "They're just hay bales. We're covering them with blankets in the morning, so if they get a little raggedy it's no big deal. They can't mess with the arch, though."

As she marched off to talk to Bruce about that, I let out a short, sharp whistle that caused all chatter and motion to stop. Meeka stood with her front paws on a bale and searched for me. "Come!"

She looked from me to the girls as though deciding what to do, then started my way.

The middle daughter, Talia, complained, "Don't go, Meeka," while the youngest, Audra, burst into tears. Bruce shot me a look that said he wasn't happy I was taking their plaything away. I wasn't happy my dog was being used as a plaything. Every few weeks, we got guests that rubbed me the wrong way. No one was horrible, we'd never had to ask anyone to leave, but we did get some who were entitled or spoiled or just plain challenging. I couldn't decide which category this group fit into. And it wasn't all of them, but after little more than an hour, I had to be honest, I was already looking forward to Sunday when they'd pack up and head home. And I was grateful we'd limited Pine Time Parties to one major event per month. Two smaller ones if they only required the backyard for one night.

I let Meeka inside so she could calm down from all that running around and then went to see Reeva.

"This is an interesting group," she said while rearranging the food on the platters. She was using her Private Investigator Reeva Long voice.

"What's your definition of *interesting*?" I snatched a deep-fried bacon-wrapped cheese curd from a tray. "This is fantastic. What's in there?"

"Jalapeno cream cheese. Yummy, hey?" She laughed when I took another. "Just stand here with me and listen. The complaints and jabs at each other don't stop. Talk about your dysfunctional family."

As if on cue, Colton started arguing with Mamie again about how Sunny always got what she wanted.

"Nice way to talk about your wife, bro," Tex muttered loudly enough that everyone could hear him.

"Ask her." Colton flung a hand Sunny's way. "She tells people every day about how spoiled she is."

"I don't say spoiled," Sunny objected, sticking up for herself. She snuggled Clyde who was napping on her lap. "I say I'm blessed, because I am."

"All I know," Colton said while taking another beer, "is that I can't afford everything she wants."

"You should be able to," Tex said. "We've got plenty." The insinuation being that the Alexander family was loaded. Tex confirmed my interpretation by adding, "Oh, that's right. Me, Josh, and Zeke have money because we work our tails off. You're too busy doing . . ." He scratched his head. "What do you do all day, Colt? You're sure not helping at the ranch; I know that."

"Guys," Mamie chastised in a gentle tone. "Can we not do this? Not here. Not now."

Victoria frowned at her—for scolding her sons?—but didn't object. I got the impression that despite not liking each other much, these families spent a good amount of time together. They spoke as though they knew each other well. Or maybe that was just the *small town where everyone knows everyone's business* effect.

I leaned close to Reeva. "Maybe we should arrange for a divorce attorney to come instead of the minister."

She clamped her lips between her teeth to stop herself from laughing out loud and shook a finger at me.

"You're not spoiled," Mamie said to her daughter. "Being spoiled is having every little thing you want. That hasn't been true for you for years."

"What's that supposed to mean?" Colton challenged. "That she's not happy with me? Then why is she spending all this money to show you all how in love with me she is?"

How in love she was with him. Not him with her? I'd seen people who were in love, and this couple wasn't. So good question on Colton's part. Why spend all this money on a display of love? Maybe it was one of those unexpected things couples on the verge of divorce did. Like buying a house in the hopes of creating the perfect family nest. Or going on an extravagant vacation to spark passion. Or getting pregnant thinking a child would bond them.

"A man owns up to his mistakes," Ty said, working the joystick on his wheelchair to move into the shade.

Colton looked at Sunny and Clyde, and replied to Ty, "That's what you told me four years ago. I did my part. Where'd that get me?"

Sunny handed Clyde to her mother, then stood and took the beer from her husband's hand. "I think you've had enough."

Angry, he reached for the bottle but knocked it out of Sunny's hand and it broke when it hit the ground. "Don't tell me what to do." He stormed across the yard to the boathouse.

I made a move to clean up the glass, but Reeva stopped me. "I've got a broom and dustpan right here." She winked at me. "It's been a while, but I remember how events like this can go." She elevated her voice. "Everyone, stay where you are while I clean this up. Watch your tires, Mr. Swenson."

Rosalyn looked at a complete loss as to what to do about the interaction. But *should* she do anything? Her role was party planner, not therapist.

Seemingly thinking the same thing I was, Sunny went to Roz's side and put an arm around her shoulders. "Unfortunately, this is how we are. You know those married couples who argue all the time but insist their marriage is strong and they always kiss and make up afterwards?"

Rosalyn nodded.

"That's not only me and Colton, it's our whole beautiful, nasty extended family. We're fine."

Did she honestly believe that? I really wanted to ask her. Her husband was rude, her mother-in-law disrespectful, her brother-in-law took joy in poking at Colton, and the rest of the group didn't seem to care much. Because they were wrapped up in themselves? Because this was, as Sunny said, how they were?

"Maybe it's too much togetherness," Sunny pondered, more to herself than my sister. "All four Alexander sons work and live on that ranch. Granted, we're spread across ten thousand acres, so it's not like we're next-door neighbors or anything. My parents' farm is significantly smaller, only one hundred acres, but we're all involved. Bruce helps Dad with operations. Nell sells some of the produce at the farmers' markets. I help Mom with the books." She nodded in a *coming to a realization* way. "Separation would probably be a good thing."

Separation from family members or a separation from her husband?

She took her son from Mamie's lap. "I'll go get him ready for dinner."

"I'll do that." Victoria held her arms out to the boy, and he climbed into them. "He is staying with us, after all. They gave us the Jack-and-Jill rooms, so he'll have his own space all weekend."

Sunny started to object but seemed to feel it was easier to just let her.

"You've got the Jack-and-Jill?" Bruce asked Victoria. "I'm sorry, but we've got five of us crammed into one room and a three-year-old gets a room to himself? Probably a queen-size bed."

It was a king, but I let that information slide.

Victoria brushed Clyde's bangs off his forehead. "Luck of the draw, darling. The owners assigned our rooms."

"The Jack-and-Jill rooms only accommodate two people per room," I explained when Bruce turned toward me, apparently wanting an explanation. "The Alcove is actually bigger, and two of your girls can sleep on the queen mattress on the bottom of the bunk bed, and the third can use the twin up top."

Victoria smiled cattily at Bruce and then kissed Clyde's neck. "Let's go get ready for dinner, okay?"

The boy giggled and hugged her tight. Mamie's mouth tightened into a straight line.

"You need to talk to Colton," Nell told her husband and motioned for their two older girls to follow them inside.

"Why me?" he asked, propping the youngest on his hip.

"Didn't you hear any of what he said?"

"No." Bruce pointed at the dock. "I was a little busy making sure our children didn't fall in the lake."

"Please don't raise your voice at me."

That was Bruce's version of a raised voice? I nearly burst out laughing. I'd had to strain my ears to hear what he said.

Nell continued, "You know the agreement. Weekends and whenever we're away from home are my breaks and your time to be on parenting duty. Anyway, Colton is being unreasonable about this gathering. He should be a little grateful for all that Sunny did."

She didn't say anything about Colton calling his wife spoiled or how upset he got about the money. In fact, everything Nell did say could be applied to herself. I didn't see her show any gratitude that Sunny involved the families and bought them a long weekend in Whispering Pines. She could have jetted herself, Colton, and Clyde off to Bali and had a beautiful wedding on the beach surrounded by strangers who would be happier for them than their family members were.

And strangers wouldn't know the dirty little secrets. Or the filthy-dirty big ones. Maybe there was a good reason the group wasn't over-the-moon happy for this couple. Was it really a renewal ceremony Sunny wanted, or was she looking for something else? Nell commanded a lot of attention, as did the rest of the family. Maybe Sunny was looking for a little time in the spotlight too. Or maybe, like her older sister, she was trying to create the life she wanted. Fake it 'til you make it? Build it and they will come? Show him how much you love him, and he'll love you back?

But did she love Colton?

Sunny confused me. In my very short time observing her, she struck me as being different from the rest of the group. She was the only one who didn't have a gripe or complaint or bad word to say about anyone else. Combining that fact with the way her family reacted to her gesture, I felt a little bad for the woman. Then I remembered the hug.

My mind was exhausted from all these ping-ponging thoughts. And I'd only been around the group for two hours.

Once everyone had gone to their rooms to get ready for dinner at Triple G, Rosalyn and I took the surprisingly little amount of leftover food from Reeva and brought it to the kitchen. There we found a note from Tripp on the refrigerator.

Went for a walk. Took Meeka.

Why didn't he ask me to go with them?

Be the bigger person, Logical Jayne told me.

Right. Thoughts had to be bouncing around in his head, too, and walks were always good for sorting things out.

We put the food away and then helped Reeva take down the table and bring items to her vehicle.

"Thought you weren't going to help," Rosalyn gently teased once Reeva had driven off.

"Guess I wanted to be around someone normal for a few minutes."

She placed her hands over her heart. "And you chose me?"

"Well, Tripp went for a walk, and Reeva left." I grinned at her as we took seats on the patio. "The last couple hours have my head spinning. The whole thing with Sunny and Tripp, Colton being such a jerk, and the way everyone else acts? I've never seen a family like this one. They remind me of those soapy family TV dramas from the 80s. I can only imagine what daily life on the ranch or farm with these folks must be like."

Rosalyn nodded but said nothing.

"Not that we were the family to use as an example of well adjusted," I continued. "I mean, Dad and Gran feuded for almost twenty years. Mom and Dad barely interacted for much of that time. He and I were pretty normal, but you and Mom were a lot to handle."

"Ha-ha," Rosalyn replied. "Maybe I'm being tested. The Universe is giving me a big challenge straightaway. If I can handle this one, I'm golden. And as Reeva said, my job is to put on the party I'm hired to organize, not fix what's broken with my customer."

"I was thinking the same thing."

"If they're meant to be fixed, the village will handle that. Maybe that's why Sunny saw my social media post. Whispering Pines summoned her." When I didn't respond, she pressed, "What's wrong? You're used to people behaving badly. Is it really that hug, because you know how much Tripp loves you."

"I do, but if these people are really just a group he met while passing through Fargo, why is he shutting down like this?"

"Going for a walk isn't shutting down. It's processing." Rosalyn studied me for a moment. "You think there's more to it."

"There has to be."

"Maybe he'll feel like talking after his walk."

"Maybe. Other things are off around the village too. Don't you feel it?"

She pointed at her head. "You saw my hair. I've been immersed in event planning. What's wrong in the village?"

I told her about the crows, crabby tourists in the commons, and how unhappy the residents were. "Shouldn't the villagers be settling in to the changes around here by now? It's been more than a year. And do you think Martin's been acting differently?"

She leaned back in her chair, head resting against the back. "Again, I've been focused on event planning so out of touch with everything else. What's wrong with my Marty?"

"Nothing major. It just seems the tourists are aggravating him more than usual. He's been around them his entire life, and it surprised me to hear him be so irritated by them."

Rosalyn waved the worry away. "That's normal. He vents about them a lot. It's more likely because he's the sheriff now. You had your share of crabby days when you were sheriff . . . What? Why are you shaking your head?"

"Hear me out on this. What if by blessing The Well, we made things worse rather than better?"

She closed her eyes. "That sounds like a question for Morgan, Briar, or Reeva." An alarm sounded from her watch, and she groaned. "Break time over. Dinner reservations in half an hour. I've got to make sure everyone is ready and give them directions for getting to Triple G. Don't let things weigh on you so much, sis. It's not your job to save the world."

No, but Gran decided long ago that it was my job to save the village, and two years later, it didn't appear I was any closer to that goal.

Chapter Six

Tripp and Meeka walked through the front door right around six thirty. She ran straight for her water dish as he carried a rotisserie chicken into the kitchen.

"Is that from Sundry?" I asked.

He held up the chicken in a box as though he forgot it was there. "Yeah." He placed a quick kiss on the top of my head. Not the greeting I was used to receiving, but I'd take it.

"You walked all the way to the grocery store and back?" No wonder Meeka was so thirsty.

"No, we walked there. One of the Sundry employees gave us a ride back."

As I watched, Tripp took celery, red grapes, pecans, and mayonnaise out of the refrigerator. My stomach growled; he was making chicken salad sandwiches for dinner. Chicken salad on his rustic bread was one of my favorites.

"It's quiet," he noticed once he had everything laid out on the counter. "Is anyone here?"

"Just me and the cat." Half white and half black Janus sat in a window and made a chirruping sound at birds or squirrels or whatever was running around out there. "Roz went to hang out with Martin for a while, and the others are having dinner at Triple G." I paused to watch him chop pecans. "I can't remember the last time I was alone in this house."

I paused again to see if, since no one was around to interrupt us, Tripp would open the topic of Sunny or any of the family members. He didn't say a thing.

"Patio or rooftop?" he asked when the sandwiches were ready.

"We rarely get to eat lakeside during the summer. How about out on the dock?"

The walk to Sundry combined with the three Lockwood girls chasing her around the yard appeared to have exhausted Meeka. Normally she took any opportunity she got to jump in the lake and swim around. Tonight, she lay down between us and immediately fell asleep.

I dangled my feet in the water while we ate and glanced around at the trees and boaters still out on the lake. No matter how long the sun lit the sky, quiet time on the lake started at seven. Canoes, kayaks, paddleboards, and battery-operated motors were okay, but loud jet skis and gas-powered boats were silenced until nine in the morning. Instead of engines, we could hear the distant murmur of the Litha crowd. And beating drums. Why was there always a drum circle at these celebrations?

We'd both finished our sandwiches, and Tripp still hadn't said a word other than, "We should get the breakfast prep done."

"Hang on," I said before he stood. "There's obviously something heavy weighing on you. I'll give you time to sort through whatever this is, but understand that the longer you go without giving me at least a hint, the worse this becomes in my mind."

He took my hand and met my eyes. The look I saw there —pain mixed with anger . . . and regret?—made my heart stutter. How long would he make me wait to hear the story?

"I hear you and appreciate your patience. This doesn't

affect us, I promise, and I will tell you about it, but I need to unpack and sort through a lot of things in my head before I say anything."

A lot to unpack. That didn't exactly ease my mind. How big was this container, and what would happen when he got to the bottom?

"But it already is affecting us." I tapped my head. "My imagination is in overdrive, and it's coming up with scenarios I don't like."

"Jayne?" He waited for me to give him my full attention. "I love you. Nothing will change that."

He leaned over to kiss me properly, but as he did, the new unwelcome thought spinning through my mind was that people walked away from those they loved all the time. And people who met in passing didn't greet each other with the kind of hug Sunny gave him. Was their connection—oh, God.

"Tell me one thing," I begged. "How long ago did you meet them?"

"Four years," he answered immediately.

Clyde was three. Plus nine months' gestation . . .

Was Tripp wondering the same thing I was? Was he also about to puke up his dinner?

The sound of car doors slamming and children laughing broke through the awful dome that had settled over us. We both looked to find Bruce, his girls, Boone, and Dinah walking from the parking lot to the front door.

"Let's go take care of breakfast." Tripp's voice was gentle, the look in his eyes softer now.

Maybe I'd asked exactly the right thing with my one question. Sunny and Colton were married. Regardless of whatever she may feel about Tripp, it was highly unlikely she'd end her marriage because she ran into him unexpectedly. Being a child's parent, however, was a lifelong commitment regardless of one's feelings for the other parent. Or it certainly should be. Then again, the best thing for a child—

Stop it, Logical Jayne snapped at me. *Those are awfully big leaps from wondering when he met them.*

They were. But they weren't unreasonable.

In the kitchen, we worked in silence mostly so we could finish as quickly as possible. Our normal nighttime chatter slowed breakfast prep dramatically. Tonight, our silence also allowed us to hear the arguing and complaining from our guests as they returned.

"Dinner was okay."

"I thought it was fantastic."

"The venue was nice."

"Like eating in a stranger's house. It was weird."

"The village is cute."

"Too many people."

"Yeah, it was so crowded."

"The beer was too warm."

"Some people like warm beer."

Fifteen minutes later, we were on our way up to our apartment and overheard two men talking in the sitting area at the top of the stairs. I stopped to listen. And since I stopped, Tripp and Meeka did too. Janus was nosey, though, and walked on up and took a left into the sitting area.

"Hey, kitty," one of the men greeted.

It took about three seconds for me to know it was Bruce complaining to either Boone or Tex. He was still worked up about Victoria and Harlan taking the Jack-n-Jill rooms.

"They would be perfectly comfortable in our room," Bruce said. "Nell is relaxed for the first time in months, but the girls are like five feet away. A little private time with my wife would have been nice while on vacay."

He thought Nell was relaxed? What was she like on a normal day?

"You think this is a vacation?" From the slight Hispanic accent, I presumed that was Boone. "With the whole family here, less Josh and Zeke, this is not a vacation. Not my version of one, anyway. Dinah is excited about the village, though, so we're going to explore tomorrow morning. I'm guessing she's already planning for the two of us to come back."

Okay, Boone and Dinah were on my nice list.

"Go on," Tripp whispered in my ear.

I cleared my throat, a little louder than necessary, and said, "What a long day. Time to chill for a while."

The guys' conversation halted as we walked straight ahead at the top of the stairs. We were almost to the door to our apartment when I heard Nell's shrill, "Bruce! I could use a little help getting the girls in bed."

Yeah, she sounded perfectly at ease.

In the apartment, Tripp hopped in the shower, and Meeka sat at the bottom of the ladder to the rooftop deck and whimpered.

"You can climb the ladder." I pointed toward the top.

The drama queen flopped to the floor, rolled onto her side, and whimpered again.

"Do you want a ride?"

She leapt up and jumped into the basket we used to haul food and other supplies to the roof. She stood with her front paws on the edge, her tail wagging so fast it was a white blur.

"You have to sit."

She did.

As I pulled on the rope, I said, "I think I'm being played. We walk way more than five miles around the village most days."

She sneezed.

I changed into boxers and a T-shirt and met Meeka and Janus on the roof. A few minutes later, Tripp came up. I handed him a bottle of Spotted Cow ale, and he sat close enough to me that our legs and arms were pressed together. He didn't say anything, and I didn't want to push him. If he wasn't ready to talk, I'd give him more time. How patient did I need to be, though? When he finally did talk to me, it had better be something big to be worth all this buildup.

No, that's not quite what I meant.

We sat in the silence, drinking our beer and listening to the sounds coming from the village and the cries of animals in the distance. In about an hour, the sun would set and bazillions of stars would blanket the sky. On Sunday, three days from now, the moon would be dark and fully in its new phase. Our favorite way to end a day, even in the winter but for a much shorter length of time, was to come up here and stargaze. Unlike the ever-changing moon, the stars were permanent. Yes, the visible constellations changed as the Earth rotated, but from our view, a star was a star.

"What does a star look like?" I wondered out loud. "We should get a telescope."

"Good idea. One powerful enough to see the rings of Saturn."

"Can you really see them?"

"Oh, yeah. It's remarkable. The Swensons had one on the farm—"

He cut himself off. Maybe because he had started talking about his time with Sunny, or it might have been the sound of angry voices floating across the backyard and straight up to us.

I went to the edge of the deck and saw Colton and Sunny on the boathouse's sundeck.

"Jayne, come back here," Tripp whisper shouted. "You don't want them to see you."

He was right. Because if they saw me, they might stop talking. Yes, I was being a super snoop tonight, but I'd take any bit of information I could get about these people. If Tripp was going to insist on being a shut-mouth, I'd use my detective skills and figure things out for myself.

"The acoustics are really odd tonight," Tripp noted. "We never hear conversations like this. Usually just murmurs."

"First, they're not conversing," I corrected, "they're

arguing. Loudly. Second, our guests aren't usually angry enough to put on public displays of unhappiness the way these people do."

They were talking about the ceremony, of course, and it seemed Colton still couldn't accept Sunny's surprise as it was offered. Whatever that meant. I still couldn't figure out her angle.

"I was cool with coming here because I really needed the downtime." Colton's words slurred. Seemed he'd had a few more beers at dinner on top of those he drank on the patio. "Now, because you needed to make some grand gesture of . . . whatever, I have to be on display. You know how hard it is for me to change tracks once I'm set in a direction."

"I know. You can still have your downtime. The ceremony will only take up half a day. You're free to do what you want with every other hour."

Tripp was right. The acoustics *were* weird tonight. Colton's voice was raised, but Sunny was speaking at a normal volume, and we could still hear everything she said.

Colton remained silent for a few seconds. I imagined his chest heaving with anger. "Is this really how you want to do this? You say you always wanted some big, fancy dream wedding. Is this it? Doesn't seem very fancy, and it sure isn't big. And do you really want to renew your vows to a man who doesn't want to be here?"

Beside me, Tripp stiffened.

"You don't want to be married to me?"

The pause between her question and his answer felt endless.

"That's not what I meant. I'm talking about all that money. You know how much it would help. My truck needs tires and brakes. The deck is about to fall off the back of the house. Clyde grows out of his clothes every month, and you seem to think you're entitled to something new every time he gets something. Don't get me started on how much you spend on your hair and nails." He released a groan of frustration. "That's just the first things that come to mind. I could list a dozen more. Like replacing our twenty-year-old furnace."

"Until a few hours ago," Sunny began, "you didn't even know about this money."

"That doesn't mean you blow it on a party."

"My parents have always followed a strict budget. Dad decided what was most important for the farm, and Mom took care of household stuff. To make sure they didn't go over budget, they only used cash and reserved their one credit card for things they couldn't pay for with cash. Anything Mom had left over at the end of the month went into these accounts for Nell and me. I knew she had them but didn't know how much was in mine until a couple of months ago. She said I could use it for whatever I wanted, but her intention was that it be for a wedding. Or vow renewal in this case. That's what I wanted too."

"You've been planning this for months? Did it ever once occur to you to let me in on it? We could have planned it together."

Sunny laughed. "You would have planned a ceremony with me? Mister go where the wind takes you? You never plan anything."

His voice tensed. "Always have to have things your way, don't you? Put on your little Sunny Sunshine smile and get everything you want."

This time, she paused before answering him. "You haven't paid a single bill in the almost four years we've been together. Don't stand there and profess you know how much I spend on things. If the money's available, I'll get something off the deep discount rack once or twice a year. My haircuts and highlights are *free* in exchange for cleaning the salon's disgusting bathrooms. Didn't know that, did you? And my nails? That's what we do at our girls' nights every other week. All it costs me is a new bottle of polish now and then. I've gotta keep myself looking good for my husband, or he'll go find a new wifey to put beer and burgers in his belly every night. You think I get everything I want? Not even close."

The challenging tone in her voice combined with his temper was not a good combination. Tripp slid to the edge of his seat like he might storm across the yard and defend her honor.

Voices from below on the patio floated up to us next. He joined me at the railing then, and we saw everyone except Ty, the children, Boone, and Dinah gathered in a cluster to watch the performance on the sundeck. Thankfully, we hadn't turned on any rooftop lights, but I still pulled Tripp down so we for sure wouldn't be seen.

Sunny called out, "And there they all are, sticking their noses into our business again. You don't want to do this ceremony because you'll be on display? Don't make me laugh. When aren't we on display?"

I peeked over the railing to see her storm into the apartment, slamming the door behind her. Colton drained whatever was left in the bottle in his hand, then went to stand by the sundeck railing. Over his shoulder he called out, "Show's over. Go back to your rooms."

All the proper family members were here to celebrate what should have been a joyful occasion. Except no one but Sunny and Mamie seemed happy about this weekend. Why? Was there an ulterior motive for the event Rosalyn had so carefully curated based on the bride's explicit instructions?

I glanced at Tripp. Was he unwittingly involved?

Chapter Seven

WE WOKE TO THE SOUND OF MEEKA BARKING, WHICH WAS highly unusual. Maybe the guests were arguing again, and they woke her up. I peeked at the time. Four thirty. The alarm was set for five thirty so we could get up and get breakfast ready. I rolled over to see if Meeka had wakened Tripp, too, and found his side of the bed empty. That could have been what set her off. Tripp snuck out quietly enough that neither she nor I heard.

Not likely. Falling dust specks would wake her, and she might whine about it, but she wouldn't bark.

As if on cue, she barked again.

"Meeka, shush. What's got you so worked up?"

She stood with her paws on the mattress and panted her dog breath in my face.

"Yuck, get down."

I gave her a gentle shove and debated trying to go back to sleep. There was no sense, I was wide awake now, so I rolled out of bed with a groan and shuffled to the bathroom. After a quick shower, I laid my uniform and accessories on the bed. My duty belt, Glock, zip-tie handcuffs, gloves, pepper spray, flashlight, badge, watch, ring, and cellphone were all ready for when I came up to change at seven o'clock. I took everything out of my belt and pockets at the end of every shift, so I was never without the things I needed. It would be super embarrassing, for example, to try to place someone under arrest only to find no zip-tie cuffs. Not that I would ever do such a thing . . . more than once.

For now, I pulled on shorts and a lake-blue Pine Time Bed-and-Breakfast T-shirt then headed downstairs.

As expected, I found Tripp in the kitchen preparing breakfast. Pine Time's breakfast had received rave reviews from our guests since day one, but Tripp wanted to kick it up a notch. He now served three individual courses instead of family-style platters. First, a starter such as a poached pear with a drizzle of honey and sprinkle of granola, or a small cup of steel cut oatmeal with a warm fruit compote. Second, the main dish. Today it was a vegetable frittata with candied bacon, roasted potato wedges, and a thick slice of his toasted rustic bread. The final course was a pastry, some of which he made himself and others we commissioned from Sugar at Treat Me Sweetly. He also had children's options. Guests told us about their kids when reserving their room, so we were sure to have the items available when they got here.

"How long have you been up?" I asked and headed straight for the coffee.

"I was wide awake at four," he answered, "so just got up. I didn't wake you, did I?"

He'd been up for nearly forty-five minutes, but it looked like he'd only just started with the morning's tasks. Maybe he sat outside for a while.

"You didn't wake me, but Meeka did. She was barking."

"Barking? That's weird."

"That's what I thought. Did you hear anything?"

He shook his head and pointed at his ears. "I was listening to a podcast about bed-and-breakfasts. This couple travels around, stays in the ones rated the best, and then discuss what they liked and didn't like about them."

"And what is something they like?" Along with the new breakfast presentation and the option of a wine and cheese tray in the rooms, he'd made changes to our amenities. In addition to a plate of cookies on the foyer table, we now placed small boxes of chocolates in the rooms that the guests could either nibble or bring home as a souvenir. The three of us always wore a T-shirt, polo, or button-up shirt with the Pine Time logo on it as well.

"In case they forget where they're staying?" Rosalyn had deadpanned.

Tripp hadn't found that as amusing as I had. He'd claimed it was so they could see what the shirts looked like in case they wanted to buy one from our merchandise cabinet. And it made us look more professional.

Regarding the podcast, Tripp said, "I think we can push breakfast a little later. Eight instead of seven thirty."

"As a guest," I answered, "I would like to sleep in a little later. As a part-time deputy, that will mess with my schedule. I'd have to clear it with Martin."

"It's only a half hour. You help me with the prep, and I can handle bringing out the plates."

"What about offering breakfast from seven thirty to eight thirty or nine?"

"That could work too. Pretty much everything I make will be fine if kept warm for an hour."

As he worked, he talked about other things the B&B podcasters mentioned, how he wanted to ask Reeva for more breakfast menu items so guests who stayed for a week weren't served something more than once, and that we needed more coffee.

"I'll stop by the Grinder and pick some up," I told him while loading the dishwasher.

We usually worked quietly in the mornings, so after

another half hour of Tripp's constant chatter, it became obvious it was not only his excitement over improving our business but also him preventing me from bringing up the Swensons and Alexanders.

For the first time in a long time, I was eager to get on patrol. The house, despite how big it was, felt claustrophobic right now, and this group of guests was overwhelming me.

At five fifteen, Rosalyn appeared in the kitchen. "Happy wedding vow renewal day! Time to decorate."

She looked between us while she added cream to her coffee, shrugged at our lack of excitement, and headed out to the front yard.

Five minutes later, Mamie came in through the patio door and asked about coffee.

"There are carafes of regular and decaf in the dining room," I informed her, "along with hot water for tea, creamers, and sugar options."

"Perfect, thank you."

"You were up early," I noted.

"I'm always up with the birds," she replied. "I didn't want to wake Ty, so I went for a walk up the driveway and around the campground. There are a surprising number of people awake at the crack of dawn. I chatted with one woman who was trying to figure out how to use this tiny portable camp stove. What a cute little thing. The stove, I mean. Although, she was a cutie too. I also stopped to learn a few tai chi moves from another woman and then paused briefly to say hi to a man who seemed to be thoroughly enjoying his book and coffee by the campfire. What a wonderful way to start the day. The early morning air is so fresh. Except for the campfire smoke. And the smell of all that pine! You're so fortunate to live here."

I grinned, amused by Mamie's enthusiasm, and agreed with her. We were very fortunate.

Mamie watched approvingly as Tripp sprinkled seasonings

over the potatoes. She smiled and seemed about to make a comment but only said, "I should go grab that coffee and see if Ty is up yet."

As Mamie headed for the dining room, I realized that her opening one of the doors so early could have been what made Meeka bark. The security system was programmed to beep if anyone opened the front or patio doors before we were up at five thirty. I rarely heard it all the way upstairs, but Meeka did, and Rosalyn said she usually did too.

Not five minutes later, Nell came downstairs wearing a swimsuit, swim shoes, and something that looked like a small, neon-yellow pillow attached to a belt around her waist. She paused by the patio door and looked over her shoulder at me. "Don't go to the right. Right?"

"Correct. How good a swimmer are you?"

Naturally, this offended her. "I medaled in high school, and it's my main form of exercise."

"I check with everyone because the lake gets deep after thirty yards or so. I suggest you head straight out. The marina is around the bend to the left and there can be a lot of fishing boats heading out at this time of day. Wouldn't want you to get hit."

"That's what my buoy is for." She pointed to the pillow thing on her belt. "Boaters can see this, and I can use it as a floatation device if necessary."

"Very cool," I praised, trying not to offend her again. "I've heard of those but haven't seen one before."

She gave me a tight smile in return. "Straight out. Got it."

At six, Boone and Dinah asked if it was safe to go for a run along the highway.

"Traffic is always unpredictable here," Tripp cautioned. "Your safest route is to go up the driveway, cross the highway, and go right for a short distance until you get to the parking lot. Then cut straight through the lot and you'll see a sign for a hiking trail. Stay on the trail and you won't get lost in the woods."

"Excellent," Dinah said while stretching her legs.

"Breakfast is at seven thirty?" Boone clarified.

Tripp confirmed that and glanced at me. "But you can stretch it to eight if you'd like. I'll keep your frittata warm until you get back."

"She could run for hours," Boone said of Dinah, "but I don't have her stamina. We'll be back before seven thirty."

Bruce and Audra showed up a few minutes later. The six-year-old was carrying a pink plastic pail. "I'm gonna gather rocks."

"She's our early bird," Bruce explained of their youngest. "And don't worry, we'll put the rocks back before we leave."

There were approximately six gazillion rocks on our beach. We wouldn't miss one pail full, but it was a nice, ecologically responsible gesture that I appreciated.

"Holy moly," I said when father and daughter slipped out the same door Nell had used. "We never see this many guests this early."

"They're farmers and ranchers," Tripp reminded me. "Like Mamie, they're up with the birds."

Harlan entered the kitchen next. "I'm here for coffee and tea. Victoria and Clyde are exploring the front yard. Okay if I bring a mug out to her?"

"Of course," I answered and directed him to the sideboard in the dining room.

Looked like Tex, Arizona, and the older Lockwood girls opted to sleep in. Or maybe they were just chilling in their rooms. And other than Nell, who still had a bit of an attitude, the group seemed less crabby this morning. Perhaps they'd been tired from their drive yesterday. Or it could be the Whispering Pines effect kicking in already. It typically took three days within the village's aura for guests to start declaring they never wanted to leave or promised to come back. A good night's sleep was always an excellent way to start, but for the guests who had been summoned here, the village's magic sometimes kicked in sooner.

Shortly before seven, Tripp told me everything was set. That meant I was free to get dressed for my other job. I only needed a few minutes to change clothes and load my belt with my tools of the trade. Except, for the last few weeks I'd been taking a few additional minutes to sit and collect my thoughts before shifting into Deputy Jayne mode. The first time I only made it two minutes, then three, and now I was up to five before my brain got squirrelly. Morgan called it meditating. I called it appreciating nature.

"Purposely sitting in stillness," she had told me, "and focusing your thoughts, even for a few moments, counts as meditation. A quiet mind leads to a calm and happy body."

I'd probably never be able to *sit in stillness* for twenty or thirty minutes the way she, River, and Briar could, but I admit to feeling calmer and ready to continue my day after those five. I opened my eyes and smiled to find Meeka sitting perfectly still in front of me with her eyes shut.

Softly, so as not to startle her, I asked, "Ready to work, Deputy?"

With her eyes still closed, she let out an equally soft *ruff*. That appeared to mean yes, because she yawned, stretched, and then raced down the stairs.

By the time I got back downstairs, all the guests, except for Sunny and Colton, were gathered in the great room, waiting for breakfast. They looked up when I entered and reacted—mouths dropping open, eyes widening, statements of "Are you a cop?"—when they saw my uniform.

"I was the village sheriff for a year," I explained, "then decided to spend more time running the B&B with Tripp. As you saw last night, the village gets really busy in the summer, so the owner convinced me to continue working part time as a deputy. I patrol the village in the morning and help out during extreme situations."

"The owner?" Boone asked.

"Yes, Whispering Pines is a privately owned village. A man named River Carr purchased it from my family a little over a year ago."

"What would qualify as an extreme situation?" Dinah asked in her Portuguese accent.

Before I could answer her, we heard a loud scream come from somewhere in the backyard.

"Was that Sunny?" Mamie leaped to her feet to go to the floor-to-ceiling windows that made up the back wall of the house.

"It didn't sound like her," Nell said and followed her mom to the windows.

An instant later, Rosalyn burst through the back door, her eyes wide with panic. She scanned the room, spotted me, and rushed to my side near the threshold of the foyer and great room.

"It's Colton," she whispered.

"Colton?" Victoria demanded. "What's wrong with him?"

Roz looked to me for the okay to say what she wanted to say. They were all family, so I gave her a nod. Still keeping her voice low, she said, "He's in the lake in front of the boathouse. I think—" She lowered her voice even more. "He might be dead."

Chapter Eight

I grabbed Rosalyn's hand and pulled her toward the patio door. "Show me where he is." Then I hollered, "Tripp!"

The urgent tone of my voice was enough to bring him running from the kitchen. "What? What's wrong?"

"Come with me, please."

As we raced across the backyard to the boathouse, the members of both the Alexander and Swenson families followed us. When we got there, I relaxed the slightest bit. Rosalyn said he was in the water, so I assumed that meant face down and floating. Colton was wearing a long-sleeve plaid shirt over a T-shirt, and it appeared that the outer shirt had snagged on something on the boathouse's foundation. His head hung forward, but his face was not submerged.

"Call Unity," I told Rosalyn. "Ask them to come with the ambulance. Then call Martin and tell him what happened, but he should wait to summon the medical examiner until we know Colton's status."

There was no cellphone reception in the village, except for individual businesses private Wi-Fi, but I still carried my cellphone with me in case I ever needed to photograph a scene. I handed the phone to Tripp and asked him to take pictures.

"Lots of them. Start with a bunch of shots of Colton from as many angles as you can safely get and then back up and get the entire boathouse if possible."

He understood what I wanted. One night this past winter when we had no guests at Pine Time, Martin had come for dinner and stayed when a snowstorm hit hard, fast, and earlier than expected. To keep ourselves entertained, he and I staged a crime scene for Tripp and Rosalyn to solve. We discussed taking photos and how a crime didn't have to be gory to be upsetting.

"Look around or past the victim rather than directly at them," Martin had explained, using the tip I had given him the first time he took pictures for me as my deputy.

The boathouse's foundation was larger than the building and created a four-foot-wide walkway along three sides of the structure. The fourth side, the one closest to the house, was approximately ten feet wide to also accommodate the staircase to the apartment above. It also served as a swim platform with a ladder hanging over the side for climbing out of the lake or a boat. Tripp went to the edge of the platform, the closest he could get to Colton, and took pictures. That was also where Boone stood, about to jump in and go to his friend.

"Boone, no!" I hollered. "I'll get him from the inside." I entered the boat garage through a side door. Boone, Harlan, and Tex tried to follow me, but I stopped them and quickly explained, "I need you all to stay away until I've investigated the scene."

"The scene?" Tex frowned disapprovingly. "You make it sound like a crime happened. He was probably drunk and fell in."

His unemotional reaction to his brother possibly being dead made me pause. "Until I determine exactly what happened and can rule otherwise, I need to operate under the assumption that this *was* a crime and preserve the scene. So stay out unless I say you can come in."

Meeka sat before them like the world's smallest bouncer, keeping everyone outside. Sure, any one of them could easily pick her up and set her aside or step over her, but they'd do so at the risk of a painful nip to their wrist or an ankle attack. Good girl.

This lower section of the boathouse was just like a car garage, but instead of slots for cars, it had slips for boats. I pressed the buttons next to the side door to open both of the boat doors, then walked down the deck between the two slips. Colton was between the two doors. His shirt had snagged on a boat cleat bolted to the foundation. How had he ended up here? I assumed he fell, but what were the chances of getting snagged on a cleat that way?

I knelt beside him and pressed my fingers to his jugular vein. It was weak, but there was a pulse. As well as a nasty wound on the left side of his head. Blood was caked in his hair and had run in a dark trail down his neck where it soaked into the collars of both shirts. Had the wound happened during his fall? Or had someone hit him and pushed him off the sundeck?

"He's unconscious but alive," I called out to everyone. "Tripp, have you taken enough pictures?"

"Give me ten more seconds." He stepped back as far as he could, presumably to get shots of the building as I requested.

"Okay, then come help me with him."

"I'll come," Boone offered.

"No," I replied immediately. "Tripp will do it."

I was concerned about Colton's head wound and therefore his neck. Tripp would be calm and listen to me. Boone was emotional and would likely just want to yank Colton out of the water. We needed to be careful and not cause further injury.

"What's going on?" came a voice from above.

I glanced up to find Sunny looking over the railing.

"Oh my God, Colton? What happened? Is he—" She didn't finish the question as she disappeared again. Surely on her way down here.

"He's got a bad head wound," I told Tripp when he got to my side. "We'll have to be really careful of his neck."

"We should wait. Drake and Jola will be here any minute. They'll have a neck brace and can safely move him."

He was right. Waiting was best.

"Let's at least keep him still. I don't like the way the water is making his head bob around. And I'm worried his shirt might tear."

Tripp dropped to his belly, hooked an arm around Colton's torso, and held him securely against the foundation. I knelt next to him, ready to assist if necessary. When we didn't immediately start pulling him out, Sunny and Victoria, both equally hysterical, demanded to know why. I explained about his head injury and our concern over his neck.

"An ambulance is on the way," I assured them. "The health care center is only minutes from here. We're trying to keep him still until they get here."

As we waited, I scanned the surroundings and came up with a few possibilities.

Like Tex coldly suggested, Colton could have been drunk and fell from above. He'd had a lot to drink yesterday.

Did he decide to go for a swim and jump in? Fully dressed. That much alcohol consumption could lead to any number of stupid choices. If so, he could have hit his head on the foundation, attempted to climb out, slipped back down, and snagged his shirt on the cleat. Except, he was only wet from mid-chest down, indicating he hadn't fallen all the way into the water, and I couldn't see any blood on the foundation.

Did he jump and get snagged on the way down? Did someone push him? When did this happen? How long had he been here like this?

It felt like a really long time but was probably only a minute or two until the Unity crew arrived. Since many injuries around here happened from people diving off boats into too shallow depths, landing on other swimmers, or swimming too far out and not having the energy to get back to shore, many villagers became certified lifeguards. Drake not only held a Doctor of Nursing Practice degree and was the one in charge at Unity, he was also head of the lifeguards.

When they got to us, Drake jumped into the water, which was about four feet deep at that spot. He got a firm grip on Colton then gave Tripp the okay to let go. Jola assessed the situation from the deck. She pulled out a pair of heavy-duty scissors from the kit she'd set nearby and when Drake gave her a nod, she cut Colton's shirt, freeing him from the cleat. Drake carefully lowered him into the water on his back and supported his head. Jola jumped in next and pushed a backboard beneath Colton. She strapped him to the board then placed foam supports on either side of Colton's head and ran a strap beneath the board, around the supports, and across his forehead.

Even though Colton was unconscious, they talked to him the entire time, asking if he knew what had happened and assuring him that they were taking good care of him. Once Colton was secure on the board, they floated him around the boathouse to the shore where a gurney was waiting to bring him to the ambulance. The wedding group followed along the platform, moving like a single unit.

"We'll bring him straight to Unity," Jola explained to Sunny after I'd identified her as Colton's wife. The others gathered nearby and listened. As had the group of villagers here to help Rosalyn set up the reception tent for the vow renewal ceremony.

"Are you equipped to handle this?" Victoria demanded. "Shouldn't you take him directly to a hospital?"

"Who are you?" Jola asked.

Victoria straightened as though offended by the question. "I'm Victoria Alexander, Colton's mother."

"I assure you, Mrs. Alexander," Jola said calmly, her attention on her patient, "we are more than qualified to assess Colton's injuries. We're always extra concerned when there's a head injury, however, so if we decide this is severe or that it isn't a situation we can treat here, we'll move him. The closest hospital is more than an hour away, though, so it's best to assess him and then do what we can *en route* if that is the decision."

"What about calling for a helicopter?" Harlan asked.

Jola shook her head. "Waiting for a copter to get here wouldn't be any faster. We need to go now."

"We're coming with you," Victoria stated.

"Not in the ambulance." Jola left no room for argument. "And don't ask us to wait for you. Jayne, Tripp, or Rosalyn can give you directions to Unity. It's easy to find."

As Jola and Drake rolled the gurney across the yard, tragic events from last summer filled my mind. Rae Crain had received a horrendous head injury while trying to rescue her daughters, Jola and Lily Grace, during a kidnapping situation. In Rae's case, they immediately knew they wouldn't be able to help her and took her directly to the hospital for treatment. She hung in for a few hours but ultimately didn't survive.

Then, in September a new fortune teller, Elody, was staying in Lily Grace's vardo when it caught fire. She suffered burns and smoke inhalation and ultimately didn't make it either.

And now Colton.

It was still happening. Even though we blessed The Well and sent Flavia away, horrible things were still happening to people here. Did we *not* get rid of all of the evil? Did something or someone return? Did some new nastiness move in?

It could be a simple case of a drunk guy doing something stupid, Logical Jayne suggested.

I'd agree with that if this was someplace other than Whispering Pines. How could a place be perfect and cursed at the same time?

"I called Martin," Rosalyn murmured to me as they loaded Colton into the ambulance. "He said to call him at home." She tilted her head and studied me. "Are you okay?"

I blew out a breath. "Remembering—"

"Rae. Me too."

Rosalyn had been there. I could have lost her that day too. "Martin wants me to call, got it. I'm going to talk with Sunny first."

She pressed her shoulder against mine. "I'll let him know."

I turned my attention to the family members and caught a glimpse of Gus Lewis in the driveway, peeking at us from around one of the pickup trucks. Maybe he saw something. I'd talk with him after Sunny. At the moment, my attention was drawn to Mamie and Harlan who were trying to convince Victoria that the clinic was no place for Clyde.

When Victoria refused to release her hold on the little boy, Harlan urged, "Vickie, be reasonable."

What was that woman's obsession with Clyde?

Mamie softened her approach. "Go do what you can for your son. Your full attention should be on him. I will take care of Clyde."

Finally, Victoria nodded, then glared at Sunny. "We're leaving as soon as I get my purse. Be ready if you want to ride with us."

At least she offered.

I waited until the others walked away and told Sunny, "I'd like to talk with you for a couple of minutes. If they leave without you, we'll get you over to the clinic."

"Okay." She was in shock, so I helped her over to an

Adirondack chair on the swim platform as Tripp almost magically appeared with a bottle of water for her.

I smiled at him and gave a small nod of thanks, but his eyes were on Sunny.

Don't read into it, Deputy Jayne ordered. *Stay focused.*

After he left, I took my notebook and voice recorder out of a pocket, stated Sunny's name, the date and time for the recording, and then placed the device on the arm of my chair.

"I know you want to get over to the clinic," I began, "but I need some answers."

"No, that's all right. You're doing your job."

"Good, thank you. Like Jola mentioned, Colton has a pretty bad head injury. I'm trying to figure out if it was an accident or—"

"You think someone did this to him?" Sunny, suddenly alert, looked incredulous. "As in hit him then pushed him off the deck? Who would do that?"

"You tell me. Do you have any idea what happened?"

"What happened," she repeated, stared at the bottle of water in her hands, then slowly shook her head. "I have no idea. I must have been sleeping at the time."

"That shouldn't prevent you from having an opinion. I won't pretend I haven't noticed the tension between you all. From the moment I met everyone, there's been arguing, anger, and pettiness."

"Yeah, we're not a great blend," she offered, and I wondered if she meant the group as a whole or her and Colton. She closed her eyes and shook her head. "I should have known better than to spring this ceremony on him."

"Why did you? If there's so much contention between you all, and you knew he'd hate it, why bring him and them here to celebrate a vow renewal?"

Before she could answer, Victoria called across the yard, "We're leaving." When she saw that Sunny was talking to me, she froze. Curious about what Sunny might be saying?

Harlan took her arm and practically dragged her to their car.

"Go ahead, I'll be a few minutes behind you," Sunny called back and then focused on me again. "Colton had a lot to drink last night. Like he does pretty much every night."

Whether it was intentional or she simply forgot, I noticed she didn't answer my question about the ceremony. "Tripp and I heard you two arguing last night." I pointed to our roof. "We were on the deck up there so couldn't help overhearing the things you said to each other. Sounds like there are some money problems?"

One of the top ten reasons for committing murder.

"Yeah, everyone thinks we're loaded because the rest of the Alexander family has money. We don't. Honestly, it gets scary-tight some months." She glowered. "He has no idea how closely I manage every single penny that hits our account. He's a spender, and to keep us from sinking further into debt, I have to be a miser." She took a drink of water. "You probably heard, but he was saying some cruel things last night. A lot of it was just his normal level of nastiness after too much beer. Other things he's never said before, and they really hurt."

"Your final comment to Colton before you went inside was something about the family 'sticking their noses into our business again.'"

Sunny shrugged it off. "That's partly why Colton's not happy about this ceremony. He hates everyone looking at him. He thinks they're judging him. In this family, they probably are. On the other hand, if there's something he wants everyone to know, they'd better keep their mouths shut and focus on nothing but him."

"Let's get back to last night. You went into the apartment around ten and left him on the deck."

She took another long drink of water. "Before I went to sleep, I went outside to bring him to bed and found him passed out on the loveseat. So I covered him with a blanket and went back to bed."

"Do you have any idea what time that was? Establishing a timeline could help me figure out what happened."

She sat back and stared out at the lake or into the trees. A wind blew through the boughs, but I only heard the crows cawing in the distance.

"When I went inside after our argument, I texted with some girlfriends back home. They knew about the ceremony and swore to keep my secret."

"About the ceremony?" Could she mean something else? Did Sunny have other secrets? "Did they keep it?"

She nodded. "Far as I can tell, they did. Gotta have those people in your life that you trust completely, you know?"

Tripp, Rosalyn, Morgan, River, and Briar. "I do."

"I think it was around midnight when I came out to bring him inside. Let me check." She pulled her phone out of a pocket and started tapping.

I held out my hand. "Mind if I take a look?"

Her fingers froze in place. "Um, sure." She leaned toward me and pointed out the group chat on the screen.

I scrolled through the conversation she'd had with Makayla, Sydney, and Taylor. The chat started with Sunny telling them, "You won't believe how drunk he is." All three friends immediately assured her that they could believe it because why would tonight be different from any other. There were lots of OMGs, f-bombs, and strings of emojis I wasn't sure how to decipher. I didn't see any comments in this string, or others prior to last night, that would implicate Sunny in this crime. I handed the phone back to her.

"The girls calmed me down," Sunny said. "I wanted to talk things over with Colton, hoping we could still have a nice ceremony, so I went out to get him." Her eyes flooded with tears that she blinked away. "Like I said, he was passed out. I tried to wake him, but he wouldn't budge."

"You didn't hear anything out here after that?"

She shook her head. "The bedroom is at the back of the apartment, and I had the windows closed. Even used my earplugs in case Colton came to bed and snored, which he tends to do when he drinks like that."

It would have been hard to hear a splash in that case.

We had the windows wide open last night. Maybe Colton falling in the water was what made Meeka bark at four thirty.

"I'm usually up early," she continued, "but since Victoria wanted Clyde to stay with them, I thought I'd give myself the luxury of sleeping in. That means my alarm went off at seven so I wouldn't miss Tripp's breakfast. He's a pretty good cook."

She said it like maybe I didn't know and winced at the tight smile I gave her. Then she mentioned something he'd made one time, apparently wanting to have a discussion about my boyfriend. I didn't. That had nothing to do with my investigation. Besides, any words I heard regarding the two of them needed to come from him first.

It was approximately seven twenty when Rosalyn told me Colton was in the water. Nearly seven thirty when Sunny looked over the railing to see what was going on below.

"Your alarm went off at seven," I repeated, keeping us on track. "Did you get up right away or stay in bed for a while . . ."

"I checked my texts first." She twitched a finger at the phone sitting on her knee. "As you saw, I sent the girls a text this morning, complaining that Colton didn't come to bed and asking why they let me go through with this ceremony. My mom was the only one who thought it was a good idea."

"You didn't think it was? You seemed excited while telling everyone about it yesterday."

She sighed. "I always wanted a big wedding. Instead, we got married in front of a justice of the peace with only our parents standing by looking all somber. When my mom mentioned the money and having a vow renewal, I agreed."

Her expression darkened. "Even though I figured Colton or his mother would ruin it."

"Why do it, then?"

She shook her head. "I don't even know now. To make my mom happy, maybe?"

That felt like a throwaway answer.

Sunny continued, "Mom noticed we've been fighting more and more lately. Like plenty of people do when they have money problems. Colton *really* doesn't do well with unexpected bills. As you heard last night. Mom tried to play therapist with us and talked about how troubles can be worked through and actually make us stronger. She also said a vow renewal could rekindle our romance." She shook her head. "I could be wrong, but doesn't that imply there was romance to go back to? My husband is *not* a romantic guy."

It was probably my imagination, but I swear she looked past me at the house. At Tripp? I shifted positions to draw her attention back to our conversation.

"Our fourth anniversary is coming up," she continued. "I thought instead of getting mad at him for not doing anything, I'd plan something this year. Try to rekindle romance like Mom suggested." She wiped away a tear sliding down her cheek. "I should have gotten him new tires for his damn truck. That would have sent him over the moon. Of course then he'd want to know where the money came from and still be upset that I didn't tell him about the savings account."

"Can't win, hey?"

"Sometimes," she whispered so softly I almost didn't hear, "I think marrying him was a mistake."

"But it's better for Clyde to have his father around, right?"

She waited a little too long before answering. "Right." She pushed herself out of the chair. "I should get over to the clinic. If you want my opinion on what happened, I think he was drunk and fell over the rail sometime after midnight and whenever he was found by . . ."

"Rosalyn. She was out here getting ready to put out the decorations."

Sunny nodded absently before climbing the boathouse stairs.

I couldn't help but notice her dismissive conclusion and the distinct lack of emotion over her husband being potentially fatally injured. And she had almost no sense of urgency to get over to Unity to be with him. The only real emotional reaction I got from her came when I mentioned Clyde's father.

What did I know after talking with her? I knew there were plenty of people angry at Colton or tired of his antics. Tired or angry enough to hit him on the head and push him into the lake?

What about opportunity? Rosalyn came inside around seven twenty to tell me she'd found him. Who had been outside here before then?

Mamie went for an early walk and came back in through the patio door at five twenty. Nell went for a swim in the lake at five thirty. Bruce was in the backyard with Audra at six o'clock. All of them were within eyeshot of the boathouse. None of them glanced over there in curiosity, wondering how things had gone between Sunny and Colton after he ordered them all to go to bed? In her defense, Nell could have been focused on her goal of swimming, which would have been in character for her. Bruce's attention would surely have been on his daughter. So it's possible that neither of them looked over here. I had no idea about Mamie.

Boone and Dinah left through the front door to go for a run, and Victoria and Harlan were in the front yard with Clyde. The lake side of the boathouse wasn't visible from there. To my knowledge, Tex, Arizona, Ty, and the other two girls were either sleeping or in their rooms at that time.

Sunny came back down the stairs, purse in hand. "The decorations. This is a nightmare. This is going to sound selfish, but I mean it to be positive. Would you tell Rosalyn I asked that she continue with the setup? I mean, maybe things aren't as bad as they look. Maybe he'll be okay, and we can have the ceremony tomorrow instead." She grimaced. "There's no way to make that sound good, is there?"

"I understand what you're trying to say." But no, her wanting to have a party didn't sound great. If this had happened to Tripp, I'd be hysterical. Or at least highly emotional. I'd answer questions, but I'd be fidgeting and eager to get to him.

Boone and Dinah spotted Sunny as they headed for their car.

"You're still here?" Dinah accused. "Come on. Tripp told us how to get to Unity. We'll drive."

Without another word, Sunny went with them.

The way Dinah said Tripp's name . . . It felt like she had known him four years ago too. This was one tightknit group. How exactly did he get into and out of it?

Chapter Nine

After Sunny left, I looked for Gus Lewis to ask him if he'd seen what had happened to Colton, but couldn't find him anywhere around the house, boathouse, or garage. I'd find his tent and talk with him there later. First, I needed to inspect the sundeck and take pictures of the presumed scene of the crime.

I found nothing out of place. None of the furniture had been disturbed as it might have been if Colton had fought with someone. The blanket Sunny had presumably covered him with lay half on and half off the loveseat. There wasn't one thing to indicate anything unusual had happened there.

What bothered me about the scene was the lack of blood. There wasn't a single drop on the deck or railing, but the wound on Colton's head had bled a lot. What had he hit his head on? Or, more likely, what had hit Colton on the head?

"Hey," Martin greeted when I called him at home from Pine Time's office. "I was about to leave for the station. How's everything going over there?"

I explained Colton's condition and all the steps we took to help him. "They're evaluating him at Unity. I'll be shocked if they don't take him to the hospital. I've got a few more things to deal with here so will be a little late for my shift."

"Don't worry about it. Jagger is covering morning patrol. Stay and take care of things there today if you need to."

I considered that for about two seconds. In that time, the look on Tripp's face as he handed Sunny that bottle of water and then the look on hers as she scanned the yard, presumably looking for him, flashed through my mind. If I was going to conduct an investigation into whatever this was, I needed to do so rationally. And I did not feel rational right now. Going into the village and getting a little distance from the drama here should help. I'd talk with Mamie and Ty first, Tex and Arizona, too, if they were around, and get their thoughts on what could have happened.

"I'll be in later," I told Martin. "You can talk through things with me."

This caught the sheriff's attention. "You think this was something other than an accident?"

"I do." I gave him a quick rundown on what I knew.

"Even if this was an accident, we need to do a formal processing of the scene."

"We do. I'll cordon off the area."

"And I'll send Jagger over to handle this one. He worked obsessively on his skills during the off-season but hasn't had a chance to officially use them yet."

"Sounds good. See you in a while."

I left the office, searched for Tripp to let him know Jagger was coming, and spotted him on the patio. He was sitting with Ty while Mamie and Clyde played in the yard. She hovered near her grandson, ready to catch him if he fell as he walked along the row of hay bales and leaped from one to the next. Meeka followed behind him, liking the leaping game.

Fortunately, Tripp left the patio door open, so I could easily hear what he and Ty were talking about. Colton's accident was the topic when I started listening, but within seconds, it changed to the reason for their visit to Whispering Pines.

"I give my daughter credit for trying to create some happiness," Ty said. "Mamie told me that's why Sunny wanted to do this vow renewal nonsense."

Sunny wanted to do it? Sunny said it was Mamie's idea.

Ty continued, "If Sunny was looking for happiness, she could have taken the three of them on a grand vacation. Or just the two of them could've gone somewhere, and the little guy could've stayed with us. Gotta say, I'm confused. The money is Sunny's to do with as she pleases, but Mamie wanted her to use it to open the hair and nail salon she's been talking about for years now."

Yesterday, Mamie said Sunny could use the money for whatever she wanted. During their fight, Sunny told Colton it was Mamie's intention that it be used for a wedding. The stories weren't jibing here.

"I don't know why," Ty continued, "we all have to be so involved with everyone's personal lives all the time. Not that Mamie and I don't care, but they're adults. What they do is none of our business. If someone messes up, well, life is about making mistakes, figuring it out, and bouncing back. As you well know."

Those last words were said slowly and purposely.

"Yes, sir, I do," Tripp replied.

"Everyone struggles a bit at some point, but you work on it. You seem to have bounced back nicely."

"Thank you, sir."

"Nothing ever got handed to me, and I don't hand things to my girls. Honestly, I was a little upset with Mamie when I first learned about these savings accounts. Then again, I'm old-school and believe it's my responsibility to pay for my daughter's wedding, so it was nice to find out the money was sitting there ready for that day." He chuckled. "I'm talking in circles, aren't I?"

Tripp laughed softly. "A little."

I'd heard Tripp talk with our guests before, but the easy,

unforced way these two spoke, like they'd had many conversations before, hit me. *How* did Tripp know these people? This was really starting to eat at me.

"That's a bit of Colton's problem," Ty went on. "Harlan and I get along well enough, but we disagree on money. The Alexanders have a good deal of it and pass it right along to their boys. Colton, being the youngest, is also the most spoiled. He grew up not needing or wanting anything important, and that, in my opinion, has not served him well. As I've said a thousand times, a man owns up to his responsibilities."

"Colton isn't worthy of Sunny." Tripp's voice held a growl. The tinge of regret I heard earlier was mixed in there again as well.

Ty softened. "Would I have chosen him for my daughter? No, I would not. There were better options."

Another statement said pointedly. I didn't want to hear any more. Any information about Tripp's relationship with Sunny, or with any members of this clan, needed to come from him first. I didn't want their viewpoint tainting my understanding of his past.

I stepped outside and acted surprised to see them there. The slight narrowing of Tripp's eyes said he wondered how much I'd heard. Maybe that would get him to talk to me.

"Hi, Mr. Swenson. I'm on my way to patrol the village, but I'd like to ask you a few questions before I leave."

He gestured at the spot on the loveseat next to Tripp. "By all means. I hear they took Colton for evaluation."

"They did," I answered. "I expect to hear something soon. That's actually what I wanted to talk with you about. Do you have any idea what might have happened? Or who could have been involved?"

He echoed Martin's earlier question. "You think this might not have been a drunken fall into the lake?"

"I don't like to make assumptions without gathering as

much information as I can first. That's what I'm doing right now."

"Good answer." He nodded. "Other than Colton upsetting pretty much everyone last night, I have no idea what happened. The boy likes his beer far too much, and unfortunately it loosens his mouth. Good that they tucked us outside and in a corner at that pub last night, but he still managed to draw attention. Sunny says she's going to stop over and apologize to . . . Marge?"

"Maeve."

"That's right. Maeve. Nice woman. I told Sunny she shouldn't have to apologize for her husband." He seemed to choke a little on the label. This man did not care for his son-in-law. "Anyway, as annoying as Colton can be, on a scale of normal to *what's the matter with that boy*, last night was closer to normal. As for how he ended up in the lake, not sure I can be much help there. We went straight up to our room after dinner. I was beat from the drive and being out of my routine. Did some reading, then turned out the light. That's really all I can tell you."

"All right. Thank you for your thoughts." I stood and nodded toward his wife. "I'm going to talk with Mamie now."

She started out telling me pretty much the same thing. That Colton was spoiled and lazy. "I've told Sunny, Nell, and their men that marriage isn't always easy. Tough times, however, can create a foundation that will help you get through anything."

We both glanced at the patio where Tripp stood, shook Ty's hand, and then went inside.

Mamie caught Clyde as he jumped off the last hay bale in the row. "Why don't you go sit with Grampy for a little bit. When I'm done talking to Ms. Jayne, we'll get a snack."

"Okay, Gammy," Clyde said and skipped off in his cowboy boots.

Mamie grew quiet for a minute then asked, "Can I tell you something?"

The shift from strong, no-nonsense farm woman to someone meeker made me pay closer attention. "Sure you can."

She sighed, her shoulders dropping as she exhaled. "I'm a little scared of Colton. Both for Sunny and myself."

"Scared?" I repeated. "Is he abusive? As in physically? Has he done anything? Do you have a legitimate reason—"

She silenced me with a hand on my arm and tapped her belly with the other. "Instinct. I feel it in my gut."

I liked this woman. "Well, I'm never one to ignore a gut instinct."

"To my knowledge, he's never hurt Sunny, but the man has a temper. I've heard rumors of outbursts at the local hangouts. He's broken a few pool cues at the bars and spent many nights in a jail cell cooling off. I fear it's only a matter of time before he takes his anger out on Sunny. If he hasn't already and she's hiding it from me. He blames her for—" She cut herself off.

"What? What does he blame her for?"

Her gaze darted to the patio. Was she looking at her husband or her grandson?

When she brushed off the comment with a shake of her head, I asked, "Have you talked with her about Colton's anger problem?"

"I have regarding her safety. She insists she's fine, but at least it's in her head now. Hopefully her instincts will kick in if things ever ramp up. I mentioned it to Ty too. He didn't dismiss it exactly but said Colton knew better than to hurt her."

Had Ty threatened Colton? "What do you think he meant by that?"

"He meant there would be a gang of men who adore our

Sunny ready to take care of him if he ever laid a hand on her."

Were any of those people here right now? "It's good you said something to her. What do you know about Gus Lewis?"

My abrupt change of topic didn't faze her. "You mean do I know he's here?"

"Right. This doesn't seem to surprise you."

She shook her head. "He knew we were all going somewhere for the weekend and kept harassing Sunny about it until she finally told him. As for your concern about him, Gus is a gentle soul who wants to be Sunny's best friend. He takes it upon himself to check in on her every day and make sure all is right in her world."

"Any reason in particular he feels the need to do this?"

"In particular?" She thought about that. "I think *he* thinks he's protecting her. Not because she's in danger, but more in the way Sunny takes care of Clyde."

"So he's mimicking her?"

"That could be. Either way, in Gus's opinion no one could be good enough for our Sunny. We feel the same way."

That's basically what Ty had said to Tripp. *"Colton isn't worthy of Sunny."*

Reeva pulled up to the house then. Presumably to set up the food tables. Did Rosalyn forget to tell her things were on hold?

"That's the caterer," I told Mamie. "Not sure where Rosalyn is, so I should go talk to her. And I may have more questions for you later."

"That's fine, honey. Sorry. Deputy. I'll be here until Sunny says we can leave. Or you kick us out."

Not to be insensitive, but we had reservations next week. The wedding people would have to leave as scheduled on Sunday.

I whistled for Meeka, who had decided to join Clyde on the loveseat. She jumped down, stretched, and trotted over to me. By the time we got to Reeva's side in the driveway, Rosalyn was standing next to her.

"Oh, that's awful," Reeva was saying when I got close. "I hope he'll be okay."

"Sunny asked me to give you a message," I told Rosalyn. "She says you should move forward with setting everything up. She's being optimistic that Colton's injuries aren't as bad as they appear to be."

"All right," Rosalyn said. "At least that way she'll get to see what she paid for. The contract says there are no refunds less than thirty days from the event. I'll give twenty-five percent back if it's ninety days out and half if it's six months. It's in my AICMM clause."

"Your what?" Reeva asked.

"Accident, Injury, Changed My Mind. In a situation like this, it feels brutal, but I understand it's industry standard."

"It is. I did the same thing when I ran my catering business." Reeva stared at the boxes and pans full of food in the back of her SUV. "What should we do with all this?"

"To the basement, I guess," Rosalyn decided. "It's all Sunny's so she can take it home with her if she wants it."

"You have a basement?" Reeva looked shocked. A few of the cottages had root cellars, but none of them had basements.

I laughed at her reaction. "According to Gran's journals, digging it wasn't easy. Clearing all the tree roots took weeks. Something the builder didn't tell her until they were half done. She told them half was enough, so it's not a full basement, but we're grateful for what we've got. That's why none of the other cottages have one. Too much work and too disruptive to the land. When we opened Pine Time, we put a second refrigerator down there. Then Rozzie added another for Pine Time Parties."

"Food!" Rosalyn blurted. "I forgot to call Maeve, Violet, and Honey. Jayne, can you give Reeva a hand?"

"Sure." That gave me an opportunity to talk to her. "Give me two minutes to rope off the boathouse first."

It took six trips to bring everything from her SUV to the basement. By the time we were done, my hands were freezing from carrying all those refrigerated stainless steel pans, and my arms ached. My legs were strong from all the walking I did, but I needed to lift weights or do pushups or something to build up my wimpy arms. After putting all the food in the Pine Time Parties refrigerator and setting the non-perishable items on a folding banquet table, I offered Reeva a beverage.

"What's on your mind, Jayne?" Reeva unscrewed the cap from her iced tea. "I can tell something's bothering you."

I pointed at the sofa there in the basement. The one Tripp used to sleep on while working on the B&B renovation. "Do you have a few minutes to talk?"

"Sure I do." She took a seat. "What's going on?"

"Where to start? Crabby tourists, crabby villagers, or the flock of crows?"

"The crows are unusual," she agreed and waited for me to say more.

"While watching Jola and Drake wheel Colton off to the ambulance earlier, I couldn't help but think of Rae."

Reeva's hands went to her heart. She and Rae had been best friends as kids.

"Thinking of Rae," I continued, "brought back memories of all the people who have lost their lives since I moved here." I paused, giving them all a moment of silence.

"You are not the reason they died, Jayne. If that's what you're thinking."

I shook my head. "No, I know it wasn't because of me." Although, if I could have fixed the problems sooner like Gran wanted me to . . .

You can't fix five decades of troubles in one year, Logical Jayne said.

"This thing that happened to Colton doesn't feel like an

accident." I tapped my belly, echoing Mamie's earlier gesture. "It's possible one of the other guests did this to him, although I have no proof of that right now."

"Say what you're working up to," Reeva urged.

"Okay. Do you think the blessing we performed on The Well worked?"

"You think these things are connected?"

"I do." How to explain? "It feels like the blessing reset things, but not the way I expected it to. It's not like I thought we'd set off a magical pulse and create an instant utopia, but things seem almost worse in ways. Whatever happened to Colton only intensified the feeling."

She nodded thoughtfully. "Remember the mess you made here while renovating the house?"

Dirt and debris everywhere. "I remember. There was a point where I thought we'd made a horrible mistake."

"And a few months later, you had a beautiful home."

I got it. "Same thing for the village?"

"Similar thing. We got rid of the evil—"

"Are you sure?" I blurted. "Yes, we got rid of . . . *her*, but it feels like something is still here. Like maybe some of her followers are still lurking or something new has taken her place."

"It's okay to say her name."

I shook my head. "I prefer not to. Doing so gives her power."

She thought about my comments for a minute. "Do you remember how Briar compared blessing the well to prepping the ground for an organic garden?"

I did because it made a lot of sense. "She said it can take years of leaving the ground fallow to leach the chemicals from the soil and make it truly organic. The same concept would likely be true regarding the toxic negativity in The Well's water."

"Right. I think you may be on to something with your

reset theory. What we're feeling could be the growing pains of Whispering Pines changing."

"We? You feel it too?"

"There have been grumblings of dissatisfaction in the coven, which is unusual. Mostly it's the Maidens thinking their new Wiccan ways are better."

I told her about the group I'd spoken to in the commons yesterday.

She nodded. "They're trying to take over and push out me and the other Crones and our old-fashioned ways. Those in the Mother stage, they're kind of stuck in the middle."

"What do we need to do?"

"*We* don't need to do anything. I understand River's directives to be that Martin and Jagger will take care of tourist problems. Your job is to deal with the non-witch villager issues. Mine is to handle wayward witches."

I glanced at the beautiful triple moon goddess pendant she always wore. A gorgeous gray moonstone represented the full moon and was flanked by two silver crescent moons. Small pentacles and tiny silver dots around the moons stood for stars and planets. Her pendant was far more intricate than the star I always carried in my pocket or clipped to my waistband, but it was just as much a badge. First Dulcie, then Briar, then Morgan, now Reeva. The coven's High Priestess was the witchy law enforcement for the village.

"Yes," I agreed, "my task is to deal with the villagers and be the village manager." I sighed. "On top of running a B&B."

"You're young. You can handle it." She winked at me.

"This thing that happened to Colton, I'm going to monitor that too. I'll keep Martin informed, of course, but this one has a personal angle. That means I should probably stay out of it . . ."

"How is it personal?" She settled back, content to stay for

however long I needed her. "I can tell there's still more eating at you."

Reeva and Tripp had become very close over the last year or so. She hadn't quite taken over a mother role for him but had definitely become like a cherished aunt.

"Something happened between Tripp and Sunny four years ago." I gave her a quick recap of what I'd learned and what I was afraid of.

"Tripp loves and adores you."

A spot in the center of my chest warmed. "That's what Rosalyn said."

"Trust us. You need to talk to him about this."

"I tried to, but he won't say anything." I couldn't keep the irritation from my voice. "I told him I'd be patient, but I have the right to know. Don't I?"

She paused before answering. "You were engaged before coming here, weren't you?"

I released a little groan at the memory. "I was."

"Did you tell Tripp everything about your relationship with . . ."

"Jonah." It had been more than a year since I'd thought of him. "I didn't tell him *everything*. I did tell him the important parts, though."

"All at once?"

Message received. "Is this how you mothered Yasmine?"

She shrugged. "Probably."

"She was lucky to have you."

Reeva pressed her palms together. "Thank you."

"Give him time," I summarized. "Don't push for everything. At least not all at once. Got it."

"And trust in his love for you. I'm sure Sunny appearing not only at his business but at his home was the last thing he expected. It seems whatever happened between them was more than a couple of casual dates. You deserve to know some things, but only as much as he's willing to tell you. She was in his past, and as long as she stays there, that's the important thing."

I leaned across the sofa and gave her a hug. "Thank you."

"I should get back to Hearth & Cauldron." Half way up the basement stairs, she changed her mind. "You know, since I was scheduled to be here, maybe I'll take the afternoon off. Bee and Thistle can handle the shop. Or Bee can, at least."

"How's Thistle doing?"

"She *will* be fine. I hope. Right now, she reminds me of the disaster Keiko was when she first started working with me —a bit stubborn, not able to do much but wants to do everything." Reeva chuckled and continued up the stairs. "Her parents chose well when they named her. She's a pretty seventeen-year-old who can be quite prickly at times."

"You just described most seventeen-year-olds. But look at what Keiko has become."

"That's why I haven't booted Thistle out the door yet. She shows a lot of promise. Like my boarder did."

After Reeva left, I stopped in the kitchen to let Tripp know Meeka and I were headed for patrol duty. He wasn't there, though, and not in the apartment either. I taped a note to the refrigerator instead.

On the way to my car, I spotted Nell in the front yard taking pictures of their girls.

"Nell, can I talk to you for a minute?"

"About?" she asked while lining up a shot of the girls climbing all over the hay bales.

"About what happened to Colton."

Her arms dropped to her sides. "Can't you see I've got my hands full right now?" She indicated her three girls . . . who Bruce was keeping out of the tent while Rosalyn and her crew tried to set it up. Just in case. "How about later tonight when the girls are sleeping?"

Actually, I was happy with her answer. I'd rather not deal with anyone else from this group right now.

As I drove away from the house, I noticed three crows in the rearview mirror. They were standing together in the middle of the driveway. Then they seemed to follow Meeka and me, making me wonder if anywhere in this village was peaceful right now. Head into the village and deal with crows dropping pinecones on my head or stay here and get more attitude from the Swenson-Alexander clan. Prickly pinecones sounded less painful.

Chapter Ten

I ALMOST FORGOT TO STOP AT GUS'S TENT TO ASK HIM IF HE knew anything about what happened to Colton. It only took a couple of minutes to find his setup, mostly because Gus appeared to take the same route to and from his tent, resulting in a distinct pathway through the field grass and straight into the woods. So much for disguising himself by setting up deep in the trees. When we got to his tent, I was happy to see that he had at least listened to my other directions. There was no campfire, nothing sitting around the tent, no visible damage to the surrounding area.

"Gus? Are you in there?" I waited a few seconds and called his name again. "No one's home, Meeka. We'll try again later."

At the station, Martin was in his office. "Hey. Come on in and tell me what happened over there."

I settled into one of the two chairs across the desk from him. "This group is a real challenge for Rosalyn's first event."

"She called me last night before she went to bed and told me all about them."

"Oh, good. I can skip that part, then."

"What happened with our victim?"

I told him about finding Colton by the boathouse and how Drake and Jola rescued him. "They brought him to Unity to evaluate his injuries. I'll be surprised if he doesn't end up at the hospital. Before coming here, I spoke with Sunny and her parents. Sunny is the bride."

"And? What do you think?"

"It could have been an accident. Tripp and I were on the roof last night and saw him leaning against the sundeck railing. It's possible he fell, except the railing is high enough that a fall doesn't seem likely. He could have jumped in."

"But you don't think so."

I explained how he had been hanging from the boat cleat. "He was dry from his head almost to his waist. The only way that could have happened was if his shirt caught the cleat on the way down. He also had a nasty head wound." I tapped the left side of my head, right in the middle and above the ear. "There's nothing between the sundeck and the boathouse foundation that he could have hit his head on, so I don't think he jumped. Besides, the water is only four feet deep there. If he had jumped, he probably would have ended up with a broken leg or paralysis."

"Do you know what his injuries are?"

"No, I don't. I'll check with Jola or Drake."

"The most likely scenario is that someone hit him and pushed him, then."

"Yes, except there were no signs of a scuffle and no blood on the sundeck. Not a single drop. Tripp took dozens of pictures of Colton and the scene at ground level for me, and I took pictures of the sundeck."

"Good," Martin said with a nod. "Maybe Jagger will find something while processing the scene."

I nodded. "I can't believe there wasn't any blood. Colton had plenty on him. Whoever did this must have cleaned up afterward."

"Unless he didn't fall from the deck."

I blinked at him. "Hadn't considered that. Maybe he was thinking he'd take the fishing boat out and ended up in a fight with someone who hit him and then pushed him in the lake." Other possibilities started circling through my mind. I shooed them away for now.

"Okay, back to this head wound. You feel it could only happen if someone hit him?"

"If he fell from the sundeck, yes. Like I said, there's nothing protruding from the building between the deck and the foundation. *If* he hit his head on the foundation, I would have found blood there."

"Right. And there was nothing in the water he could have fallen on?"

"Correct. And like I said, he was only wet to here." I held my hand to the bottom of my ribcage. "So it's not like he landed in the water and was trying to climb out."

He narrowed his eyes, envisioning the scene. "I'll keep thinking on this one."

"And I'll keep interviewing the wedding guests."

"Should you? I mean, someone should, but should it be you? Rosalyn told me about Tripp's connection to the bride."

Of course she did. "I've already spoken with Sunny. If I was going to have a hard time being impartial, it would have been with her."

"What did you learn?"

"She was upset but not as emotional or concerned for her husband's well-being as I'd expect. I mean, she planned an event to celebrate their love . . ." My words trailed off.

"What are you thinking?"

"That I'm not sure I believe her. She planned this event, but I don't see them as being an in-love couple. Neither does Rosalyn. We can't figure out why she wanted to do this. Unless it was to prove her suspicion that Colton doesn't really want to be married to her."

"Why do you think that?"

"Because Tripp and I overheard Colton basically tell her that last night."

Martin's eyebrows shot up. "Feelings confirmed."

"*And* when I was talking to her earlier, she flat out said marrying him was a mistake."

"This was an awfully expensive way to get a divorce, if that's what she's after."

"Exactly." Why *did* she set all this up, then?

"I hear and believe you," Martin assured me, "but I think Jagger or I talking to her as well might be a good idea."

"Might be. I don't believe I will have any issues talking with the rest of them."

The look he gave me said he reserved the right to speak to them as well.

"In other news," Martin said, blessedly segueing on to something else, "we've got a crow problem."

"We talked about that yesterday. Kind of. They're everywhere. Three of them followed me out of the driveway this morning like they were going to run me off the road and steal my lunch money."

Martin chuckled at that. "You mentioned the mess they were making around The Well and Pentacle Garden, but you didn't say they're becoming a physical problem for people too."

"I did. I told you they dropped pinecones at Meeka and me. You didn't want to talk about birds, though, so I didn't get to tell you how upset India was that her customers were being bombed."

He opened a file on his laptop and noted that. "Well, they've also been harassing the circus animals and swooping at people along the midway up there. There haven't been any reported injuries yet, but the patrons are a little scared and a lot unhappy. Creed says they're going to install nets along the midway to stop the swooping."

"That's a good idea. We've got those poles in place around the commons for stringing fairy lights. We could do netting as well. That would at least take care of the commons area. We'd need *a lot* of netting, though."

"Glad to hear you've got ideas already. Check into that option and report back to me. It's officially your problem to deal with."

I gave him a salute and headed off on patrol.

With tomorrow being Litha, the crowd in the commons was growing larger by the hour. There was a line of people waiting to get inside Treat Me Sweetly. Sugar and Honey told me once that checking out those who wanted pastries or other baked goods didn't take long, but scooping ice cream was a slower process. Good thing their niece, Telly, came on board last summer. It would take the sisters forever to get through that line if it was just the two of them. They could barely keep up even with Telly's help.

Before I forgot, I headed to Ye Olde Bean Grinder to let Violet know we needed more coffee for Pine Time, except they also had a line out the door. I carried Meeka inside to prevent her paws from getting stepped on.

Basil, Violet's brother, took the steady stream of orders while she calmly prepared one drink after another. The high school boy they hired this season to keep the creamer and sugar table stocked and the small sitting area clean was also working non-stop. Like most shops did, they needed more help.

"I need to reload the pickup shelf in back," Violet told me. "I'll do that when I get a break. Take what you need and let me know how much to charge you for."

"Great. Thanks, Violet. I'll stop back when I'm done with patrol."

She gave a nod, indicating she'd heard me, then handed me an extra-large mocha with a double-pump of vanilla and extra whipped cream. My favorite drink. How'd she make it so fast? Then she added a bag of biscuits for Meeka.

One thing I loved about being a deputy and River's village manager was that I got to interact with the villagers much more than I did as sheriff. What I didn't love was hearing pretty much the same things every day. Some loved the improvements he was making, others hated them. Some appreciated knowing a multi-billionaire considered villager safety and comfort a priority. Others felt things were fine as they were and wanted him to leave everything alone. The role also helped me build trust with the residents. They knew Gran's plan was for me to take over for her and that I'd do my best to keep River on the path she envisioned for Whispering Pines. But the truth was, regardless of whether they liked his changes, it was now his village. He could do whatever he wanted.

One controversial change he made had to do with lodging. River was a businessman and knew Whispering Pines survived and thrived on tourist dollars. Last year, when the tourists' prime complaint was about the lack of lodging, he came up with a plan. Since the villagers owned their homes but rented the land the structures occupied, he offered discounts on land rental to those who left during the peak season and agreed to rent their cottages to tourists. It was such a great offer, villagers who didn't normally leave took advantage of it this year. While his plan solved the problem of not having enough lodging, it created the problem of not having enough people to work in the shops or with village services.

Coming up with a solution for this issue filled my thoughts, especially while I wandered around on patrol. I was so deep in thought about it today, I nearly collided with a tourist near one of the Pentacle Garden points. This woman was very thin in a fine-boned rather than sickly way and was dressed all in black—wide-legged flowy pants, ankle boots, long-sleeved shirt with a ballerina neckline, and a wide-brimmed hat. I could just make out strands of ink-black hair beneath the hat. Maybe she had a sun allergy and needed to stay covered up? Her skin was so pale it was almost white, which made her black lipstick and long, pointed black fingernails that much more dramatic.

"I'm so sorry," I told her, stopping just in time.

"Don't worry, no harm done." Her voice was surprisingly deep. I'd expected a higher-pitched chirping sound to come from such a bird-like waif of a woman.

Nearby, a little girl was about to pick a flower from the garden, so I pointed out the *Please Do Not Pick the Flowers* sign to her father. When I turned back, the woman was gone. Swallowed up by the crowd.

"No harm done," I told myself and returned to my previous thoughts.

We were, overall, a group who liked our privacy, and while everyone was happy to have more income, it was becoming almost too much for some of the more introverted villagers. This was true for some tourists too. People came to the woods for peace and relaxation, but according to those I spoke with while on patrol, especially those who had been here in previous years, that wasn't the case anymore. Days in the village were sometimes stressful rather than joyful, with folks snapping at each other rather than getting along.

Had providing more lodging actually backfired, or was this due to the growing pains Reeva and I talked about? Either way, we needed to try something different. I thought about limiting entrance, although I wasn't sure how we'd do that. Another option was to shorten the season to Memorial Day through Labor Day like the rest of the country. Except, our Samhain celebration in October drew witches and witch wannabes from everywhere. We didn't even have to promote that one because witches were really good at spreading word about witchy things to their witchy friends.

"And," I said to Meeka, "shortening the season by two months would really affect the businesses income."

"Talking to yourself?"

I blinked to find we were standing in front of Shoppe Mystique. Keiko had just come out, and River followed a few seconds later. I expected he would somehow know I'd been thinking about him and pull me aside to chat. Instead, he held a hand up in a wave and moved on without even a, "Good morning, Manageress." That was odd.

Meeka immediately pressed her little body against Keiko's legs, and Keiko bent to give her a belly rub.

"How's it going at the Unchurch?" I asked. "Are you tired of people asking you that?"

"A little," she replied, "but I'm happy to say they won't have to for much longer."

I gasped in excitement. "You got your license?"

She stood, held her arms out to the side, and gave a dramatic, low curtsy. Then she shot back up again. "I got the email yesterday. My certificate is in the mail."

"You're ready, then."

"The outside is done, and we're putting the finishing touches on some things inside. I'm beyond grateful for Reeva and Ruby's help with the design and can't wait for everyone to see it. We'll have an open house for the villagers next week. I thought about putting up a message on the Community Board, but then we'd get a bunch of tourists coming. Acorns & Oaks isn't for them."

A thrill rushed through me. "That's the name you decided on?"

"Yep. Acorns & Oaks Dayplace."

After numerous villagers were accused of grossly unacceptable behavior last year, River kicked them out. One of those people was Sister Agnes. When she left with little more than two suitcases in tow, her Unchurch—more a spiritual retreat center than a church—was left vacant. At that same time, River declared Keiko Shen to be our newest official villager. After a few months, she asked for permission to turn the Unchurch into a daycare for villagers' kids.

"This will be for villagers only," she insisted in her presentation. "If people are here on vacation with their children, they should be with their children."

This would help those villagers who wanted to work in the shops but had no one to take care of their little ones. After reviewing Keiko's incredibly detailed plan, River wholeheartedly approved the conversion of the Unchurch. The only hiccup along the way was that the coven had to bless the property three times to rid it of the darkness hanging around before Keiko felt fully comfortable there.

Was that the problem with The Well? Did we need to bless it again?

"I love the name," I told Keiko. "Really."

She gestured at Shoppe Mystique. "I just met with Morgan and River. Juniper and Talon are thirteen months old now, toddling all over the place, and driving Briar batty." She leaned closer to me. "Apparently the twins escaped their playpen the other day, and it took Briar an hour to find them hiding in a bean teepee. She was so frustrated she brought them over to Blackbird Cottage and left them with River. He handed them over to his assistant because he had one conference call after another that day."

I bit back a laugh. "That couldn't have gone well. Josephine's maternal skills only extend to her plants. As for the little escape artists, Briar told me she can't get anything done in the garden, so she's been pushing Morgan to hire a nanny."

"That person was going to be me, and then I decided to turn it into an actual business." Keiko pushed her shoulders back proudly. "We just signed the contract. The twins are my first official students."

"And what about the Oaks side of the business?"

"That's Uncle Krys' realm. He got so excited when I told

Reeva about my idea for the daycare, he said he wanted to set up a senior section too. It was part of his motivation to move here."

Reeva was over-the-moon excited when her uncle agreed to move to the village shortly before Yule.

"Since I don't want to deal with kids on stairs," Keiko continued, "I suggested the oldsters take over the second floor."

"I assume you'll have help."

"Yep. I hired a few villagers who also have kiddos in need of entertainment. They're not only happy for their little ones to have playmates, they're excited to be around other adults during the day. As for Uncle Krys, he says instead of hiring people, his floor will be self-sustaining. He wants a different activity in each room, like classes, crafts, games, book discussions . . . He's recruiting villagers to manage a room in lieu of a monthly membership."

"Congratulations on your new venture, Keiko. I thought it sounded like a great idea from the start. Not to jinx anything, but are there any issues I need to know about?"

"Crows."

I heard a few of them calling out from the treetops. "What about them?"

"What's it called when birds gather to sleep?"

"Roosting?"

"Right. They've been roosting on the tower. I was heading home last night and noticed the peak was a mass of black birds. River says they've been hanging out around Blackbird Cottage too."

I chuckled, inappropriately, at the irony of that as I pulled my notepad out of its cargo pocket. "Martin just assigned the crow issue to me to deal with. I'll add Acorns & Oaks and Blackbird Cottage to the list of problem areas. Speaking of that tower, I'm surprised you didn't tear it down during renovations."

"I considered it, but when Krys started talking about a senior area, we decided to gut it and put in an elevator like you did at Pine Time." She stopped talking suddenly, and then her face lit up like a spotlight had been aimed at her. "Oh my Goddess."

Chapter Eleven

Keiko gave a happy little squeal and ran past me. I turned to see what had excited her so much and watched her practically tackle-hug Lily Grace.

After her mom died last May, Lily Grace gave herself time to mourn and asked for a deferment to starting veterinary school. The college was understanding and said she could start next year instead. Then, when her vardo was set on fire resulting in fortune teller Elody's death, Lily Grace checked out to the point I was worried she'd never be herself again. She divided her time between her boyfriend, Oren, and helping at the circus. By Yule, though, she'd had enough of well-meaning villagers and smothering grandmothers constantly asking her how she was doing. She decided it was time to get out of the village and get on with her life. The college helped her out again and agreed to her entering the veterinary program during the second half of the school year.

"When did you get back?" I gave the young fortune teller a hug after Keiko released her. Lily Grace froze mid-hug, then gave me an extra tight squeeze before stepping away with a grin on her face. She had read me. "What did you see?"

"Nothing," she said in a way that clearly meant she'd seen something. "I got home about two weeks ago. Been helping Igor with the circus animals and earning internship credits. Gotta make up for lost time." She paused before adding, "And I've been working on another new vardo."

"Will you be doing readings too?" She had changed her mind on so many things so many times, I didn't know what her plans were anymore.

She shrugged. "Since I'll be interning at the circus for the summer, I figured I'd bring the vardo up there and use it as a teensy-tiny home, but who knows."

Lily Grace had a long, complicated history with the village in general and her fortune teller grandmothers in particular. I was proud of her for taking control of her life. They'd always welcome her back at The Fortune Tellers' Triangle if she changed her mind again.

"So what are we talking about?" she asked Keiko and me.

"The crow problem," Keiko answered.

"Oh, I've got a possible solution for that," Lily Grace said in a *you should have asked me* way.

"You have an answer for attacking crows?" Keiko asked. "Did you just happen to learn about them this year?"

Lily Grace ticked classes off on her fingers. "This year was statistics, genetics, journalism, and organic chemistry. I wanted zoology and physics but have to wait until next semester. Anyway, when Credence said they wanted to suspend nets over the midway, I figured that would protect people's heads from beaks, talons, and pinecones but wouldn't take care of the problem. So I did some research. That's why I have an answer."

It amused me to no end that the young woman who grew up surrounded by spirituality was such a science and animal nerd. She'd had a horse that lived at the circus with the other horses since she was ten. Something I never knew until this past winter. Sir Oreo of the Forest, aka Oreo, was a black and white Gypsy Vanner, which was basically a smaller version of a Clydesdale with a flowing mane and tail.

"Please," I said regarding the crows, "enlighten us."

"They usually attack because they're defending their territory. There have always been a few crows around here but never a flock this big. They showed up suddenly, and the attacks are happening all over instead of in a specific area, so it doesn't seem to be a territory thing."

"Unless they consider the entire village to be their territory," I suggested.

"That's possible," she agreed. "Crows will also attack if they feel threatened. I read articles about crows targeting a certain person who had accidentally killed one of the flock members. Same thing with another person who threw something at a crow that was harassing a robin's nest."

"You're saying crows hold grudges?" Keiko asked.

"Big time. Another article mentioned a woman who hadn't done anything but was getting dive-bombed every time she went out for a run. Turned out the birds were doing the same thing to other joggers who had blond ponytails."

"In other words," Keiko concluded, "someone with blond hair must have done a bird wrong and they took it out on every blond they spotted on the path."

"Right."

"This is interesting," I said, "but how does this help us fix our problem?"

"Getting there," Lily Grace singsonged impatiently. "One of the blond women decided to try to distract the birds by leaving a trail of peanuts behind her."

"Feed the birds," I murmured. "Did it work?"

"Not only did it work," Lily Grace answered, "it turned the relationship around. The birds still followed her but acted more like protectors, preventing other birds, dogs, and even random men from bothering her. Then one of them brought her a gift. It landed on the path directly in front of her and set down a candy wrapper."

I pondered this option for a moment. "That really is fascinating. And while it doesn't explain why they're suddenly attacking us, feeding them might be worth a try." Then again, if we let the attacks continue, it might reduce the tourist population. No, that's not the right answer. "This gives me some things to think about. Thank you."

Just then, Shoppe Mystique's door opened, and Briar held it so Morgan could push their double-deep stroller out. While Morgan maneuvered the twins down the ramp, Briar descended the stairs to me.

"Jayne. Blessed be."

"I was just talking with Keiko." I gave her a quick hug. "I hear this is a big day for you."

"It's a good day," Briar corrected. "The big day will come next week when I'm no longer on grandchild duty. Love the little rugrats dearly and don't mind watching them on occasion, but I'm well past this taking care of humans every day phase of life."

Briar's passion was her garden. Morgan told me her mom's energy used to be endless. Then Briar suffered a stroke about two and a half years ago and now got very tired after a day of tending plants. The only real sign that something wasn't quite right was the slight slur when she spoke. Even that was getting better, though.

"Hello, you," Morgan greeted me while giving the stroller to her mother.

"I was just about to come in and see you. Do you have a few minutes to chat?"

She kissed her toddlers then stood and sighed, disappointed. "I'd love nothing more than to talk with you, but the shop is so busy . . ."

"I understand. Everyone is swamped today." My personal problems would have to wait.

"We'll get together for tea soon. Or maybe something stronger." She glanced at the packed commons area. "I'm hoping traffic will ease a little after the Litha celebration."

"Both things would be nice," I replied. "Tell me when you've got time. Maybe we can arrange dinner."

She kissed Briar's cheek. "Try to rest this afternoon, Mama. It's okay to put them in their playpen and close the top if you need a few minutes. They'll be fine."

When Morgan had gone back inside, Briar told me, "River made a lid for the little daredevils' playpen. I know it's for their safety, but I feel like I've locked them in a cage when I use it."

"You're heading home?" I asked. When she nodded, I took the stroller and told her I'd walk with her.

"Don't you need to patrol?"

I shrugged. "I haven't gone past the Meditation Circle in a while. It's a short stroll to your cottage from there. I also need to analyze the crow problem throughout the village. Martin asked me to deal with it."

"What's bothering you, Jayne?" she asked in the motherly tone that, depending on the situation, made me feel either comforted or like a stupid kid.

"How do you—"

"I just know."

So once again I repeated what was happening with Rosalyn's first event.

"And you know for a fact Tripp and the bride had a relationship of some kind in the past."

I liked how she added *of some kind*. It softened the blow a bit. "I've never seen anyone hug a stranger or casual acquaintance that way before. And yes, I tried to talk to him."

"But he's still processing. Give him time." And with that, we were done discussing Tripp and his ex . . . whatever she was. "What else?"

We entered the curving ramp that led to the bridge that

crossed the highway. After too many near misses with tourists trying to dart across the two-lane road to get to the Meditation Circle and hiking paths, River made a change. He had village services install an aesthetically pleasing fence that would force folks to either take the bridge or walk a half mile through the woods to an open spot. Over the next off-season, they would put in the same kind of setup by the parking lot across from Unity.

As we climbed the ramp and crossed the bridge, I told Briar about my village reset concern.

Echoing almost word for word what Reeva had said, she agreed it did sound like a sort of reset but that The Well blessing did what it was meant to do.

"Patience, dear girl. Now, what's really going on? It's not The Well or that an old flame came to town. You've got my undivided attention, let's dig in. What's eating at you?"

"I . . . I don't know."

"You do. Whatever it is, it's been hovering in the background all winter. That Jayne sparkle hasn't been there."

She wiggled her fingers at me, making me laugh.

"I sparkle?"

"When you're happy, you do. Why aren't you happy?"

"I don't—"

"We're going to run out of time. When we get to the cottage, I'll have to feed, change, and put these two down for their naps. Then I'm going to lose myself in my garden for as long as possible. Why aren't you happy? What's the first word that pops into your head?"

"Guilt," I blurted.

"There we go. If you want to get your sparkle back, let's work this through. Don't overthink it. What do you feel guilty about?"

Before I could stop myself, I said, "Iris, Zinnia, and Isobel."

Iris died last year after eating a poisoned scone. Isobel died from a blow to the head with a rolling pin. Zinnia was stabbed with a pitchfork and thankfully survived but was understandably traumatized by the event.

Briar let out a soft groan. "Why on earth would you feel guilty about them?"

"I should have been able to stop those events."

"How?"

My chest tightened. "What happened to them circles back to my decision to lock Flavia in that tower. If I wouldn't have—"

"Dear Goddess, Jayne." She almost sounded angry. "How many times do we need to discuss this? You could not possibly have known."

"But if I would have done the right thing—"

"The right thing according to whom?"

"The law. If I would have sent her away after Rae died, like I should have done, those events last summer wouldn't have happened."

"Flavia wasn't responsible for those events. Her groupies were. Whether you locked her up here or let her get taken to prison, they would still have done the things they did." Briar quieted, and the sound of our feet crunching on the gravel became overwhelmingly loud. "I've seen this kind of thing happen during the off-season. We have less to keep us busy, and dark thoughts move in. This is why all of us getting together as often as possible is a priority over the winter. During this one, do you recall what you said when one of us would ask what you were up to?"

I thought for a few seconds. "Not really. I mostly did B&B things to get ready for this season. I read some books Rosalyn recommended. Tried a new weaving technique at Twisty Ruby thought I might enjoy."

Briar shook her head. "You said you were doing 'whatever Tripp or River asked'."

"What's wrong with that?"

Ignoring the question, she pressed on. "You read books *Rosalyn* gave you and did crafts *Ruby* suggested. Now you're dealing with crows because Martin told you to."

"I'm fine dealing with crows."

"Should you be? That sounds like a job for Igor or possibly Jagger. Not someone with your level of experience."

I shrugged in reply as a feeling of shame moved in.

"You became complacent over the off-season and let others make your decisions for you. When is the last time you did anything for yourself?"

"Well, the weaving—"

"Would you have come up with that if Ruby hadn't suggested it?"

I sighed in frustration. "I don't know, Briar. Maybe. I enjoy weaving. What's wrong with trying things other people suggest?"

"Nothing if they're activities you truly want to be doing." She paused, tilted her face to the treetops, and took a deep breath of the pine-scented air. Mimicking her, I did the same. "The problem is you seem to have lost confidence in yourself. Is your wand finished?"

The change in topic threw me for a moment. I'd forgotten all about my wand. After Yule, things really slowed down in the village. We had only a few guests per month at Pine Time, and while we all tried to get together on Sundays, there weren't any big celebrations. Imbolc on February first marked the spring equinox. We made a special dinner and got all excited that the days would start getting longer, but this far north, it was hard to plan gatherings in February because the weather was so unpredictable.

Rosalyn and Martin went to Reeva's house for Imbolc, and we got together with the Barlow-Carrs. While we were there, I asked Morgan and Briar about setting up an altar. Was I becoming Wiccan? I had no idea, but part of me, probably the middle-of-winter bored silly part of me, thought putting together an altar sounded like a good idea. They told me I needed to gather altar tools first and suggested I dig through Reeva's stash of estate sale items. There would almost certainly be something in there that I liked.

"Or you can make your own tools," Briar encouraged.

"Make your own wand, for sure," Morgan insisted.

"How?" I asked.

"Wands are made of wood. When you think of wood, what comes to mind?"

"Pine," I said instantly.

Morgan smiled and nodded. "Pine offers healing, fertility, and protection."

"Go for a walk in the woods," Briar instructed. "Tell the trees you want to make a wand and ask them to donate a branch. Bring it home, study it until you can see your wand, then start whittling."

Two years earlier, I would have bent over laughing at being told to ask a tree for a branch. But I did it, and after stating my intentions about two dozen times and walking a good half mile into the forest, a branch fell to the snow-covered ground behind me.

"I'm not quite done with it," I told Briar now. "And setting up an altar was something I did for myself. No one suggested it."

Briar held my gaze, the smallest of smirks turning her lips. "How much do you still have to do? Is it at least wand shaped?"

"Yes," I replied in a bratty tone. "I was technically done with it months ago. It doesn't *feel* done, though."

"Go home and sit with it. Chant the words *healing* and *protection* in your mind or out loud, your choice. After that, if the wand still doesn't feel complete, that's okay. You can do more to it later. I often add or make changes to items I've had for decades. We change over the years; it's okay for our tools to change with us. Morgan mentioned us getting together.

Come to the cottage tonight after seven. The twins will be in bed by then. And bring Tripp. River needs man time."

And with that, we arrived at the front gate of the Barlow-Carr cottage.

"Go on." She swished her hand in a shooing gesture. "My garden is calling. It's me time."

Chapter Twelve

WHEN BRIAR BARLOW GAVE AN ASSIGNMENT, IT SHOULD GET top priority, but everything considered, I checked to see if Tripp or Rosalyn needed me for anything first when I got home from patrol.

In the front yard, the event tent was fully decorated, which honestly felt a little sad. Sunflowers and wildflowers were woven into the grapevines twisted around tent poles, embellished the wagon wheel light fixtures hanging down the center of the tent, and created beautiful centerpieces on the tables. Outside, bouquets in a variety of containers were set among hay bales, on top of old oak barrels, and among other small farm equipment I couldn't identify.

"That's a lot of flowers," I noted.

Rosalyn nodded. "Sunny said there couldn't be enough of them. Ruby agreed, but I think I might have achieved peak flowerage."

"Where did all this stuff come from?"

"Sunny brought some of it from home, Reeva had a few of the pieces in her storage locker, and I borrowed the rest from area farmers."

"I see why Harlan thought they could have done this on

their ranch. I'm not criticizing. To each their own, but that's *a lot* of flowers."

"And there's more in the backyard," Rosalyn noted. "Mamie says Sunny will love it. Fortunately, I've got Ruby to consult with on these kinds of things. That woman is the living definition of more is better."

"Are you done? Is it ready if the event can go on? Not that I think it will."

I told her how I'd stopped at Unity before coming home and found Sanjay there alone.

"Drake and Jola took Mr. Alexander to the hospital," Sanjay told me. "That head injury was worse than it appeared."

"I thought it *looked* pretty bad," I replied. "Any idea what could have caused it?"

Sanjay hesitated before saying, "I don't like to make assumptions, so this is off the record, but from the position Drake and Jola said they found him in, I don't see any way that injury happened from a fall off the deck."

He was confirming my suspicions. "You think someone hit him."

"*If* that's what happened, they hit him hard."

Which would indicate anger. Or possibly adrenaline-fueled fear. Who was afraid of or angry enough at Colton to cause that kind of injury? Unfortunately, based on what I'd learned about the guy, a lot of people were. Even family members.

In reply to my question about being ready for an improbable ceremony, Rosalyn said, "There's nothing more I can do right now. Reeva, Honey, and the others are on standby if it becomes a go."

"And if it doesn't become a go? What happens to all this stuff?"

Rosalyn frowned sadly. "No refunds. Like I said earlier, it's all Sunny's, so she's free to take it. I don't know otherwise. Set out the food in the commons and let the tourists have at it?

Activate the call tree and invite the villagers over for a party and everyone is required to take home an armful of flowers? For now, I'm going to the office for my afternoon shift."

Inside, I found Tripp in the kitchen sitting at the dinette just finishing the last bites of a ham-and-cheese sandwich.

"Hi," he said with the sandwich halfway to his mouth. "I wasn't sure when you'd be home."

"That's okay. I can make my lunch."

He sighed. "I wasn't saying you couldn't."

"And that's not what I was implying." I sat next to him. "What's going on? The last time I saw you in a mood like this was when you found out that your mom had died."

From a drug overdose in a grimy bathroom in a bar somewhere in the middle of Missouri. He had been, understandably, devastated.

He shook his head and didn't reply to my question.

"They took Colton to the hospital."

"Yeah, I know. Sunny, Victoria, and Harlan stopped here first and then went to be with him."

"So no ceremony," I mused.

"Sunny hasn't seen the completed setup yet," he said with a territorial tone that might not have actually been there. "Rosalyn is supposed to leave it up."

I waited while he finished his sandwich and iced tea, then asked, "Tell me what you know about these folks."

"Told you, I met them while I was wandering the country. I stayed in Fargo for a bit. Did a few odd jobs . . ." He gave a little more information this time but not anywhere near enough.

"Look, this is becoming a legal issue. We don't know exactly what happened to Colton yet, but Sanjay felt that his injuries were not conducive to a fall. The doctors at the hospital will hopefully be able to tell us more."

"Not conducive," Tripp repeated. "Meaning someone—"

"Hit him hard with something and then knocked or

pushed him over the railing. If he dies, this will become a murder or manslaughter investigation. To save time, I'm treating it that way now. What do you know that might help?"

He pushed away from the table and took his dishes to the dishwasher. "I don't know anything. Nothing that could help with your investigation. They're just people I knew four years ago." Then softly added, "Or thought I did."

"Please tell me what happened between you and them. It seems like it was something not great."

He held onto the edge of the countertop, his head hanging forward. I thought he was working up to something, but then he muttered, "Not now, Jayne."

Time to change the subject. "We're supposed to go to the Barlows' tonight. Any time after seven."

He groaned and started to object.

"You don't have to socialize with Briar and Morgan," I snapped, growing weary of his attitude. "They're going to help me with . . . something." I didn't even know why I was supposed to go there. Just following Lady Briar's instructions to show up with my wand. "Apparently River needs guy time."

That made a difference. Seemed Tripp had had enough of the womenfolk. "Fine. I'm going for a hike."

And he left. Without asking either me or Meeka to go with him.

After changing into shorts and a Pine Time T-shirt, I was on the way to my loft above the garage when I came across Nell sitting on the back patio. She had her phone in her hands and was tapping on the screen. Posting to her social media pages, I guessed. I glanced around and didn't see the girls or Bruce anywhere. I'd hoped I might run into more wedding people to interview, so I had tucked both my notebook and my voice recorder into a pocket.

"Is this a good time to talk?" I asked gently, prepared for her to snap at me again.

"Hang on." She gave her phone's screen a final flurry of taps. "Sure, let's talk. Bruce is upstairs with the girls. He's going to take them to the public beach. Hopefully the fresh air and running around will exhaust them and they'll sleep like rocks tonight."

I got the distinct impression that Nell Lockwood didn't enjoy being a mother. Every time I'd seen her with them, however, she was taking their pictures. Her relationship with her daughters wasn't what I wanted to talk to her about, though. I took out the recorder, informed her that I was going to record our conversation, hit the go button, and stated her name, the day, and time.

"I assume you know they took Colton to the hospital," I said while setting the device on the loveseat cushion next to me.

She nodded. "Suppose your next question will be, do I know what happened to him. I don't. Not a clue."

"I couldn't help but notice how much you all argue with each other. Is it always like that or only when the two families are together? Did something happen on the way here from North Dakota?"

"No, nothing happened. Yes, it's usually like this. The arguing mostly happens when our husbands are around. Sunny's and mine."

"Bruce causes problems?" That shocked me.

She laughed in an annoyed way. "Yeah, I know, because he's such a mild-mannered guy, right? Those who have been married or in a committed relationship for longer than a couple of months always tell those who are in a new one that you can't change your partner. I never wanted Bruce to change. When we were dating, he had swagger and was a macho, sexy guy." She wiggled her shoulders imitating a macho man. "When Ellie was born, he softened. Then he softened more with Talia. When I found out I was pregnant for the third time, I prayed it was a boy who would infuse some testosterone back into the family." She shook her head. "I know how that sounds, and I don't care. Bruce is a good dad, but he's become an absolute girly dishrag of a husband."

Whoever hit Colton, if that's what happened, likely did so in anger. Nell seemed like a very angry person.

"What about Colton?"

Nell made a face, like she'd just tasted something sour. "I can't stand Colton. Never have been able to. He brings the wrong kind of energy to the family. Bruce might be a dishrag, but at least he's not lazy. If I have to give him credit for something, it's that he works really hard to take care of his family. Colton is a lazy, spoiled mama's boy."

She went on for another minute about how Colton always got others to do things for him and would get secret stashes of money from Victoria while Sunny drove herself nuts trying to pay their bills. There was definite love for her sister in both her words and tone that I hadn't seen in her actions. Had Nell taken out her anger over her own life on Colton? Was she defending her sister?

"How do you know his mother is giving him money?"

In a very hush-hush way, Nell said, "We were all together one time, and Colton was complaining about being broke. Dinah mumbled something about him getting plenty from Vic so shouldn't be, not realizing I'd heard her. I confronted her about it. Dinah does the ranch's accounting and said she noticed large cash withdrawals but had no receipts explaining what they were for. She asked Victoria. Victoria told her the truth and threatened to accuse Dinah of stealing the money if she ever let the secret slip."

"Colton gets money from Victoria," I noted, "but

complained about the money Sunny spent on this event. Does Sunny know about the money he gets from his mother?"

"She doesn't have a clue." More compassion in her tone. "All she wants is for Clyde to have a happy life. She is so devoted to that boy. Absolutely adores him. Except for her occasional girls' nights out, when she leaves him with our mom, she's home alone with him every night."

"While Colton is . . ."

"At the bar building a massive tab by buying drinks for everyone."

"Do you know this for certain?" I needed facts, not speculation or slander because of bad blood.

"I know for certain. I had Bruce go to the bar one night on a spying mission, I guess you could say. He got there early so was at a table with a beer when Colton walked in and announced he was buying 'a round for the house, put it on my tab.' Then Colton proceeded to bet on pool or poker games he challenged people to, losing one after another until the bar closed. That's what the money Victoria gives him is for."

"And he does this often?"

"Far as I know."

"Any idea why he does that?"

"Bruce thinks he's trying to buy friends, and I agree. Colton doesn't have any. No real ones, at least. He doesn't understand that flashing Alexander money around doesn't help. Not when everyone else is struggling."

She never once mentioned how badly Colton treated people, like Mamie did. Did Nell not see it? Did she not agree with her mother? Abusers became really good at hiding their anger and/or violence. Victims got really good at covering up the truth. I saw and heard Colton's temper but had no physical proof of him being an abuser. Did he hide it from everyone else but show it around Mamie? She said she was afraid of him. Did Sunny agree with her mother's concerns?

I paused for a moment to write those questions in my

notebook, and when I looked up, Nell was on her phone again. She smiled at something on the screen, then noticed me waiting for her.

"Sorry." She pointed at the phone. "I got comments on my posts."

"What did you post about?"

"The girls, of course. That's what everyone wants to see."

"How old are they?"

"Ten, eight, and six. They're a handful, but we send them to day camp during the summer. Mom watches them when they're home, because Bruce and I help Dad manage the farm. I also run a booth at the local farmers' market. Biggest one in the county. Want to see?" Before I could reply, she handed me her phone, open to a social media page.

Her booth was bigger than the produce section at Sundry. At her urging, I scrolled through a few dozen pictures of her smiling, angelic-looking girls helping Mom with the booth. There were also a few well-timed shots of Bruce doing active *manly* things on the farm. Nell's personal life may not have been what she wanted, but she had created a perfect digital one on her social pages.

"That's very impressive." Knowing I was about to get a lesson on produce stalls, I handed her phone back to her. "I don't want to take up much more of your day. Is there anything else you feel I should know about Colton? Any thoughts at all on how he ended up injured and in the lake?"

She smiled at the curated pictures of the family on her phone so longingly, I almost felt bad for her. "No thoughts. Sorry."

"You don't think anyone from the group might have confronted him?"

"You mean hit him in the head at four-something in the morning?" She went through the lineup. "Mom, me, Dinah, and Arizona, we stay clear of him when he's like that. Sunny is tired of fighting so basically walks away when he gets bad.

Boone, never. Tex . . . I can't see it. Bruce? Don't make me laugh. Dad speaks his mind if it's something serious. If Harlan has something to say to his son, he'd just say it. He wouldn't sneak around in the dark."

She seemed very sure of her claims. Would other family members back her up?

"Is that it?" she asked.

"For now. I may have more questions later. Thank you for your thoughts. You said Bruce was going to take the girls to the beach?"

"Yeah. They should be down soon."

"I'd like to talk with him before they go. Would you mind sending him down here alone? Or I could go up and send the girls down to you. It should only take a few minutes."

Nell scowled as she dropped her hand holding the phone to her lap. Because she had to step away from her online family? Or because she had to watch her kids for a few minutes? That might be overly harsh.

"I'll send him down."

He arrived a minute later with a cautious smile on his face. "You wanted to talk to me?"

I motioned for him to sit in the chair his wife had vacated, pointed out the voice recorder, and informed him I would be recording our conversation.

"Anyone but you going to hear it?" He eyed the little gadget.

What was he planning to say? What didn't he want others to know? "I might play parts for the sheriff, but this is mostly for me. I prefer to record conversations so I can listen to what people tell me. I might miss something important if I'm constantly scribbling in a notebook."

"Okay, then." He relaxed.

As before, I stated his name, the date, and time, then said, "I'm trying to understand what might have happened to Colton Alexander."

He indicated he knew Colton had been taken to the hospital but not the extent of his head wound.

"I couldn't help but notice the arguments yesterday. They started as soon as you all got here and continued until you went to your rooms for the night. Is that normal, or did something happen before you got to the village?"

"That's pretty common when the families get together."

"Any particular reason for that?"

"Colton and his brothers. They're full-grown men and constantly poke at each other like kids. Sometimes like enemies."

"There are four brothers?"

"Yeah. No sisters."

"Does the poking go all four ways or do they take sides against each other . . ."

He shook his head. "Mostly it's the others going after Colton. He's pretty spoiled."

Consistency! Maybe I was getting somewhere. "How are their parents with him?"

Bruce looked around as though making sure we weren't being overheard, then spilled his guts. "Victoria babies Colton. Harlan, as far as I understand, has always been tough but fair with all four, but Victoria doesn't like him being hard on *her boys*. Colton, being the youngest, got away with a lot while he was growing up because the others, Victoria included, were busy turning the ranch into the business it is today. Since Colton was little, he couldn't do much physical work, so he wandered around the ranch and mostly got ignored and into trouble."

I couldn't recall ever being so grateful for the voice recorder. He spoke so fast, I never would have been able to write all the details.

"In other words," I reiterated, "the brothers and Harlan have been a team all along, and Colton sees the ranch as being the thing that left him on the outside."

Bruce agreed and seemed more than happy to talk about this. Like he had the knowledge trapped in his head for a while but had no one to share it with.

"You married into the Swenson family. How do you know all of this about the Alexanders?"

"Because we all grew up in the same town, and people in small towns like to talk. They also like to think that because they know a few things about someone they know everything and have the right to speak their minds about them. There's a lot of talking in the corners, if you know what I mean."

There was some of that here. Not that I was naïve, I knew the villagers gossiped, but their whisperings mostly happened behind closed doors, not out in public.

"You're trying to figure out who from this group could have caused that head injury." Bruce settled back in his chair, crossed his muscular arms, and a bit of the swagger and confidence Nell mentioned emerged. He seemed to like having the answers and being listened to.

"That's exactly what I'm trying to figure out," I agreed. "Because if Colton dies from those injuries—"

"Someone's getting charged with murder."

"If it was premeditated. Manslaughter if it was a heat of the moment thing. Any thoughts on who might have been angry enough to do this? And what they might have been angry about?"

He blew out a breath. "Like I said, there's always bickering going on. The brothers think it's fun to gang up on Colton, but if any of the four were angry enough to hit someone in the head, it would be Colton. You may have noticed, he's got a temper."

That's basically what Mamie told me. "I did notice. But it's unlikely that Colton hit himself."

"Right," he said with a chuckle. "Let's see . . . Harlan? I've never thought of him as a violent man. Ty, well, his arms are stronger than all of ours, so he could swing good and hard, but he couldn't get up those boathouse stairs. Boone, far as I can tell, has always tried to keep, or rather *get* Colton on the right path."

"What about Gus Lewis?"

That name shocked him. "Gus? He's here?"

"You didn't see him sneaking around?"

Bruce shook his head. "I've been too busy watching the girls to notice much of anything else."

Did anyone other than Mamie see him? If they did, were they hiding the fact for some reason? "Mamie says Sunny told him about the ceremony."

"I can't see Sunny doing that."

"She said he harassed her enough about where you all were going that she finally told him."

"Ah. To shut him up, yeah, I guess I could see that. I can guarantee she didn't invite him, though. He probably followed us here."

Followed them? Gooseflesh crawled up my back. "Is he stalking Sunny? Should I be concerned about him?"

Had I made a massive mistake by letting him set up a campsite?

Bruce looked confused by my question. "You mean, is he dangerous? Nah, he's more like a lovesick puppy."

I once had an excited puppy knock me to my back and then jump all over me when I knelt down to greet her. She scratched my arms and neck with her claws and got slobber all over me, but I understood the point Bruce was trying to make.

"Back to the group," I said. "You only mentioned the men."

He propped his right foot on his left knee while he thought. "Victoria is an obvious no. Unless she's got a dark, twisty side I've never seen. Mamie?" He glanced around, his bravado slipping a little. "I'm honestly not sure about Mamie. I know she doesn't like Colton, but I can't see her walloping him. I don't think Arizona would do anything, and I don't know Dinah well enough to have an opinion about her. Sunny is plenty mad at him for obvious reasons."

"You're missing one," I nudged.

"Who . . . Oh, Nell?" He thought some more. "Nell loves her sister, but I don't think she'd put herself in legal crosshairs for her."

An interesting way to put it. Again, I was grateful I had the recorder running.

Adopting a casual tone, I said, "I noticed you're the one who watches your girls most."

"Happy wife, happy life," he repeated the phrase from yesterday, his confident swagger fading a bit more. "That's our deal when we're away from home. Nell is responsible for them the rest of the time."

That's not how she made it sound. She said they worked the farm together, so Mamie watched the girls when they weren't at camp or in school. "What's a typical day for you?"

"Up at five, home shortly after five every day but Sunday. The farm is pretty big. Nowhere near as big as the Alexander Ranch, but it's still a lot of work. Sometimes I come in for lunch, but usually Mamie brings it out to us. Nell will, too, if she's not running the stall at the market."

Regarding this couple, I had no idea what their real story was. Was Nell actually a stressed-out mother of three active young girls who got to decompress when away from home? Not a bad arrangement if Bruce was on board with it. Or was he a wimp, and she cracked the whip? Either way, he looked like the star, and she came across as the pampered princess. Maybe that's what fit with her version of the perfect family and was what she wanted people to think.

Fortunately, figuring out their personal life wasn't important to the Colton issue. I was concerned with the blended family, and Nell's and Bruce's stories jibed enough to create a believable picture in that regard.

"Thanks for your time, Bruce. If you think of anything that might explain what happened, would you let me know?"

"Of course. I'll be here until . . ."

"Tomorrow. Even if we wanted to extend your reservations, we've got new people checking in on Monday afternoon."

That meant the time was ticking for me to talk with the rest of these folks. Sure, I could call them or set up video chats after they left, but interviews were best done face-to-face. Along with Nell and Bruce, I had spoken with Sunny, Mamie, and Ty. Harlan, Victoria, Boone, and Dinah were at the hospital with them. Where were Tex and Arizona? They always seemed to be lying low.

For now, I had a different assignment to complete.

"To the loft?" I asked Meeka who had been napping beneath the loveseat.

She yawned, stretched, and then got hit with the zoomies. In the time it took me to walk to the garage, she ran two laps around the ceremony setup in the backyard then once around the front yard.

"You're going to need another nap after all that."

She slogged up the stairs in agreement.

Chapter Thirteen

ONE OF THE WEAVING PROJECTS I'D WORKED ON AT RUBY'S craft shop over the winter was an altar cloth. Her winter project was to learn how to spin and dye wool. When I told her I wanted to make a cloth, she asked what colors I wanted and then dyed a few skeins for me using lake blue, pine green, bark brown, and misty gray. When the beautiful, variegated yarn was ready, she showed me how to do a technique called leno that created a beautiful lacey pattern. Fortunately, the wool was forgiving because I'd had to undo and redo the weaving a few times before I was happy with it. The table Gran had used for her altar sat beneath a window overlooking the lake. It was now covered with the cloth I made. That's also where my wand-in-process waited for me.

I had spent weeks carefully whittling and sanding the pine branch until it felt perfect in my hand. Then I carved elemental symbols into the handle—small stick-figure pine trees for earth, wavy lines for water, a feather for air, and a candle for fire. Then I added rustic-looking hearts to symbolize my love for this village and my life. Stick-figure people represented my family and friends. The wand was covered with tiny icons and appeared ready for a final light sanding and waxing, but it still didn't feel finished, and I couldn't figure out what was missing.

After lighting a candle scented with a blend of grapefruit, bergamot, and mint—to help with focus, Morgan insisted—I sat in my comfy chair and held my wand as Briar had suggested. I turned it over and over, and suddenly a voice in my head, that sounded a lot like Gran, asked which symbol represented me.

"The entire thing is me," I replied. "All of these icons show what's important to me."

You've got representations of the elements and the people in your life, but which one is Jayne?

I thought about that until a symbol appeared in my mind.

"Too arrogant," I dismissed and searched for a different one.

Stubbornly, the image reappeared and then flashed like the lights on top of a police car. Or like a guiding beacon?

The longer I thought about it, the more it started to feel right. With the pocketknife I'd used to do the whittling, I etched a star into the flat end of the handle. The beacon had shown me a pentacle, but that didn't feel right. And as Briar said, I could always make a change and add the circle around the star later if that felt right someday. Now when I held the wand, it would be like holding on to all that was important to me while still clearly seeing myself.

"Now it's done," I told Meeka who had been watching me curiously from the floor cushion I'd found among Gran's things and set out as a dog bed. "Time to sand and wax."

I didn't want to get sawdust all over my loft. Even a light sanding would result in dust everywhere, so I blew out the candle, gathered my sandpaper, wax, and a cloth, and headed outside. I was going to sit on the dock, but then I caught a glimpse of the sundeck. The ropes I'd hung to cordon off the area until Jagger could process the scene were gone, indicating Jagger had finished the job. We were free to go up there again.

Perfect. It felt appropriate to finish the wand in the place where my Whispering Pines journey had begun.

As I rubbed the sandpaper over the wood, I thought of my first days, weeks, and months living in the boathouse apartment while we renovated the house. I didn't have much because I had only planned to be here for a couple of weeks, so it was the perfect cozy place to restart my life.

After I finished sanding, I wiped off the residue and began the final stage of rubbing in a coat of wax. I recalled Briar's instructions to chant *healing* and *protection*. I laughed, internally, when she said that, but the longer I sat in silence, chanting the words in my head as directed, I started to feel like I actually needed healing. From what, though? The bad decisions I'd made in the past? Despite Briar's earlier scolding, I couldn't stop myself from thinking about Iris, Zinnia, and Isobel. Guilt once again settled over me. Maybe *forgiveness* was the better word to chant. I needed to forgive myself.

Protection was Briar's other word. What did I need protection from? Both Reeva and Briar felt The Well blessing had worked, and the turmoil we felt was the village going through a change. Maybe I needed protection from whatever was coming next? From the onslaught of thoughts that refused to leave me alone? They went all the way back to Frisky Fox . . . No, to the night Rosalyn was kidnapped at age fifteen.

The more I rubbed in the wax, the more the pine wood started to gleam. When I felt the wand was done, I looked up and saw my beloved trees swaying insistently despite the lack of wind at ground level. They were trying to tell me something, but I still couldn't hear them. Or was it that I didn't understand them? If that was the case, if I couldn't understand my trees, something really was wrong. With me? With the village? Both?

I could have sworn I'd seen three crows, probably the same ones that had followed me earlier, clinging to the branches in one of the swaying trees when a voice startled me, making me jump.

"Here you are." Tripp crossed the deck to where I sat in the corner farthest from the stairs. "I checked the office and your loft . . . What are you doing up here?"

I held up my wand like an offering. "This felt like the right place to finish this."

He took it, inspected every little carving, and smiled as I explained what each one meant. Then he looked deep into my eyes. "I'm sorry I've been so crabby lately. I shouldn't be taking things out on you."

What *things?* Instead of pressing, I simply nodded, accepting his apology.

"Dinner's ready," he said. "Or will be soon. I just put some salmon filets in the oven to poach. And I made a salad."

I wanted to ask him to talk about the past, but more than that, I just wanted to be with him. For us to be us again because we weren't right now. He was my safe place. My happy place. Usually.

"Let's go eat, then." I'd let the past go for now. "Don't let me forget to bring my wand tonight. Briar's going to teach me a spell or something. Apparently she feels I need to learn how to trust myself again."

Tripp didn't comment, but the slight acknowledging tilt of his head said he agreed with her. What did they see that I didn't?

He held out a hand to help me up from my cross-legged position, and we both stood there for a moment staring at the loveseat and chairs where we spent so many nights gazing up at the stars. We talked, got to know each other, and did our best to figure out the village.

When I looked away, the railing caught my attention. Specifically, the spot where Colton must have gone over. I looked down at the cleat his shirt had snagged on.

"New perspective?" Tripp asked, his voice tight. He

couldn't say even two words regarding Colton without anger seeping in.

"Yeah," I answered. "I came up here this morning to see if there was any evidence to collect, but I didn't look over the railing."

He took a step back rather than joining me.

"There's nothing he could have hit his head on," I mused, "except the edge of the foundation which would mean a head-first fall. That lines up with the injury being on the left side of his head. But the only way he could have gotten snagged on the cleat the way he did was if he descended feet first. That would explain why the top half of his shirt was dry."

"In other words, he jumped."

"Why would he do that, though? I know he was stupid drunk. Did he decide to go for a swim fully clothed? I mean, he still had his boots on."

Tripp murmured something about that wouldn't have been the first stupid thing Colton had done, then said, "Maybe someone picked him up and tossed him over. Bruce, Tex, and Boone are strong." A thought or memory of some kind clouded his face. "You'd be surprised how strong folks get working on a farm or ranch. Hay bales are surprisingly heavy. Full feed sacks are too." He let his words fade away.

It didn't escape me that he mentioned the guys' names like they were people he hung out with all the time. Or used to hang out with. I could accept that he knew about hay bales because he helped Rosalyn place the ones in the yard, but how did he know about feed sacks? Did he actually work on the Swenson's farm or the Alexander's ranch?

Stay on target, Deputy Jayne chided.

Right.

I leaned far over the rail. "If he went head first, he could have hit his head, but then he would have had to bounce backward and flip upright toward the building to end up snagged the way he did. Not possible."

An alarm sounded from Tripp's pocket, and he seemed grateful for the interruption. "The salmon is done. Let's eat."

"I'll be right there." I bent to gather my supplies and nearly pushed my tin of wax over the edge. I grabbed it and looked down at the water. If someone hit Colton, and it was looking like someone had, where was the weapon? Did they toss it in the water? Hide it in their car? Pitch it into the woods? Throw it in our garbage can or stuff it in a hay bale? The options were overwhelming.

If someone hit him, why wasn't there any blood on the deck? Head wounds bled like crazy. Did they wash the blood away?

Tripp was taking the lid off the pot when I walked in through the back door. "I have to call Martin quick. I'll be back in two minutes or less."

Fortunately, Martin was still at the station. "It's a holiday weekend during tourist season. Of course I'm still here."

"Jagger processed the scene over here, right?"

"He did. Yes, he found traces of blood using luminol. It was really faint since the sun was shining, but he made some kind of miniature darkroom and was able to see it that way."

"Creative thinking on his part. Where did he find it?"

"Near the middle of the deck, closer to the railing than the building. And on the railing near the stairs."

I paused before replying, "Those two spots aren't near each other. Did he douse the whole sundeck with luminol?"

Martin chuckled. "He said he needs to order more, so I think he might have. Looks like whoever hit the victim tried to wash the blood away with just water."

"I wondered if that's what they did. We should have divers come over and search the area around the boathouse."

He understood where I was going with that. "You think they tossed the weapon in the lake?"

"It's possible, so better for us to be on top of it."

"True. Okay, I'll call the marina and talk to Gil or Oren.

One of them should be available to do a search. Will you be around there tonight?"

"Briar told me to report to their cottage after seven."

"And we don't question a Briar directive. I'll come over there during the dive."

"You'll let me know if they find anything?"

"Of course."

I hung up, and my head felt muddled, like the clogged feeling in my ears had spread through my skull. The blood on the railing by the stairs would almost certainly be Tripp's. That's where he'd been standing with Colton before the initial gathering on the patio and somehow scraped his knuckles. Had Colton been responsible for Tripp's injury? Had Tripp gone back at four in the morning to confront Colton and things got out of control? No, that wasn't possible. Tripp would never purposely hurt anyone. Not over a scrape.

Not the Tripp I knew, at least.

What had happened between those two? Not just now but four years ago. Their dislike bordering on hatred for each other was obvious.

My stomach seized, and I felt like I was going to vomit.

Goddess, help me. I had no choice. I had to put Tripp on my suspect list.

Chapter Fourteen

TRIPP HAD POACHED THE SALMON WITH LEMON SLICES, seasonings, and some sort of kitchen magic that made it savory and fall-apart perfect. The salad was crisp and refreshing with a citrus dressing. We brought it up to the rooftop deck with Meeka and Janus alternating between begging for scraps and chasing each other all around. Tripp seemed to relax as we ate and sure didn't strike me as someone who had recently hit a man hard enough to nearly kill him. Meanwhile, my desperate mind spun to come up with a legitimate reason to not put the man I loved on my suspect list. The problem was, he wasn't in bed with me when Meeka woke me up at four thirty, and would only say he was wide awake at four o'clock when I asked him about it.

Despite Deputy Jayne's concerns, Regular Jayne decided to trust him. *He didn't do anything. The truth will come out as soon as he talks to me.*

"I swear," I said while plucking Meeka off the ledge, "you're going to fall three stories to the ground." I held her so she could see how far that was. "There's nothing down there for you to land on, so it would hurt. Don't make us put up a net."

"No net," Tripp said with finality. "We just won't let them come up here anymore."

The furry pair stared at him. There's no way they understood his words, but they acted like they did.

I checked the time after we finished washing the dishes. "It's after seven. We should get over there."

"All right, but I still have to do breakfast prep, so we can't stay long."

How long could it take to learn a spell?

As we headed toward the highway, I thought about Gus Lewis again. I didn't have time to talk to him now, the Barlow-Carrs were expecting us, but I could ask him to stop by the house in the morning so we could chat.

"Stop the truck," I told Tripp when we got to the end of our woods.

"What's wrong? What are you doing?" he asked when I got out. His jaw dropped when I told him. "Gus Lewis is here in Whispering Pines?"

"You know him?"

He gave me a half shrug, half nod.

"Should I even ask how?" I held up a hand as he opened his mouth. "I know, you met him when you passed through Fargo. Yes, he's here. He was looking for a room, but everyplace was booked. He asked if he could pitch a tent in the yard, and I told him he could set up inside the tree line as long as no one could see him from the road or campsite."

I didn't wait for Tripp's response to that. Instead, I marched through the field, and he followed me. The tent was still there, but once again, Gus wasn't. I could leave him a note . . . but I didn't have paper or a pen.

"I don't like this, Jayne," Tripp scolded as we headed back in the truck. "It's not safe."

"It's not my best idea," I agreed, "but it's no more dangerous than letting strangers stay in our home."

He had no comeback for that.

Then I thought about Gus following everyone from North Dakota and hiding around corners. Did Tripp mean letting Gus camp in our woods wasn't safe, or that Gus himself wasn't?

"Are you mad at me?" I asked, reaching for his hand.

"Is there something I should be mad at you about?" When I replied with a sigh and pulled my hand away, he said, "No, I'm not mad at you, babe. It's just . . . we don't have time to get into it now."

He turned left onto the road to the Meditation Circle then took a right on the other side of the bridge that crossed the creek. We were at the Barlow-Carr cottage a few seconds later.

Meeka squeezed through the hedge to play with Pitch the rooster, and Morgan met us at the door, wearing flowing black lounge pants and a snug black tank top that read *Salem 1692: Never Forgotten* in a witchy font. She told Tripp, "River is in the garden. He's not himself lately. I think it has something to do with all these crows, but he won't say why."

Tripp flashed a glance at me, then told Morgan, "I'll talk to him."

She touched his arm with the tips of her fingers. "Thank you, Tripp. He's got a bottle of red wine out there, but if you'd like something else—"

"No, that's great." Then he went to the garden for guy time.

"What was that look he gave you?" Morgan asked while leading me back to the conservatory.

"Tripp has also not been himself lately. Not since the wedding party arrived."

"Ah. Mama told me about the bride."

"I don't understand why he won't talk to me. Everyone— meaning Rosalyn, Reeva, and Briar—is telling me to give him time, but the longer he waits, the more my mind is spinning this into something horrible." I blew out a shaky breath and told her about Clyde.

"The boy is three," Morgan repeated, "and Tripp last saw this woman four years ago. You think he might be Tripp's son."

"It's possible, but I don't know." Tears stung my eyes and threatened to fall. "If he is, what does that mean for us? Will Tripp want to move to North Dakota to be with his kid? Am I supposed to upend my life and go with him? Would he even want me to?"

And on top of that, he might be the one who hit Colton, a thought whispered in my head.

Morgan placed her hands on my shoulders, looked me in the eye, and took a deep breath. A moment later, she exhaled and nodded for me to follow along. Three breaths later, I still felt like crying but wasn't spiraling toward hysteria.

"Hard as it is, try not to skip that far ahead." She took my arm, and we continued toward the back of the cottage. "I think Mama asked you here at exactly the right time."

The conservatory, with its full walls of windows and glass ceiling, was loaded with plants that needed protection from the outdoors either because they were still sprouts or simply couldn't tolerate the environment. Morgan and Briar gardened in here when the weather wasn't tolerable for them either and also used it as their altar room.

Briar met us with a mug of tea for me. "Focus blend."

I scowled. "Tripp gets wine, and I get tea?"

"You can have wine later," Morgan promised. "*After* you've done the spell."

Briar inspected my wand, praised it as being "simply lovely," and pointed at the wingback chair placed before the table that served dual purpose as a surface for potting plants and performing rituals. "Sit. Tell Morgan what you told me earlier. About your feelings of guilt surrounding Iris, Zinnia, and Isobel."

I repeated for Morgan everything I'd been feeling along

with new concerns that I wouldn't be able to figure out who attacked Colton.

"Combine that with your concerns over Tripp possibly having a son—"

"What?" Briar demanded and twirled a finger counterclockwise. "Back up. I didn't hear this part."

So I repeated that too.

"I agree with Mama," Morgan said gently once I finished. "Your confidence is shaken, and you need to restore trust in yourself."

"How do I do that?" With every minute that passed, the more I wanted to curl up in bed with the covers over my head or wander off into the woods and search for fairies with Mallory.

"You start by performing a moon spell to release your fear," Briar replied. "The new moon phase is about reducing or releasing and starting fresh. The spell isn't difficult, but I've written everything down, so don't worry about having to remember the steps." She took a scroll of paper tied with a yellow ribbon from a pile of items on the table and placed it in a small basket.

"We won't actually perform the spell. That way all intentions remain yours alone." Morgan took a black and sky-blue votive candle from the pile and set it in the basket. "Black for banishing, and blue for healing." Then she handed me something wrapped in a square of cloth. "Aquamarine is for courage, protection against negative energy, easing fears, and for overcoming judgement. Hold the stone now to infuse it with your essence, use it during the spell, and then carry it with you until you know the spell worked."

I unwrapped the slightly lumpy, light-blue-green aquamarine. The stone was about an inch in diameter and nestled perfectly in the palm of my left hand. "How will I know it worked?"

"You'll know," Morgan answered with her usual confidence.

Next Briar placed lilac incense in the basket. "To drive away evil. You'll also need your wand and a pin or small knife."

"Is blood involved?" I meant it as a joke to ease my tension, but I remembered overhearing someone say blood rituals protected people from negativity. Granted, it was a tourist, and they often got things wrong regarding Wicca.

Briar fixed a look on me that was somewhere between amused and exasperated.

"Listen now," Morgan directed with a slight scold, "and we'll teach you the spell for releasing fear. This is best done during the waning or dark phase, and we are within that window. And it's Friday."

Which was apparently important, but I didn't ask why.

"Where will you perform this spell?" Briar asked. "It should be someplace you won't be disturbed."

I'd love to do it on the sundeck, but Sunny could come back or one of the other guests could go up there. The rooftop would also work, but I felt a little self-conscious about this and didn't want Tripp to overhear me. "I think in my loft." That made the most sense anyway.

"Perfect," Briar praised. "To begin, it would be best to take a cleansing shower, but you may also smudge yourself. Once you're physically ready, turn on some soft music, light the incense, and sit in quiet meditation until you feel ready to start. Then gather the candle, a lighter, the knife or pin, and the aquamarine and cast a circle with your wand. Alternatively, you could cast a triangle which represents the trinity—mind, body, spirit or maiden, mother, crone, etc. It's your choice, but a circle is all-encompassing and probably best for this spell."

A little thrill over being able to use my altar cloth and

wand rushed through me. Not to mention, I was going to cast my first solo spell.

Morgan took over. "If you cast a circle, sit in the center. Sit at the base of the triangle if you choose that formation. Whichever you cast, face west." She took another scroll from the table. This one tied with an indigo ribbon. "Read this affirmation aloud within your formation before you begin the spell."

"Now you're ready to start," Briar said. "Choose the word that defines your fear."

"You keep saying *fear*. I'm not afraid."

The mother and daughter duo cast matching looks at me.

"Are you sure?" Briar asked.

"Think about that," Morgan encouraged.

Constant worry about making yet another wrong decision that would lead to someone else's death. Unsure I was doing the right things or doing enough for the village; that was my purpose here, after all. I was also terrified that I might be losing Tripp.

The word that defined my fears was *failure*. I was afraid I would fail at everything I tried.

Morgan picked up the candle. "Scratch the word into the top near the wick, not on the side. Light the candle and, while waiting for the wax to cover the letters, state the incantation written beneath the affirmation statement. When you're ready, say *so mote it be* or *blessed be* or whatever closure feels appropriate, then extinguish the flame and let the smoke carry away your fear."

I closed my fingers around the aquamarine. "That sounds like a lot."

"It goes faster than you think it will." Morgan waited for me to look at her. "Remember, spellcasting is about intention, and intention comes only from the caster. Focus on what is important to you."

They walked me through the spell once more and then—

because the twins would be up and active before the adults were ready, Tripp needed to prep for breakfast, and I had a spell to perform—we headed home at nine o'clock.

"How's River?" I asked him. "Morgan said the crows were upsetting him."

He shrugged. "Yeah, and the villagers' complaints are getting to him too."

I knew that much, but Tripp wouldn't say more. Fine. What was said between the dudes stayed between the dudes. If there was something I needed to know about, River would summon me to his office.

As we got out of the truck, again I told him, "I'm supposed to do a spell."

He gave me a crooked grin. "If we lived anywhere else, I'd probably question that. Breakfast prep shouldn't take me long. If I'm not in the kitchen, I'll be on the roof."

"Okay." I went into the house with him and explained, "I'm supposed to take a cleansing shower first."

"Another statement I won't question."

As he headed for the kitchen and me for the stairs, I called out, "I love you, you know."

He closed the gap between us, put his arms around me, and held me close. Something he hadn't done since before the North Dakotans descended on our lives. "I love you, too, babe."

With my little basket of supplies in hand, I rushed upstairs and did the showering thing, then went to my loft. As I pulled aside the area rug that covered the circle Gran had burned into the floorboards long ago, I glanced around at all the things in the room that held special meanings for me.

First was Durga. Dad had given me a statue of the Hindu goddess of strength and justice. She was also the protector of positivity and harmony. And considering she rode a tiger, had eight arms, and carried a tool for fighting evil in each hand, Durga was a badass.

Second, the stang or staff made from a hawthorn branch that Morgan, Briar, and River made me for my birthday last year. As with so many things around here, the stang was loaded with meaning. The wood represented earth or the Underworld and stood for grounding. Branches reached high into the sky and represented the Upper World or air. They carved icons for fire and water into the branch. The stang was where I got the idea to do what I'd done with my wand.

Finally, I centered myself by thinking of those who had blessed my space with their presence. Briar and Morgan swept it to get rid of any lingering bad energy. Dad and I performed a little ritual together up here. Mom declared it perfect and said every woman needed a space of her own. Gran was everywhere I looked, of course. Tavie and Silence, the girl who nearly died from a stab wound, slept up here. Rosalyn hung out with me now and then. Meeka was almost always up here with me.

As though knowing I was thinking about her, Meeka's tail thumped against her cushion on the floor, but she didn't budge otherwise.

With the rug out of the way, I gathered all my tools. I placed my cloth in the center of the circle then held my wand and stood facing east. As I turned clockwise, I paused at each elemental direction and envisioned a circle of energy building around me. Then I sat, facing west, and followed the instructions Briar had written for me. As the candle burned, the wax slowly filled in the letters F-A-I-L-U-R-E I'd scratched into the top, and I read the incantation.

"As the candle burns, my fear of failure becomes no more; I ask Hecate and Durga to hear what I implore. Trust in myself and protection from this dread is what I beg you to grant me. This spell is now complete; as I have said, so mote it be."

I don't know how long I sat with the aquamarine in hand, watching the candle well fill. When I felt ready, I extinguished the flame and watched the smoke float my fears to the rafters. Then I stood, faced north, and turned counterclockwise. I again paused at each direction, thanked the element for the protection it offered, and envisioned the circle fading away.

An unexpected sense of pride filled me. "I just did my first spell, Meeks."

Her tail flapped lazily in celebration, and it was clearly time for my tired pup to go up to bed.

I must have been in the loft far longer than I'd anticipated. Or Tripp was more tired than he'd thought, because he was sound asleep when we got up to our apartment.

I stripped off my clothes, climbed in beside him, and smiled at my achievement as I drifted off to sleep as well.

A few hours later, I woke with a jolt and sat straight up in bed. A very clear voice demanded, *Check the security camera.*

I hadn't looked at the recordings because the cameras were pointed only at the house. There was one by the patio, however, that focused on the backyard. On the dock in particular.

"In case a guest ever has an accident," River explained as his team installed the Blackbird Industries equipment, "and you need to defend yourselves in court."

I didn't think that camera would also pick up activity around the boathouse, too, but it was worth checking out.

After sliding out of bed and creeping down two flights of stairs, I went to the office, brought up Thursday night's recording, and started it at the ten o'clock mark. That's when Sunny and Colton were arguing on the deck. The camera did catch the boathouse, but the recording wasn't clear from that distance. I zoomed in a little, but too much resulted in nothing but a big blur. I could make out Sunny's long blond hair, however, and knew the person with her was Colton but only because we'd watched them from the rooftop, not because I could make out his features.

What I saw on the video matched what she'd told me, but

there was one thing she hadn't mentioned: Colton took a swing at her. That must have been after I'd pulled Tripp down, not wanting them to see us on the roof. Colton missed her by a lot but had clearly intended to hit his wife. This was when she stormed into the apartment. I checked the timestamp: 2217 hours. As we'd seen him do, he leaned against the railing and then lay down on the loveseat about five minutes later. Two hours after she'd gone inside, at 0013 hours, Sunny came back out to check on him. She stood by him for about a minute, probably trying to wake him up, then covered him with a blanket and went back inside.

I let the video play at super-fast speed until around four in the morning, when Tripp claimed to have woken up. Colton hadn't moved even once during that time. Then at 0428, right around the time Meeka had started barking, someone crept up the boathouse stairs. Either a noise or some other sensation startled Colton. He woke up, got to his feet, and appeared to say something to the person. Their body language—leaning toward each other, arms flinging out to the sides, turning away and then right back—made me believe they were arguing, and it appeared quite heated. Not surprising with those families. Then near the middle of the deck, across from where Colton had been found below, the person swung and hit him on the head. I couldn't make out anything long, like a pipe or baseball bat or tree branch, but they must have hit him with something hard because Colton collapsed to the deck an instant later. Without a second glance, the person turned and left.

How did he end up in the water? Would he come to, stumble around, and fall over the railing? Would the person come back?

With eyes glued to the screen, I watched, waiting for the answer. I almost fast forwarded but didn't want to miss anything.

About five minutes after the person left, they returned. No, this wasn't the same person. I'd need side-by-side screenshots to tell for sure, but this person appeared bigger, as in rounder, not taller, than whoever hit him. This person was also big and strong enough to pick up Colton by wrapping their arms around his torso, swing his legs over the railing, and drop him. Then they left.

I kept watching. There had to be blood on the deck in the spot where Colton lay at that point. And possibly on the person's clothes. It hadn't rained last night. Would one of these two come back to wash it off?

A little more than three minutes later, one of them did. It appeared to be the second person. They had a bucket tied to a rope that they dropped over the side into the lake and pulled back up. Then they dumped the water on the deck. After doing this four more times, they must have decided they'd washed away all the evidence. Except water doesn't wash away everything. As Jagger proved when he sprayed the deck with luminol.

I needed to view the video again on a bigger screen. I wanted to see those two people side by side to verify it was, in fact, two people. The laptop screen was just too small, and I couldn't zoom in close enough to help. The big screen in the interview room at the station should take care of that problem.

Before going back up to bed, I checked one last thing. Our security system kept a record of card swipes for those who entered the house when the doors were locked from ten o'clock at night until five thirty in the morning. I ran a report starting Thursday morning at four. The only swipe recorded was someone in the Grand Suite at 0521. That would have been Mamie when she came in through the back door. More than an hour after Colton had been tossed into the lake. I couldn't imagine the tiny woman was strong enough to lift him, but could she have hit him hard enough to knock him out? She made a point of telling me about the people she'd met at the campground. She could have hit Colton and then gone on her walk. A scenario that sounded especially cold to me. Hit someone in the head, possibly killing them, and then go for a stroll. I needed to stop at the campground and find out if any of the campers had seen Mamie there yesterday morning.

As for leaving the house, that didn't require a swipe. Rosalyn was up and out in the yard around 0515, and Nell went for a swim around 0530. Both after Colton was in the water according to the video. We didn't see anyone else until after 0600 when the doors would have been unlocked.

What about Tripp? Logical Jayne asked.

The facts were, if he left the house after waking up at 0400, he could have been the person who climbed the boathouse stairs at 0428. If he was the second person who dropped Colton over the railing and cleaned off the dock, he would have had time to do those things and get to the kitchen to start breakfast before I came downstairs around 0500. Tripp, Rosalyn, and I didn't use key cards to swipe in. We entered a code into a keypad outside the doors. Our entries weren't recorded by the system. We didn't see the need since we were the only ones who knew the code.

This doesn't exonerate him, Logical Jayne said sadly.

No, it didn't.

Watching the video provided some answers, but I still had a lot of questions. What I now knew for certain was if Colton died, someone was going to be charged with murder.

Chapter Fifteen

I woke to Tripp's five o'clock alarm feeling groggy from my middle of the night video viewing. He gave me a little nudge as he got up, and I grunted that I'd be down shortly. Not wanting to risk falling back to sleep, I forced myself to get out of bed right away and into the shower.

As the water pounded down on me, I thought about the security video and wondered again if Mamie could have been the one who hit Colton. She hadn't been shy about her feelings regarding her son-in-law. Then again, no one in the group seemed to hold back in that regard. The timing ate at me, though. She claimed to go for a walk right around the time the attacker had struck. As I'd reasoned last night, she surely wasn't strong enough to lift Colton, but she could have hit him. Although, she admitted to being afraid of him *and* she was angry about how he treated her daughter. Two emotions that caused adrenaline to spike and could increase strength. For now, I'd reserve any accusations until after I'd interviewed the campers at the campsite and re-viewed the video.

I dried off, towel-dried my hair, then slathered on some moisturizer and sunscreen. Then I laid out my uniform, my watch, the aquamarine Morgan gave me last night, and my . . .

"Where's my ring?" I asked . . . the empty apartment. Meeka had gone downstairs with Tripp.

Not this past Christmas but the one before, Tripp and I gave each other matching silver bands engraved with *I promise to always love you*. Promise rings we'd each purchased at Shoppe Mystique. Morgan, the sneaky witch, had encouraged us individually to come in because she had something to show us.

As he slid it on my finger, Tripp vowed, "Someday I will ask you to marry me. From the start, we've taken things slow and enjoyed every moment of the journey. The last thing I want to do is rush anything now. But I also want you to know how much I love you and that I'm not going anywhere."

Did he still feel that way? Was he still enjoying every moment? Because right now, since these people invaded our home, he didn't seem to be enjoying much of anything.

"*That's* not important right now," I scolded myself. "Finding your ring is."

It got loose with soapy water and since I usually washed some dishes during breakfast prep, I didn't put it on until I dressed in my deputy's uniform. My morning routine rarely changed. After my shower, I dressed in Pine Time clothes and laid everything out on the bed. I always set my ring inside the curve of the watchband. Did I wear it yesterday? When something became standard procedure, it was easy to assume that, yes, I must have put my ring on. But *did* I?

I searched our small apartment from wall to wall with no luck. To figure out what could have happened to it, I reviewed all I'd done yesterday, starting with the most recent event.

Morgan answered the phone with concern in her voice. "Jayne?"

"I'm sorry to call so early."

"You know one of us is always up at this time. Miss Juniper is still an early riser. Is something wrong?"

Her concerned tone made me feel ridiculous. Calling someone before six in the morning regarding a piece of jewelry. But the damage was already done, so I might as well ask. "Did you notice if I was wearing my ring last night?"

She made a little humming sound that let me know she was thinking. "No, I don't believe you were. Is it missing?"

"I can't find it anywhere. I'm probably overreacting, but I feel horrible. Along with everything else I told you last night, this almost feels like—"

"If you're about to say it's a sign, don't. I'll look around here for it but take a minute and sit in silence. Maybe you'll remember when you last had it on."

I thanked her, hung up, and sat cross legged on the bed with my hands on my knees. I continued yesterday's reverse timeline. Before going to see Morgan and Briar, we had dinner. I put the dishes in the dishwasher and Tripp washed the few that couldn't go in. Before that, I worked on my wand. Little chance it would have fallen off doing that. I interviewed Nell and Bruce, walked Briar home, and spoke with Keiko and Lily Grace in the commons area while on patrol. I reviewed everything regarding Colton with Martin at the station. I couldn't imagine it just falling off my hand in any of those situations.

Before heading into the village, I helped Reeva move the food downstairs. A shiver of hope ran up my back. My hands got cold while carrying those pans, so my fingers would have shrunk. I shook my hands a few times to warm them up again. That had to be when it slid off, and because my hands were so cold, I didn't even notice.

I shoved my feet into some sandals and went down to the basement. Reeva and I had only been in the one room, so I checked the floor around the refrigerator and inside it. I looked beneath the sofa and between the cushions. I looked under, around, and on top of everything else in the room. Nothing.

If I had dropped it between the basement stairs and the patio doors, Holly would have found it when she vacuumed yesterday. Maybe it fell off outside.

As though processing a crime scene, I methodically checked the route between the back door and where Reeva's car had been parked on the driveway. Then I searched the grass for five feet on either side of the sidewalk in case it bounced and rolled. No luck. It could have fallen off as I reached into the back of Reeva's vehicle.

I called Hearth & Cauldron planning to leave a message, but Reeva answered.

"Oh, how upsetting," she replied. "I rode my bike this morning, so I'll check my SUV as soon as I get home tonight."

I thanked her and decided the only other possibility was that I somehow dropped it while on patrol. That didn't seem likely, though. If that was what happened, my chances of finding it were practically nil.

Heartbroken, I went to the kitchen where Tripp greeted me with a kiss. "How did your spell go last night? Sorry I was asleep when you came up. I was wiped out."

While he organized the ingredients for Eggs Benedict, I assembled fresh fruit cups and told him about the spell.

"Failure? You still can't get past the Flavia thing?"

I couldn't talk about her again, so I switched topics. "I heard a voice in the middle of the night . . . or had a dream . . . or heard a voice in my dream. Whatever. It told me to check the security video."

"In the hopes of finding . . ."

"Whoever hit Colton. I don't even know what time it was, but I got up and watched it."

He paused before asking, "What did it show you?"

As she had yesterday, Mamie appeared at the back door with her keycard in hand.

"I'll tell you later." When she stepped inside, I asked, "Up with the birds again?"

She gave a trilling little laugh. "If I lived in a place like this, I'd be out for early-morning walks every day. It's perfectly flat by us with not much more to look at than fields full of crops and trees planted strategically as windbreaks. Remember, Tripp?"

He froze with his whisk suspended over the saucepan of Hollandaise sauce. A couple of seconds later, he cleared his throat and began whisking. "I remember."

Mamie's face went blank. "Did I say something wrong?"

"Of course not," I replied. Although that depended on whether she'd said something he didn't want me to know about for some reason. "Did you chat with any more campers this morning?"

"I did." She smiled but her bubbly exuberance of a few moments ago had lessened dramatically. "I've never been interested in camping, but those folks seem to be enjoying themselves so much, I'm almost tempted to give it a try."

"Maybe in one of those tour buses celebrities travel in?"

She pointed at me as though I were on to something. "Then Ty could still drive, and we wouldn't have to worry about pitching a tent." She gave a little finger wave. "I'll let you two continue with your cooking."

Tripp had shut down after her comment about the farm fields and gave me little more than two or three-word instructions as we finished breakfast prep. I was trying to give him time, I really was, but my patience was wearing very thin.

Rosalyn came out of her room at six thirty to eat with us before the guests were served. Or rather, to eat with me. Tripp burned the first batch of sauce and had to make more.

"What's wrong with him?" she whispered once she settled into the chair next to me at the dinette.

"I have no idea. Something to do with our guests, but he won't say anything other than he met them in North Dakota."

"Well," she began while spreading jam on half an English muffin, "Nell told me—"

"Stop. I don't want to hear anything from anyone until I've heard it from Tripp first."

"Fair enough." She stared out at the backyard while munching her muffin and sighed. "It looks so nice, doesn't it?"

She meant the arch setup.

"It does. You did a great job. Things obviously didn't go as planned with this one, but I think you've got a real talent for this."

She gave a happy wiggle. "Thanks, sis. How long do you suppose I should keep everything up?"

"You haven't heard from Sunny?"

"Not a peep." She sipped her coffee. "Since she basically paid for the entire B&B for the weekend, guess I'll leave it until either checkout time tomorrow or she gives me the okay to take it down. I'd really like her to at least see it first."

While we finished eating, I told her about my moon spell. She also disapproved of me choosing the word *failure* but thought the rest was cool.

"A spell to release fear," she mused. "Suppose it would work on spiders?"

Before I could answer, Boone and Dinah appeared in the kitchen.

"Good morning," Tripp greeted with a warm smile. Was he forcing cheer, or had he given himself a pep talk while remaking the sauce? "Did you just get back?"

"No," Dinah answered, "we got here around two in the morning."

I knew that because I was logged into the security system at that time, and an alert popped up on the screen that someone staying in The Treehouse suite had just scanned in.

Boone looked heartsick. "We stayed at the hospital to offer moral support and be there in case Colton woke up or at least showed signs of improvement. Eventually, we figured Sunny and the Alexanders might want time to discuss . . . things."

His voice broke, so I assumed by *things*, he meant what would happen if Colton didn't make it.

"We know breakfast isn't until seven thirty," Dinah said, "but is it possible for us—"

"Of course." Tripp handed her two of the fruit cups I'd assembled. "Go have a seat in the dining room. Coffee and tea are available. We'll bring the rest out to you."

I brought my dishes to the sink and waited for Tripp to assemble their main course plates. Then I delivered them.

"Take your time eating," I told the couple, "but I'd like to talk with you both when you're done. I'll be in the sitting room." I pointed across the hall.

Twenty minutes later, they met me. Normally, I'd talk to them individually, but they'd had more than enough time together to sync their stories if that's what they were going to do. I started by informing them I'd be recording our conversation.

"How is Colton doing?" I asked.

"Not well," Boone admitted. "The doctors aren't optimistic about him recovering. When we left, they were talking about transferring him to a hospital closer to home. Victoria, naturally, wants him at the ranch where she'll hire onsite care." He gave me a tight smile. "That's not really what you want to know, though."

"It's not, but I do care about what happens to him." And not just because it would make a difference in how charges were filed. In the very short time I had known Colton, he struck me as a conflicted man. He needed help, not a blow to the head. "I believe that Colton's injuries weren't due to an accident."

"You mean someone did this to him," Boone clarified.

"Right. Do you have any idea who that person could be?"

"That's the million-dollar question, isn't it?" Boone blew out a breath. "Honestly, there are more than a few people back home who aren't fans of his, but from this group? I could see him and Tex getting into a scuffle. Tex and the other brothers . . . that's complicated. They wish Colt wasn't the way he is."

"Meaning?"

"All they want is for him to do more around the ranch."

"They feel like he doesn't pull his weight," Dinah added.

"Right." Boone continued, "Harlan and Victoria have made it clear their sons will be given equal shares of the ranch when they pass. Each of them has different skills, so keeping it in the family shouldn't be hard. Josh will oversee the business side. Zeke is the animal expert. Tex makes sure the grounds are maintained. They hoped Colt would step up for guest relations—"

"Because he can be a real charmer," Dinah said.

Boone laughed. "That's not going to happen, though, because Colt just can't get it together. I'm sure the others have told you he's lazy. I hate to say it, but he is. Harlan is about done giving him chances to prove himself. I think he'd like to cut him out of the ranch altogether, but Victoria won't hear of it."

"Do you feel Tex could have done this?"

Boone sat forward on his chair, eager to keep talking about this. "He could have, but it would have been an accident. I've never once seen the brothers fight with that kind of anger. This happened pretty early in the morning, right?"

"Right."

"Yeah, I can't see Tex getting out of bed at that time to pick a fight with his brother." He paused to think. "Mamie and Ty are furious at Colt over how he treats Sunny. So is Nell."

She was? I didn't see anything from her to indicate that.

"I think," Dinah offered, "something happened between Nell and Colton. A while ago, I mean. There are times when her anger at him seems personal, not just that she's defending her sister."

"Do you have anything to back up that feeling?" I asked.

"As in evidence? No. It's just a feeling. If Ty wasn't in that wheelchair, I'd say look strongly at him."

Boone agreed. "From the moment Sunny announced she was pregnant, Ty was all over Colt to do the right thing and marry her. 'A man owns up to his mistakes.' That's got to be Ty's favorite saying."

"And by *mistake*," Dinah injected, "he means the pregnancy was unplanned. Everyone loves Clyde."

"If I had to narrow the suspect list," Boone said, "I'd say look at Sunny or Nell."

That wasn't what I expected to hear. I knew for a fact Sunny hadn't done this. There was only one way out of the boathouse apartment, and she never left it from the time she covered Colton with a blanket at midnight to stepping outside when we were rescuing him from the lake.

"Do either of you think Sunny and Colton love each other?" I asked. "There are plenty of married people who fight like enemies but are actually very much in love."

"*Love?*" Boone echoed. "I wouldn't use that word to describe them. There was obviously an attraction at one point, but Colt has a wandering eye, as the saying goes. Far as I know, he never wanted to get married. He's crazy in love with his son, though."

I looked at Dinah for her thoughts.

"I moved to town and started working on the ranch about five years ago."

"What do you do there?" I asked.

"I manage guest relations. The position they hoped Colton would take over. Until Boone and I started dating about a year after I got hired there, my involvement with the family had been strictly as an employee. To me, Colton seemed angry at Sunny for getting pregnant and messing up his life."

"Colton didn't want to marry her?"

"No," Boone answered without hesitation. "Everyone

expected him to do the right thing by her, though. Even Victoria stood on that side of the situation."

I understood what he/they meant, but there was something misogynistic about this that rubbed me the wrong way.

"She did," Dinah said, regarding Victoria. "I've worked pretty closely with her from the start. She liked Sunny well enough four years ago. I remember her saying Sunny was as bright as her name and a joy to be around. I think Victoria saw her as a positive influence for Colton and hoped Sunny and the baby would help settle him down."

"Her feelings obviously changed," I noted.

"Yeah, Colton started saying all these hateful things about Sunny. Victoria took his side and called Sunny a gold digger who was only with Colton for the money. She even claimed at one point that Sunny got pregnant to set Colton up. I never thought that was true."

"Colt liked being single," Boone stated. "They both felt pressured to get married, but I don't think either of them really wanted to."

"It would have been better," Dinah mused, "if they co-parented Clyde and had separate personal lives."

And how did Tripp play into this? Was he the one Sunny would have preferred to be with? Had he wanted to be with her? Was Clyde really Colton's son, or was Tripp his father and, for some reason, the families didn't want him involved? Or did Tripp leave town not knowing Sunny was pregnant? The questions wouldn't stop coming.

We were wrapping up the interview when the front door opened and Victoria and Harlan walked in.

Boone jumped to his feet. "How is he? Any change since we left?"

Victoria looked devastated as Harlan reported, "He took a slight downturn. We want to move him to Fargo, but the doctors say that would be risky right now. We're here to shower, change clothes, and get something good to eat. The hospital's food is lacking. Then we're going back."

"Breakfast is ready," I told them. "Take a seat in the dining room and I'll get it for you."

Minutes later, from the hallway, their breakfast in hand, I heard Victoria saying, "She's never been good enough for Colton."

"That's not true, Vic," Harlan replied. "Sunny has been a grounding influence for him, but we always knew that would be a mighty big battle. The truth is, we paid more attention to the ranch than him as he was growing up."

"That's not—"

"It is true, and you know it. That's why you baby him so much now. And why you're trying to get a do-over with his son."

Victoria grumbled something I couldn't hear, then said, "She's a very good mom to my grandson. I won't take that away from her. She's too pushy and demanding of Colton, though."

"So Colton says. We've never talked to her about her version of things. She wants a good life and isn't afraid to ask for it. If you hadn't done the same thing to me thirty-some years ago, the ranch wouldn't be what it is today."

Their food was getting cold, so I brought in the tray loaded with fruit cups, plates of Eggs Benedict, and small plates with pastries. "Here you go. We normally do this in courses, but I'm guessing you'd rather eat and get back on the road."

"We would," Victoria agreed. "Thank you."

"Did Sunny come back with you?"

"No," Harlan answered. "She didn't want Colton to be alone. Once we're back, she'll come here to check on Clyde and freshen up."

"Is she planning to drive herself?" I asked. "Is she okay to do that? We could always send someone to get her."

"She's not alone," Harlan answered. "Gus Lewis is there. He'll drive her."

Gus was at the hospital? That explained why I hadn't seen him lurking around the house or at his tent. I set their plates in front of them, took the tray back to the kitchen, and then rushed upstairs to The Treehouse. I knocked on the door, and Dinah opened it, looking startled to see me there.

"I have some more questions," I said without apology, my voice recorder in hand.

She pointed over her shoulder. "Boone just got in the shower . . ."

"That's okay. What can you tell me about Gus Lewis?"

She opened the door wider so I could come inside. "Gus works for the Swensons as a fieldhand. He's nice enough but a little mentally slow, if I'm honest."

"He knew about the renewal ceremony. We were told only Sunny and Mamie knew the details, so we should keep quiet about it. Do you think one of them would have told him?"

Dinah started nodding in understanding before I finished the question. "Gus has a huge crush on Sunny and was really upset when she told him we were all going away for a long weekend. It's a safe bet that he pestered her for details until she finally told him and then he followed us here."

That basically lined up with what Bruce said. Although, he said he couldn't see Sunny telling Gus about the ceremony.

"A crush," I repeated. "Would you call him obsessive? Is Gus dangerous?"

"He's definitely obsessed with her. He shows up at their house and sits on the front porch like a stray cat looking for food. But when Sunny tells him it's time for him to go, he leaves. Is he dangerous?" She gave that question serious thought. "Not to Sunny. He's gentle as a newborn with her."

"What about with Colton? Could Gus have attacked him?"

She blew out a slow breath. "I really want to say no, but

there was a night a few months back . . . It had been a long, hard day on the ranch, so a bunch of us, Colton included, decided to go to a local hangout for dinner. Sunny met us there, so of course Gus showed up. There are times when, I swear, he's like her second shadow. As usual, Colton had too many beers and got rowdy. Sunny grabbed his arm to take him home, and he took a swing at her. He missed, thank God."

Just like on the sundeck last night. Sounded like a pattern of abuse to me. No wonder Mamie disliked him so much. Had one of his swings ever connected? Did Mamie know?

"Gus saw and went ballistic," Dinah continued. "He got in three hard blows before Boone and the bouncer pulled him off Colton. Fortunately, Colton only suffered some nasty bruises and no breaks, but Gus had to sit in a jail cell for the night and then a psych ward for a two-day hold."

"This was in Fargo?" I pulled out my notebook and wrote the name of the hospital she gave me. "Do you know what the outcome of the hold was?"

"I know they put him on some meds, and he seems better since starting them. He's also been going to anger management therapy. Colton wanted to press charges, but when half the bar said they'd seen him take that swing at Sunny, he backed off. He could use some therapy too. And AA."

"Last question. Harlan told me Gus is at the hospital with Sunny. Is there any reason to worry about that?"

"You mean for Colton's safety?"

I was worried Sunny might be in danger, but her point was valid too.

Dinah shook her head. "Colton's in the ICU, and they won't let anyone but family in. It's probably worth a call to caution them about Gus, though."

"Sunny is planning to come back here to check on her son and change clothes once Harlan and Victoria return to the hospital," I mused aloud. "Are you and Boone going back too?"

"We were planning to wander around the village today and get a little distance from the group. Sorry if that sounds cold. Why do you ask?"

I told her I was concerned that Gus would likely be the one to bring Sunny back here.

"And you're worried about her being alone with him." Dinah sighed and looked disappointed at the sudden change to their plans. "It's only a few hours. We can wander the village once we're back with her. Better safe than sorry."

Chapter Sixteen

B<small>EFORE LEAVING THE HOUSE</small>, I <small>CALLED</small> M<small>ARTIN AT HOME</small>.

"What time is it?" he asked, his voice croaky.

"Just before eight. I know you were at the station until late last night dealing with tourists, but I need to discuss the attack on Colton."

"I was there until early this morning." He groaned, muttered something about three hours of sleep, then said he'd be there. "But I'm not gonna rush. Take a walk around the commons. The Litha celebration wound down as the sun rose; make sure there's nothing that needs tending to."

"Yes, sir. See you in a bit."

Meeka and I found Tripp in the kitchen, cleaning up the breakfast dishes.

"Heading to the village?" He flipped a piece of Canadian bacon to Meeka, then let Janus lick the Hollandaise off a spoon. The cat let us know shortly after adopting us she was not okay with Meeka getting special treatment.

"Yeah. Along with patrolling, I have to talk to Martin about what happened to Colton."

"You mean what you saw on the security video?"

"Right." I stepped closer to him and softly said, "Someone

hit him, Tripp. They knocked him out cold, picked him up, and tossed him over the railing."

He shook his head as though sorry to hear that. "Sounds like this was purposeful."

"Sure does. And it seems awfully coincidental that the attacker wandered up to the sundeck at four thirty in the morning as Colton lay passed out on the loveseat. They had to know he was out there."

According to the video, Sunny never left the apartment. But she had a cell phone. Had she called or texted the attacker and gave them the go-ahead?

"What are you thinking?" he asked.

"You said you were wide awake at four o'clock. Colton was attacked not even half an hour later. You're sure you didn't hear anything out there?" The boathouse was maybe fifty yards from the house. Not that far away.

"Are you accusing me of something?" Tripp took a couple of steps away from me. "Because it's starting to sound like you think it could have been me."

That was the last thing I wanted to think. "Whoever did this was either *really* angry at Colton or *really* cared for Sunny. I don't know which side of that line you fall on because you won't talk to me."

He sighed. "Jayne—"

"I need to get my head on straight and work through this with Martin. When I come home, I'd like it if you would finally trust me enough to tell me what the hell happened between you and these people." I spun on my heel, walked out of the kitchen, then turned around and went back. "I need bread."

Tripp blinked, confused. "Bread?"

"I need to leave the crows a gift. Lily Grace said it might help. Long explanation."

He went to the pantry and came back with a gallon-size zip-top bag filled with thick bread loaf heels. "I was going to make croutons, but you can take these." He didn't let go of the bag when I grabbed it. Instead, he pulled me close, looked me in the eye, and said slowly and intensely, "I love you. Don't doubt that."

Loving me didn't mean he wasn't guilty. My throat clenched with emotion, and I couldn't respond. I could barely breathe so just nodded and walked away. On the front porch, I bent forward, hands on knees, and took a moment to get my emotions in check and shift from Regular Jayne to Deputy Jayne before getting in the car.

"Jayne?" Rosalyn rushed over to me from the event tent. "What's wrong? Are you okay?"

Still bent forward, I looked up at her. "Tripp wasn't involved with this, was he?"

"With . . . the attack? No. He wouldn't do that."

I wanted to believe that, but a comment Tripp made when he found me on the sundeck before dinner last night kept playing in my head. I was looking over the railing, wondering aloud if Colton fell, was pushed, or had jumped.

"Maybe someone picked him up and tossed him over. Bruce, Tex, and Boone are strong."

What were the chances of him knowing exactly what had happened? Was it a lucky guess? A logical possibility? An admission of guilt?

"Jayne, *no*," Rosalyn repeated emphatically.

My moon spell was meant to help me get past my fears and trust myself. Except Regular Jayne was far too emotional right now. And Deputy Jayne had a bunch of details but no logical timeline of events so was a bit scattered. I needed something to hang on to right now, and what I knew for sure was that Rosalyn would never do or say anything to purposely hurt me. So until I could trust myself again, I'd trust my sister. I straightened and gave her a hug.

"Why would you think he was involved?" she asked gently.

"Because he won't tell me anything, and as much as I hate

to admit it, some of the evidence I've gathered indicates he could have been." My voice dropped to a whisper. "He's on my suspect list, Rozzie, and I really, *really* want him off of it."

"You're going to talk to Martin?"

"Right."

"Good. Go and come back with a clear head." She glanced down. "Why are you carrying a bag of bread?"

"It's an offering for the crows."

She didn't ask for a further explanation. "There are three that have been hanging out around the yard. They tried to steal things off the tables in the tent. If bread will appease them, by all means give them some bread. I think they're over by your car."

Sure enough, I found the trio hopping around my Outback. One was on the roof.

"Get off of there," I scolded and tore a bread crust into three pieces and tossed them into the grass near the driveway. "These are for you. Please don't steal our stuff or drop anything on our guests. They've been through enough."

One of them cawed at me. Then one by one, they snatched up a piece of bread and flew to the roof of the garage.

"Hopefully Lily Grace was right," I told Meeka while she jumped into the back of the car. Before I could close her cage door, she stood on her back legs, paws on my chest, and licked my cheek. I gave her a hug and ear scratch in return. "Thanks, girl. I needed that."

We drove through the campground on our way to the station, and I spoke with two campers who were outside their tents. First, a man reading a book by the fire, who said he had indeed chatted with a lovely woman named Mamie. At the second site, a woman was sitting on a blanket in lotus pose and meditating.

"Sorry to disturb you," I said softly, "but I need to ask you a question."

"Cool, as long as you keep your voice down. They're still sleeping, and I'd like them to stay that way." She gestured at the two tents behind her. I assumed she meant kids, although it could have been friends she was camping with.

The woman said she had also met Mamie yesterday and even walked with her for a short while.

Satisfied that Mamie's story checked out, I went to patrol the commons.

With my bag of bread in hand, I found the village service's crew on cleanup duty again. The good thing about a raucous celebration going on all night was that the birds left less of a mess. The humans, however, trashed the place. Along with food containers all over the ground, despite there being barrels every few feet, they'd left behind plenty of personal items— clothing, pricey travel mugs, and a surprising number of cell phones. I instructed the crew to bring the items to the station; we would act as the Lost and Found. Then I gave them some slices of bread.

"Leave them around the commons when you're done," I instructed, "and tell the crows that there will be more if they quit harassing us."

Half the crew looked at me like I'd lost it, while the other half shrugged in compliance.

"It was out of control," Laurel told me as we stood in front of The Inn. "River has to do something about these events. We had to lock the doors at eleven last night. Even though we told them the restaurant closed at ten and the crew had gone home, people were insisting we feed them. I was worried they were going to storm the kitchen and raid the refrigerator and shelves."

"The volunteer villagers were here, weren't they?"

"Yes, but that wasn't enough. Martin finally called Creed

and asked him to send the carny patrol down here to help. I've never seen a crowd like that here before."

"You're right," I told her. "Someone's going to get hurt. Or worse. I'll talk to River."

I heard a similar complaint from Maeve. "They wouldn't leave the deck. We closed the dining room and shut down the kitchen at ten as planned and decided to stop serving alcohol shortly after that. I didn't want to contribute to the chaos."

Maeve normally served drinks and pre-packaged snacks on Triple G's deck until midnight, but she was right to stop early. "Good call. I told Laurel I'll talk to River. I'll tell him what you said too."

Litha was historically the most chaotic of our celebrations. The tradition was to keep the party going until the sun rose to welcome the Oak King to the throne. Or give him a sendoff as he vacated the throne. Whichever. Regardless, most of these people were just here to party, and that wasn't what Wiccan celebrations were supposed to be. Not the ones in this village, at least. Maybe it was time to end the Litha celebration at midnight like we did all the others.

And the tourists weren't the only problem this morning. A few villagers who wandered into the commons, now that the party was over, complained that they had to kick the Maidens out of their gardens last night. So Elliana and Thistle carried through with their plan to harvest herbs at midnight. Many of the green witches had put nets over their gardens to keep the birds from tearing them up like they had the Pentacle Garden. Too bad the nets wouldn't keep out the Maidens as well. As for the crows, villagers reported they had started stealing things from their yards. Anything shiny, colorful, or happened to catch their attention and was small enough to fit in the crows' claws or beaks was getting snatched. I told them to try leaving bread or nuts out for them.

Knowing the passageway to Biblichor had become a favorite pinecone bomb location, Meeka and I went there to leave an offering. I'd gone about halfway down the path when seven crows in the canopy of tree branches called out as though performing a round.

"I have something for you." I set seven pieces of bread on the red brick walkway. "You're welcome to stay, and I'll bring more but only if you stop harassing the tourists, tearing up our gardens, and leaving such a mess all over. Deal?"

Was I seriously negotiating with birds?

A few of them cawed in reply, but the problem with crows was that their cries made it sound like they were laughing.

"Okay? No messes and no harassing, and you get more bread."

"Deputy O'Shea?"

In my slightly sleep-deprived state, I thought for an instant that one of them actually spoke to me. Then I realized it was Martin calling over my walkie talkie.

"Deputy O'Shea here. Are you at the station?"

"I am."

"Be right there."

As I headed his way, I saw the woman dressed in black again. This time, she was sitting at a table outside Ye Olde Bean Grinder enjoying a cup of coffee. Again, she was in a chic, all-black outfit: a floor-length skirt, tank top, long gauzy blouse, flat shoes, and the same hat.

"Hi," I greeted.

She wore round, silver framed sunglasses, even though the sun wasn't an issue yet, so I couldn't tell if she was looking at me or not until she gave me a nod.

"Good morning, Deputy."

"Looks like you've got the best seat in the house," I commented.

She glanced from the crowd slowly gathering around the Pentacle Garden to Shoppe Mystique on her left and back to me. "I think you're right. I can see almost everyone from here."

She had a sophisticated air about her and a slight accent I couldn't identify that made me think of . . . someone. I couldn't figure out who.

"You've been here for a couple of days. Are you planning to stay in the village for a while?"

"That depends on whether my plans come together quickly or require more time. Fortunately, I was able to book one of the lovely cottages here for a month. Just in case."

A month? Was she here with someone? What plans did she have? "I'll probably see you around, then. I hope you have a wonderful day."

She inclined her head. "You as well."

The woman was so intriguing, I would have loved to stay and learn more about her. I was eager for Martin's input, though, and to get a handle on the Colton Alexander situation before everyone left the B&B tomorrow. The clock was ticking faster.

Chapter Seventeen

The station was quiet. As in, not even a hum from a computer or an overhead light quiet. If not for the desk lamp illuminating Martin's office, I wouldn't have known he was there. I found him in his desk chair, eyes closed, hands clutching a really big travel mug of coffee.

I whispered, "Are you awake?"

"Barely. I'm waiting for the coffee to kick in."

Giving him a few more minutes, I went to the main room and made myself a cup. When I returned, his eyes were open, and he agreed I could turn the ceiling lights on.

"Ready?" I asked.

"Yep." He groaned as he stood and moved to a chair in front of the portable whiteboard. "Okay, what do you know?"

Using a blue dry erase marker, I drew a horizontal line across the top of the board. At the left end, I drew a short vertical line. Above it I wrote *Thursday*, and below it *1500* and details about what had happened at that time.

"The guests arrived Thursday at three o'clock and were already bickering. Once they were all checked into their rooms, they met on the patio. Sunny Alexander, the bride, announced the surprise vow renewal ceremony, which kicked the bickering up a notch."

"What were they arguing about?"

"Nothing important, in my opinion." I ticked things off on my fingers. "Nell Lockwood is Sunny's sister. Nell complained she hadn't brought appropriate clothing for herself or their girls because Sunny kept this a secret. Nell's husband wasn't happy that Mr. and Mrs. Alexander got the Jack and Jill rooms for three people while they have five in The Alcove. Once Sunny announced the ceremony, it grew worse. Colton, the groom, felt blindsided or foolish for not knowing about his wife's plans. Harlan, Colton's father, felt that, since Sunny went with a farm theme, they could have held the ceremony at their ranch even though everyone agreed they wanted a vacation and this was the week to do it. Colton and his mother, Victoria, didn't feel vow renewals were important at all. And when Sunny revealed that she had paid for the whole thing, using money her mother had started setting aside when Sunny was a little girl, Colton got really angry. He felt the money could have been used for more practical things."

"Hang on." Martin's eyes were wide, and he didn't seem to be blinking. "You're talking really fast and there are a lot of players. Make a list of everyone and their connections for me, please."

On the right side of the board using a green marker, I wrote:

Sunny (Swenson) Alexander – bride
Colton Alexander – groom
Clyde Alexander (3) – son
Mamie and Ty Swenson – bride's parents
Nell and Bruce Lockwood – bride's sister and brother-in-law
Eleanor (10), Talia (8), Audra (6) – Lockwood children
Harlan and Victoria Alexander – groom's parents
Tex Alexander – groom's brother

Arizona Heller – Tex's partner
Boone Gonsalves – groom's friend, employee at Alexander Ranch
Dinah Yubero – Boone's partner, employee at Alexander Ranch
Gus Lewis – employee at Swenson Farm

"Thank you." Martin tipped his mug toward the board like a pointer. "Continue."

I drew another vertical line on the timeline. "Around 2200 hours Thursday night, Tripp and I overheard an argument between Colton and Sunny. We were on the roof, and they were on the sundeck. They argued mostly about money. Not just about how much the ceremony cost but also how Colton felt Sunny spent far too much on unimportant things like her hair, nails, and clothes."

Martin inhaled sharply but said nothing. He knew when it came to Rosalyn, that kind of controlling behavior could end their relationship. Fortunately, moving to Whispering Pines settled her spending habit greatly. I never asked but was pretty sure she had at least two maxed-out higher-limit credit cards when she came here.

I drew a new vertical line, wrote *Friday* above it and *0515* below. "Rosalyn grabbed a coffee and went to the front yard to prepare to decorate the tent." Another vertical line. "At 0520, Tripp and I were working on breakfast when Mamie entered through the back door. She said she'd walked up to the campground, wandered around, and talked with a few people. I stopped there on my way in this morning and was able to corroborate that claim. Mamie chatted with us for a few minutes, then went upstairs to see if Ty needed help getting dressed. He's disabled and uses a wheelchair." Another vertical line. "At 0525, Nell left for a swim. Half an hour later, Boone and Dinah went for a run, Bruce took their youngest daughter to the shore to gather rocks, and Harlan took a mug of coffee to Victoria in the front yard where Clyde was playing. That tells you what everyone was doing and where they were."

Martin scanned the list of names. "What about Tex, Arizona, and the other girls?"

"When we saw Tex and Arizona, they said it was a treat to sleep in until seven and have breakfast ready for them when they came down. The older Lockwood girls were, I believe, in their room."

"Gus Lewis?"

"He's not staying at the B&B." I left it at that for now and would deal with the tent in the woods in a minute. I drew a longer, thicker line and wrote *0720*. "That's when Rosalyn reported Colton was in the lake, and she presumed he was dead."

"All right, so you heard Colton's voice at ten Thursday night, and Roz found him nine hours later at seven twenty."

I went to the left side of the board and drew a red line I labeled *2217*. "At ten seventeen, Pine Time's security video showed Colton attempt to hit Sunny. He swung so hard, he spun himself around. Sunny went inside at that point. According to her statement, and the video backs her up, she came outside again around midnight, 0013 according to the timestamp, to bring him inside but he was passed out cold on the loveseat. She covered him with a blanket and went back to bed." I drew two more lines and labeled one *0400* and the other *0428*. "Tripp said he got up at four. Right around four thirty, Meeka started barking and woke me up. The timestamp showed that at 0428, someone, who I'll call A, climbed the stairs to the sundeck. Either A called out to Colton or the sound of them climbing the stairs and crossing the deck woke him up. They argued, and then A hit Colton with something hard enough to knock him unconscious. A left and approximately five minutes later, a different person, B, went to Colton, picked him up, and tossed him over the side. At least I believe it was someone different. B appeared to be bigger than A. The distance from the camera to the sundeck is kind of far, and our laptop screen is too small for me to see the images clearly when I zoom in."

Martin waited until he was sure I'd finished speaking and somberly stated, "Let's make a suspect list."

Next to the full list of event guests, I wrote:

Sunny Alexander
Bruce and Nell Lockwood
Bruce Lockwood and Tex Alexander
Bruce Lockwood and Gus Lewis
Tex Alexander and Gus Lewis
Gus Lewis
Mamie and Ty Alexander and Gus Lewis

"Those are the people I think could be responsible and possible pairings."

"Why them?"

"Bruce, Nell, Mamie, and Ty," I began, "are fed up with Colton's mistreatment of Sunny. He's degrading, disrespectful, and possibly violent. The video showed two people, or the same person twice, with two healthy legs so obviously not Ty. He could have, however, instructed Bruce to put Colton in his place. That's why he's on the list."

"Fair enough."

"Mamie was so angry at Colton, I could see her knocking him out and then getting someone else to dispose of the body, so to speak. Same, potentially, with Nell." I tapped Sunny's name. "According to the video, Sunny never left the apartment, but she could have contacted someone via cellphone to take care of Colton for her." I placed a finger next to Gus Lewis's name. "He's an obvious possibility because he has a huge crush on Sunny, but he's almost *too* obvious. Tex and the other Alexander brothers are fed up with their pampered youngest brother. They feel Colton is lazy and does nothing but still gets money from their mother to cover his gambling debts and massive bar tab." I took a step back to study the list. "That's it."

Martin compared the list against my timeline. "The four o'clock time slot shows that's when Tripp woke up. Is he on your suspect list?"

"He is." My heart sunk, and my hands shook horribly while I wrote Tripp's name on the board. "Tripp and Colton have a relationship that I haven't been able to get specifics on yet, but I will."

Thankfully, Martin left it at that. "You said it looked like two people were involved with the attack. Let's discuss that."

"Like I mentioned, it appeared the person who hit Colton was smaller than the one who picked him up. I sent a copy of the video to my email here so we could watch it on the big screen."

"Let's do it."

While I cued up the video in the interview room next door, Martin made more coffee for us.

He handed me my refilled cup and took a seat while I stood next to the screen with the remote control in hand. As I'd hoped, the larger screen helped tremendously.

"This is just before the attacker appears at the top of the stairs. You can see Colton wake up as the attacker comes into view."

The black-and-white infrared recording was high-quality enough that, when I zoomed in, we could make out important details even from the distance. The first person who approached Colton had short hair and a trim build. They wore jeans, a plaid shirt left unbuttoned, and a cowboy hat, which covered enough of their face that I couldn't make out who it was. Boone, Tex, and Bruce all wore plaid shirts and cowboy hats. The video showed Colton and the person arguing for a short time, and then the attacker pulled back their arm and swung it forward hard.

Martin leaned toward the screen, elbows on knees, and instructed, "Back it up to the point where they bring their arm back and pause it."

I did so.

"What is that in their hand?" he asked, squinting. "A horseshoe?"

I stepped closer to the screen. "I think you're right. Did Gil do the dive search?"

"Owen did it. He swam around for almost an hour, checked a fifty-yard arc in front of the boathouse, and found nothing. Well, nothing that would be considered a weapon but plenty of aluminum cans, plastic bottles, and things like lost swim goggles. He's going to organize a villager dive at the end of the season to clean up the lake floor. I can't even guess when we last did that."

"Good plan," I said absently and returned to the topic of horseshoes. "Considering the only horses around here are at the circus, the weapon probably came from the back of one of the farm or ranch trucks. Since it wasn't in the lake, they either put it back in the truck, in our trash, tossed it in the woods . . . or disposed of it in any other number of ways."

"If you can't get them to agree to voluntary searches of their vehicles and don't find it in your trash, I'll call for a warrant. Meeka and Tyrann can search the woods without a warrant."

Meeka perked up when she heard her name and the word *search*. She loved looking for things.

We returned to the video. Colton had slumped to the deck a heartbeat after being struck, and the attacker left.

"About five minutes after the attack," I began, "someone comes back to the sundeck. It's easy to see on this screen that this isn't the same person."

"Not the same," Martin agreed immediately and listed, "different clothes or at least no plaid shirt, a baseball hat—"

I didn't hear what he said after *baseball hat*.

"Jayne?" From his tone, Martin had clearly called my name a few times.

"Sorry. What?" I blinked at him.

"You checked out. Why?"

"The hat." I paced around the room thinking of the contents of our bedroom closet. "Tripp has exactly one baseball hat. He won it when we went to an outdoors show." I tapped my forehead, trying to remember the logo. "Some camping gear manufacturer. I can't remember the name, but the point is he *never* wears it. He has like two dozen beanies of varying thicknesses and rotates between those. Sometimes he'll change things up and wear a bandana when he's cooking or he'll tie his hair back in a stubby ponytail. Since the day I met him, I have never seen him wear a baseball hat."

Martin gestured at the screen and offered me an additional ray of hope. "Let's look closer for details. This video is remarkably clear. Blackbird Industries equipment, I assume?"

"Yeah," I murmured while stepping up to the screen again.

"Look at the person's physique."

This guy's T-shirt fit snug, and he had broad shoulders. He picked up Colton like he weighed nothing instead of a good one hundred eighty pounds of dead weight. Or unconscious weight as the case would be.

My throat felt tight as I said, "Hay bales are surprisingly heavy. Full feed sacks are too."

"What?" Martin looked confused.

"That's what Tripp told me when we were discussing how Colton could have ended up in the water. He was telling me how strong people who work on farms can be." I pressed my finger to the man on the screen. "Tripp is lean and muscular. That guy is broad and bulky." I looked at Martin, tears of relief threatening to spill. "That's not Tripp."

"It's not." He seemed equally relieved. "Do you know who it could be?"

I studied the man closer. "I can't be sure. They all—Tex, Bruce, Boone, and Gus—have all worn hats at some point, but not the entire time. I would have sworn that Boone wasn't involved, but I think he had a baseball hat on when he and Dinah went out for their run yesterday. Colton and Harlan both wore cowboy hats. Sunny even told Colton he could wear his during the ceremony."

"Sounds like hats are a big deal to these guys," Martin mused. "Can we get something specific about the one this guy is wearing?"

I backed up the video. Just before scooping up Colton, the man on the screen turned his hat around as though to prevent it being knocked off his head. "What is that? Looks like a circle with . . . I can't tell what the thing in the middle is." I zoomed in even closer, and the image blurred, so I backed off a bit again.

"Looks like a brand," Martin stated and stood next to me. "As in, what they use on cattle."

"Okay, I can see that." I looked longer. "An *A* in the middle with the line extending out on both sides."

Martin stood and tapped the left side. "That looks like an *H*."

It did. "And that's a sideways *V* on the left. To make it look like an arrow? Alexander, Harlan and Victoria. It's their ranch brand."

"Which of them would wear that?"

I groaned. "Boone, Tex, Gus, or Harlan."

"Are you adding Harlan to the suspect list?"

I considered that, then shook my head. "He's a big man and is probably plenty strong, but he walks with a limp. Bad knee, I think. Both guys in the video walked smoothly. Besides, while he seems frustrated with his son, I don't see him wanting to harm him. So not Harlan or Ty."

Martin offered me a small smile. "And we eliminated Tripp."

We went back to the whiteboard in his office and with a much steadier hand, I drew a line through Tripp's name. Thank the Goddess.

"The first person had a trim build." I crossed off Mamie. "She's a little on the plump side, and I don't think she could have lifted Colton. We already discussed that Ty couldn't have climbed the stairs."

"Unless the two of them hired someone to do this," Martin reminded me.

I added that possibility as a note next to their names. "Nell is on the tall side, and while she could have hit Colton, she has a much smaller build than the first person on the video. Although, in the social media pictures she showed me of her at her huge farmers' market stand, she's almost always wearing a pastel plaid shirt. It's like her uniform."

"Add a little padding . . . I'm not sure we can eliminate her."

"She could have worn padding, but that seems like a stretch at four thirty in the morning." This was our rule for brainstorming: no idea was to be held back no matter how improbable. Since there was potential doubt about Nell's involvement, I added a note next to her name too. Then I underlined Bruce, Tex, Boone, and Gus. "That leaves us with these four. Boone and Gus are both on the bulkier side so could have tossed Colton over the railing."

"Lean doesn't mean not strong," Martin noted with a hint of offense in his voice.

"Point taken. Guess I need to ask some more questions."

"Start with Tripp," Martin instructed. "Sounds like he could supply some answers. It should help that you no longer see him as a suspect."

"It does. And I've got an idea for how to get him to talk."

In unison, our walkie talkie units blared out three loud

beeps—River's signal that we were to call him. Two beeps meant call the Barlow-Carr cottage. Three meant he was at his office at Blackbird Cottage.

Martin hit the speaker button on his desk phone and then the button for River's office.

"Good morning, Sheriff Reed," River greeted. "I'm looking for Deputy O'Shea. Is she there or on patrol?"

"I'm here," I called out.

"Excellent. As soon as possible, come to my office, please."

"We're just finishing here," I told him. "I can be there in half an hour or so."

"Very good." He disconnected without another word.

"Did we cover everything?" Martin asked.

I checked over the timeline I'd written on the board and underlined Sunny's name. "I'm not convinced she's completely innocent here."

"That may be because you have *feelings* surrounding her and Tripp."

"I've been trying to think more reasonably about that. Until a few weeks before coming to the village, I was engaged to Jonah. Tripp is entitled to past romances." Much as I hated to think of him with another woman. "Back to Sunny. When I spoke with her, she seemed more eager to vent her marital frustrations than discuss who could have done this to her husband. If I question Bruce and Boone further, and manage to track down Tex, maybe they'll clear her. Or implicate her."

"Don't forget Gus Lewis."

"He's at the hospital with Sunny right now. After speaking with Dinah about him, I convinced her that she and Boone should go get Sunny and bring her back. I didn't like the idea of her being alone in a vehicle with Gus. Meeka and I will stop at his tent on the way home. Maybe he left a window unzipped and I'll—"

"His tent?"

Time to fess up. "Literally everywhere in the village was

full, and I was pretty sure he'd sleep in his truck rather than drive twenty or thirty miles for a room. I told him he could set up a tent in my woods deep inside the tree line by the field near the campground where no one could see him."

The more I explained, the deeper Martin's frown grew. "Do we need to discuss that decision?"

"No, we do not. He suckered me and made me feel sorry for him. I won't let that happen again."

"Okay." Martin's tone indicated we were done. "If you think of anything else, let me know. If you want to make an arrest, I can come pick the person up. In the meantime, you'd better get over to River."

"Will do. Wonder what he wants me to do now." I mentally began to shift to Village Manager Jayne mindset.

"By the way," Martin called out as I left his office, "why is there a bag of bread on your desk?"

I explained Lily Grace's idea of leaving gifts for the crows.

"An easy solution to a serious problem?" he asked. "I'm doubtful but glad to know you're trying something."

Chapter Eighteen

I ALMOST DROVE TO BLACKBIRD COTTAGE BUT WANTED TO clear my head of suspects—and Tripp not being one of them! —before talking with River, so Meeka and I walked instead. As we approached Shoppe Mystique, Morgan stepped outside.

"Blessed *quiet* morning." She exhaled a relieved sigh and gave Meeka a scratch with her short fingernails. She used to wear them long until she accidentally scratched Talon during a diaper change and immediately cut them all off.

"What are you up to this morning?" I smiled at Meeka's moment of bliss.

"Restoring order to my shop."

"Did you have chaos last night too?"

"Somewhat. Mostly I'm reveling in the peace of the moment. The only quiet I can find lately is in the garden or while walking between home and here. As for chaos, there's always a certain amount that comes with the tourists, but I agree there seems to be more of it with this group. Ironically, they come here to participate in a Wiccan celebration and are less respectful of our traditions than those who are simply here for vacation."

"This is only my second year, so I don't have much to compare to, but I agree that this group seems rowdier than others have been. We shouldn't blame everything on the tourists, though. I mean, we can't throw parties and then get upset when things get messy. Not if we don't announce and enforce some rules." Hopefully I could talk with River about this today. "In other news, I performed my spell last night."

"And how did it go?"

"Good, I think." I pushed my shoulders back proudly. "I feel very accomplished. Now I'm waiting for it to kick in."

"Patience, Jayne."

"Easy for you to say." It had been late April since we'd chatted even this long. Last night was almost entirely devoted to my spell. I can't recall asking about her or the twins even once. "How are my babies? I didn't get to kiss their cheeks last night. Or even ask about them. I'm a terrible aunt."

"You're a wonderful aunt," she assured. "Before you got there last night, they gave us a glimpse of their twin connection. Now we know what it means when they sit close, stare at each other, and get very quiet. It seems they're formulating a plan."

"Really? What did they do?"

"Juniper distracted us by crying over a non-existent injury while Talon grabbed a fistful of their favorite crackers from the container on the coffee table."

I shook my head in a *naughty twins* way but was doubled over laughing inside. "You'll have to keep everything three feet off the ground now. Can't wait to see what they do next."

"Goddess help us."

"Much as I'd love to talk all morning, you should get back to restoring order, and I should get going. Boss Man summoned me."

Morgan made a cautioning hum sound. "Beware, he's still acting oddly."

"Guy time with Tripp didn't help?"

"I think he enjoyed talking with Tripp, but whatever is at the root of this, it's still there."

"What does 'acting oddly' mean?"

"How to explain?" She gazed at the sky while coming up with an answer. "It's like he's chanting to himself, but he stops when I get close enough to hear, so I can't make out the words. To be honest, I'm getting a little concerned about him."

"Talk to him," I advised as she had me yesterday regarding Tripp. "Before I left home this morning, I warned Tripp that we are going to talk about Sunny and the others tonight. I've been patient long enough. He has to give me something."

"And how did he react?"

I smiled. "He told me he loved me."

"You've got a good man, Lady Jayne."

"As do you. They're just going through a rough patch right now." An idea occurred to me. "You know what we need?"

She tilted her head and grinned mischievously. "I could list a number of things. What are *you* thinking?"

"Another weekend away. Not until the end of the season, obviously."

In late fall, Morgan got an email from two women named Silver and Moon. More than a year ago, the friends spent a week in Whispering Pines learning how to run a New Age shop from Morgan and Briar. They had finally opened their store, Silver Moon Apothecary, in Blackwood Grove in southwestern Wisconsin, and invited the mother-daughter duo to come see it. Briar declined, so Morgan asked if I wanted to go with her instead. I did, and we had the best time on our girlfriend road trip weekend.

Morgan's eyes lit up. "Another trip sounds like a wonderful idea. We'll need to start planning where to go next. For now, good luck with River."

I stopped next door at Ye Olde Bean Grinder to get a

mocha for me and a bag of biscuits for Meeka. When I told Violet where we were off to, she gave me her version of the goings-on last night.

"At first, I thought it was my imagination but realized they were asking for drinks that were purposely complicated. The joke was on them when they got exactly what they asked for and I wouldn't give them a refund. Honestly, some of those combinations were disgusting. And few of them seem to understand what a trashcan is for. You should have seen my dining room." She inhaled deeply to calm herself. "I'll stop there, but my point is you need to talk to River about this."

I promised I would. Hopefully today. My list of complaints was growing unwieldy.

At Blackbird Cottage, Josephine was waiting for me. I couldn't believe how much more relaxed she was now than when she first arrived in the village dressed in business slacks, a button-up blouse, heels, and a sleek ponytail. Today, she wore loose linen pants, a tank top, and sandals. Her coily black hair was long and free. I liked it when she wore it that way.

"Is he in his office?" I tossed my empty coffee cup in the bin and then headed for the stairs.

"He is. I'm going up with you. We've both been summoned."

"Both of us? I just talked to Morgan, and she says he's been 'acting oddly lately.' Any idea what's going on?"

Josephine shook her head. "He's been complaining about the crows a lot, but I have no idea why that's got him so worked up."

"Let's go see if we can find out."

We started the climb to the third floor, Meeka plodding along after us.

"Will I be able to move back into The Boathouse on Monday?" Josephine asked. "I miss the lake view."

I understood that completely. "Absolutely. I'll even ask

Holly and Arden to clean the apartment before the other rooms."

Josephine knocked lightly on the doorjamb at the top of the last flight of stairs. "Are you ready for us?"

"Yes, please come in," River replied.

Before he commandeered the cottage, this room was a frilly pink-and-white girly-girl's dream of a bedroom. Rosalyn would have loved it. Never in a million years would I have guessed Flavia Reed had a girly side. If there had been a casting call held for a sourpuss, uptight, frigid woman, she would absolutely have gotten the part.

Now, the room felt a bit like a cave. The walls were dark charcoal gray with a slight sheen to help reflect any available light around the room. River's desk had a clear glass top sitting on a wrought iron base with taloned feet like those found on a clawfoot bathtub. Blood-red pops of color broke up the black and gray—his leather wingback desk chair, a vase on a book case, and a tall slim lamp on the desk. A trio of paintings of gothic castles, mostly black with splashes of red, hung over a black leather sofa. The ornate black frames were lightly speckled with midnight purple in a nod to Morgan. He preferred red. She loved purple.

River indicated we should sit on the sofa, and he took the red tufted chair next to it.

"Before we begin," I stated, "I'd like to talk about some villager concerns, if that's okay."

He seemed almost grateful for the delay. "Things did not go well during the Litha celebration last night?"

"Unfortunately, last night is only one of the problems." As I read my list of complaints from the shop owners and villagers, Josephine took notes, and River's frown intensified.

"I agree," he said when I finished speaking, "these things need to be rectified. What do you propose, Manageress?"

His latest title for me was a mouthful. "We've got a couple

of options. We could limit the number of tourists allowed in the commons."

"Is that doable?" he wondered, mostly to himself.

"It is," I answered, "but it would mean setting up fencing with entrance gates. Not exactly practical or aesthetically pleasing. We could stop the festivities altogether and let the villagers celebrate privately."

"That would severely impact the businesses income," he objected.

"Correct. They count on the season to support them. Canceling sabbat celebrations isn't the best idea, but the shop owners are very unhappy with the tourists' behavior last night."

"I count on you to provide solutions. What else do you propose?" He was already losing patience with this topic.

"We need more than two deputies during these events. Maybe we can attract more villager volunteers with some sort of compensation. I think ending the Litha celebration at midnight, like we do with the other gatherings, makes the most sense. All-night parties are exhausting and just get rowdier as the night goes on. Also, I think we need to consider abandoning the cottage rentals." Before he could question that, I quickly added, "The idea seems to have worked too well because now we don't have enough villagers to work in the shops, which are becoming overwhelmed with the increased traffic."

River held up a hand, indicating I should stop talking. "As Morgan has informed me numerous times, the village has become too popular. An interesting problem to have." He considered this for a minute, then nodded. "Yes to bringing on more help during the events. Ask Sheriff Reed to put together a proposal, and I will review it. I also approve adding a third permanent deputy to the station."

"Regarding the cottage rentals," I added, "those villagers who stay here all season don't like having tourists next door."

He nodded slowly. "We will conclude the cottage rental experiment at the end of the season."

"Some of them are already taking reservations for next year," Josephine pointed out. "We'll need to let everyone know right away. I'll put together a letter."

"Very good. We have the start of a workable plan to address villager dissatisfaction." He waited, then asked, "Is there anything else?"

"You know what happened at Pine Time," I said.

"I am aware, yes. Tripp told me about the unfortunate turn of events when you came over last evening."

"Martin and I narrowed the suspect list." I gave him a brief recap of our brainstorming session.

"When do you expect to have people in custody?"

"This afternoon. I'm going back to Pine Time when we're finished here. I've got video evidence of the crime, so it shouldn't take much to get confessions."

"Very good. Unless there's anything else . . ."

Josephine shook her head as I said, "Nothing else for me."

He sat with his elbows resting on the arms of his chair, fingers tented. While he normally looked people in the eye when he spoke, he seemed to be purposely avoiding looking at either of us now. "As for the reason I brought you both here, I'm not prepared to discuss details. Not until, as the saying goes, I wrap my head around what's going on. Until that time, I have an assignment for each of you."

An assignment with no details? Wrap his head around what was going on? Morgan and Josephine were right; he was acting strangely. And this sounded bigger than the crows.

"The two of you are my seconds-in-command. I will need you to step up even more and help me run things for, hopefully, a short time. What I can tell you is that this is something personal, and it has left me emotional and sidetracked."

River emotional? And he was *asking* for help? Seriously, what was happening?

"Josephine," he continued, "I will compose a letter to upper management explaining that until further notice, all communication regarding Blackbird Industries, whether minor or extreme, must go through you. You will then discuss it with me and reply on my behalf. Once the letter is ready, you can review it and forward it to the appropriate people.

"Jayne, your grandmother always intended for you to take her place as ruler, for lack of a better word. Your solutions to the current problems in the village prove to me that she was correct. You are more than qualified to deal with these issues.

"Rest assured that I will back you both on whatever decisions you make, but if you feel you need my input, I'm not going anywhere. I will be either here or at home with my family." He laughed softly. "By the looks on your faces, this is a surprise for you. What questions do you have?"

"None at this time," Josephine said.

"I have more of a suggestion than a question," I blurted before I could stop myself. "I hope I'm not overstepping my bounds."

He hesitated before asking, "What is it?"

I looked him in the eye. "I stopped and talked with Morgan on my way over here. She warned me that something has been bothering you, but she doesn't know what it is. After hearing what you just told us, I think you should talk to her. She should know the full story."

My heart hammered in my chest, and Meeka, sensing my rising stress level, leaned against my leg as I waited for River to reply. Had I just made another of my signature bad decisions?

"Offering me advice," he said, his voice even. "Seems we have changed positions, Proprietress."

I released the breath I'd been holding after hearing him use the first nickname he'd given me. The one he now used only in casual situations. I relaxed further when one corner of his mouth curved up a fraction of an inch.

"I thank you for your concern," he added, "and will take your words under advisement."

Having pushed as far as I dared, I clamped my mouth shut and nodded in response.

"If there's nothing else," he said, "I have things to take care of. Josephine, please walk Jayne down and then return in an hour to review the letter. And during this time, the two of you should be in regular contact with each other."

We agreed and left his office.

"*What* is going on?" I asked when we got to the main floor.

"I have no idea," Josephine answered. "You know how private he is. I hope Morgan can convince him to let us in. Whatever this is, maybe we can help."

"Right. Did I overstep? I didn't make him angry, did I?"

"I don't think I've ever seen him angry, but on occasion he does this thing." She struggled to explain. "I can only describe it as the sort of mind control tactic hypnotists use."

I gasped. "I think I know what you're talking about. He came to Whispering Pines the weekend of Pine Time's grand opening. Another guest was the epitome of a disgusting jerk. He was nasty to everyone but especially his wife. River witnessed one of the man's verbal attacks on her while they were eating breakfast in the dining room. The guy just wouldn't stop. I watched River stare him in the eye and then draw his finger down his own throat from chin to Adam's apple. The next thing I knew, the man started choking on whatever he'd been eating."

Josephine nodded. "That's what I mean. I know it's basically a power of suggestion thing. It's not like he can perform magic. Either way, it's a little freaky."

"How often have you seen him do it?"

"Only once. No, twice. Both were similar situations to

what you described. Someone upset him, and he made them choke."

"You've proven my point. It's probably best to not anger him." I called for Meeka, who was sniffing around the cottage. "If I don't see you before, I'll see you at home on Monday."

"Home," she said dreamily and pressed her hands together in thanks.

Chapter Nineteen

GUS LEWIS DROVE A RUSTY, OLD FALLING APART FOREST-GREEN pickup truck. It was distinctive looking, so I spotted it easily as I drove past the campground parking lot. When did he get back?

Past the campground, at the tree line, I pulled over and opened the back of my car to let Meeka out.

"Let's go talk to a suspect." I tilted her furry little face up to mine. "Stay with me, girl. I'm feeling a little uneasy about this Gus guy, so don't go running off."

She hopped out and practically sat on my foot while I closed the cage and hatch again.

"Okay. Meeka, heel."

She tilted her head and seemed to scowl in a way that meant, *I heard you the first time.*

I followed the route Gus had worn through the grass and made as little noise as possible.

Wearing a baseball cap with the now easily recognizable Alexander Ranch brand on the front, Gus paced around his tent. He repeatedly threw his hands in the air as he muttered to himself, punctuating whatever thought was upsetting him. Then he pulled the hat off his head, tossed it aside, and ran his hands through his curly hair. When he dropped to the ground, lowered his head to his knees, and let out a primal roar of frustration, I decided it probably wasn't a good idea to confront this guy by myself.

Meeka never left my side, following my every move as I backtracked out of the woods. Once we were home, she sat in the middle of the driveway and stared toward the campground, as though ready to defend the property against intruders. I went directly to the office.

"Hey," I greeted when Martin answered the phone. "Is that video still up in the interview room?"

"It is. Need me to check something?"

"Yeah, does the person who threw Colton over the railing have curly hair?"

"Hang on." I heard his footsteps as he walked through the station. A few seconds later, "Yes, he does. Why is this significant?"

"Gus is the only one of the group who has curly hair. I just saw him near his tent. He was wearing that same hat."

"With the ranch's brand."

"Right. He's really agitated, and I'd rather not confront him alone."

"I told you I'd come get him."

"Yeah, I'm not sure you should confront him alone either. Okay, hurry. I'm a little worried he might run. I'll meet you at the tree line."

As I left to meet Martin, I heard voices coming from the back patio. I looked to see who was out there and spotted Tripp sitting outside with Sunny.

Trust him, Deputy Jayne urged in her logical way. *Analyze the scene.*

When I did, I realized they weren't sitting next to each other. She was on the loveseat, and he was on a chair. Their body language indicated nothing romantic or intimate was going on. If anything, they appeared a little awkward. What were they talking about?

I'd ask him later. For now, I needed to assist the sheriff with an arrest.

Martin met me about a minute after I got to the designated spot and followed me to Gus's site. As I feared, Gus was packing up his gear. If another task, even a quick one, had needed my attention, we'd be issuing a BOLO for his truck.

"Going somewhere, Gus?" I asked.

He spun around, tent spikes in his hands. Both Martin and I stiffened and squared our stances. Those spikes could easily be used as weapons.

When Gus saw it was me, he turned back to packing up his tent. "Yeah, I'm out of here. Going back to Fargo. Think it's time for me to move on from there too."

I took a step closer to him while Martin moved to the left. "You were at the hospital with Sunny. Did something happen there? You seem really upset."

Gus tossed the spikes on the ground, but they were still easily within reach. "Sunny and Victoria argued about Colton. It was bad. I've never seen them fight like that. Victoria and Harlan came back here to change clothes or whatever. When they left, Sunny talked to the doctor, then called her mom. I don't know what Mamie said, but Sunny wanted to come back here right away, so I brought her."

"What has you so upset? Did Sunny say some—"

"I don't want to talk about it." His tone elevated in both intensity and volume.

"Okay," I said soothingly. "There is something else we need to talk about, though. Would you turn and look at me for a minute?"

His head dropped back, then he turned with a sigh and snapped, "What?"

Martin and I took turns explaining what we saw on the security video. He filled in details I left out and vice versa.

Martin even thought to bring a screenshot of Gus holding Colton over the side of the railing.

"That's you," he said, "isn't it?"

Gus hesitated, searching for an explanation, then gave up. "Pretty obvious it is."

"We know from the video," I began, "that you didn't knock Colton out. Someone else did that. Do you know who?"

"No comment."

"Did that person ask you to move Colton?"

"No comment."

"Did they specifically ask you to drop him in the lake, or was that your idea?"

"No comment."

"Was it Sunny?" Martin asked. "Did she ask you to do this?"

"No," Gus insisted. "She didn't know."

"She didn't know you did what you did," Martin clarified, "or that anything was happening outside while she slept inside the apartment a few feet away?"

Gus hung his head. "No comment."

Martin took his handcuffs out of the pouch on his belt. "Hold your hands out to your sides, please."

Gus followed the order without hesitation.

While locking the cuffs around his wrists, Martin said, "Gus Lewis, I'm arresting you for the attempted murder of Colton Alexander. If he dies, the charge will change." Martin continued reading Gus his Miranda rights as he led him to the Tahoe. Once Gus was secured in the backseat, Martin told me, "I'll process him so you can deal with figuring out who the other guy is."

I nodded. "I'll write up the report once this is all over."

With his hand on the doorhandle, he added, "If you see Rosalyn, tell her I'll call her later."

"I'll give her a kiss for you too."

He smirked, gave a little salute, and left with Gus.

Back at the house, I saw Sunny carrying a suitcase down the boathouse stairs.

"Hey, Sunny," I called out. "What's going on? Are you leaving?"

She stopped at the bottom of the stairs and let out a heavy exhale. It was a big suitcase. "I'm moving in with my parents and Clyde. Colton isn't coming back tonight, and we have to leave tomorrow, so there's no sense in me staying in the apartment by myself. It's lovely, by the way. So cute the way Rosalyn decorated it. And that bed is *so* comfortable."

I smiled in thanks. "When did you get back? I thought you'd be at the hospital until Victoria and Harlan returned."

"After they left, I called my mom to check on Clyde. She said he was upset and crying and wanted to know where his mommy and daddy were. Mom said he had a bad night last night and it only got worse when he couldn't find me this morning. So I had Gus bring me back here. It would only be an hour or two that Colton would be there alone." She paused as though debating saying more and then sat on the stairs. "I made a decision. Victoria was horrible to me at the hospital."

Gus said they argued. I'd tell her about him when she was done saying what she wanted to say.

"She was nearly hysterical over what had happened to Colton, and I understood that. She's never really liked me—" She shook her head. "No more candy coating. The woman hates me. She accused me of purposely getting pregnant to get at Colton's money." She snort-laughed. "If I wanted Alexander money, I would have seduced one of his brothers. They're all hardworking and motivated, unlike their lazy baby brother. And Tex was available four years ago so . . ." She winced. "That was probably inappropriate. Anyway, after a full day of listening to her tell me what a gold-digging, horrible wife and mother I was and how her son would be better without me, I decided she was right."

"That he'd be better without you?"

She shook her head. "That my life would be better without him."

Her husband was in the hospital, fighting for his life, but I didn't get the impression she meant she had tried to have him killed.

"I'm certainly not a gold digger, and I am an awesome mom. I learned from one of the best, after all. As for being Colton's wife, I can't tell you how many times I tried to be the woman he wanted. Even while organizing this event, I kept thinking he's not going to like this. I should put tires on his truck instead. But I've always wanted a real wedding, even a tiny one. I scrimp and scrounge and manage our teensy budget pretty well, I think." A shadow crossed her face. Thinking of her husband's gambling debts? She shook her head and blinked. "I decided to be true to my mom's wish and use the money for a wedding."

"You said you'd be better off without him. What did you mean by that?"

"I didn't ask anyone to kill him if that's what you're thinking. Not to come off as a heartless wench, but I decided if Colton survives this, I'm going to divorce him. Even if he has an *I've seen the light* experience and ends up caring about me even remotely, his mother will make my life hell until she or I die. I can't do it anymore. I can't keep living my life to make them happy. I shouldn't have to. Especially because I've got a family who will support whatever I choose to do."

"I'm sorry it took a tragedy to lead you to this, but good for you." I waited a beat, then asked, "Speaking of Colton, how is he doing?"

Sunny shook her head. "They don't expect him to make it. Of course, Victoria says that's my fault. According to her, if I hadn't kicked him out of the apartment last night, he wouldn't have been out on the sundeck and wouldn't have gotten attacked."

"That's not what happened. I'll tell her if you want me to. I told you before, Tripp and I overheard the fight."

She shrugged and stared out at the lake. "I'm not sure I care either way."

"Not to overstep my bounds"—although that seemed to be my theme for the day—"but you've got to think about your son. He's also their grandson. If Colton doesn't make it, I wouldn't be surprised if they fight you for custody."

The color drained from behind her suntan. "Oh God, I didn't think of that. You're absolutely right." She put her hands over her face. "I'll never be done with them, will I?"

"No, you won't, but you may be able to come to neutral grounds for Clyde's sake. Sounds like that little boy is about to lose his daddy."

Then her anger at her husband and his parents turned into sorrow for her son. Her shoulders shook as she sobbed.

I'd tell her about Gus later. For now, I placed a hand on her shoulder, and she covered it with her own. Sunny seemed like a good person. Time to track down Tripp and learn the rest.

"I'll go get your mom," I told Sunny and slipped away.

Chapter Twenty

I TRACKED DOWN MAMIE FOR SUNNY AND THEN THOUGHT about speaking with all the guests again to try to figure out which one of them hit Colton with that horseshoe. I also thought about searching for the horseshoe. However, knowing that Sunny planned to leave Colton distracted me. Was she interested in trying to rekindle something with Tripp?

I couldn't wait any longer. The time for him to talk to me was now. I needed to know the truth about these people.

"Why are we going right?" Tripp asked as I eased the boat toward the weedy area. "I thought we were going fishing."

Between all the tourists who descended on the village and the year-round villagers, there was little of my grandparents' property that was just for the family anymore. In fact, I only owned ten of the original two thousand acres. River bought the rest from my parents. My grandfather's treasured speedboat was something that was just ours. No one else got to use it. The western-most side of Lucy Lake was another. Could people enter this area? Sure, they could, but I warned everyone not to go to the right because of the weeds. Gil and Oren also told folks who rented kayaks and canoes from the marina that the west side of the lake was off limits because it was too dangerous. A few months after I moved to the village, a man almost drowned after getting tangled in the weeds. I rescued him, but he died a few hours later. Dry drowning, Dr. Bundy, the coroner, had determined. That was when we posted buoys with big *Danger: Thick Weeds, Turn Back* signs.

"You can toss a line in the water if you want." I picked up speed, then killed the motor so weeds wouldn't get tangled in the propeller. The momentum carried us through the ten-foot-wide patch of foliage that ran the entire width of the lake and into The Secret Pond, as I'd dubbed it. The pond was surrounded by towering pines, and despite the underwater jungle we had to pass over to get here, the water in this spot was somehow perfectly clear of the pesky plants. It was peaceful and private and felt like slipping into another world.

"There aren't any fish at this end," Tripp complained and frowned at the fishing gear he'd grabbed.

I let the boat drift a little farther and then dropped the anchor. "Guess we'll have to talk, then." I'd start with an easy question and hoped he would have an easy answer. "What happened to your knuckles?"

He glanced down at his scraped but healing hand. "I helped Colton bring their bags up to the apartment, and we got into an argument. We were discussing an incident that happened a long time ago. Tempers flared, and when I held out my hand to offer an apology, he swatted it away and into the railing hard enough to scrape it." He turned his head toward me. "Is that really what you brought me out here to ask?"

No, but at least I had an answer for the blood Jagger found near the stairs. "I brought you here because I want to know about Sunny and her people. I've made that pretty clear since the hug she gave you Thursday afternoon, but you've been completely shut-mouthed about it. I told you when I left this morning we were going to talk today. So unless you plan to swim home, which would be dangerous, we're not going anywhere until you talk to me."

Meeka whimpered at the angry tone in my voice and jumped overboard. Letting her floatation vest help carry her, she paddled toward the shoreline away from the weeds as I'd taught her. I climbed out of the captain's chair, shoved the key in my pocket, and moved to the small sundeck at the bow of the boat.

Tripp sat on the built-in, cushioned bench across from mine and took a minute to gather his thoughts. "Remember I told you how I went looking for my mom?"

Progress. Thank the Goddess. "I remember. You lived with your aunt and uncle until you graduated high school, then started searching for her."

"Right. For five years, I wandered from California to Washington state, then through Oregon, Wyoming, Colorado, and Nebraska."

"Then the Dakotas and you quit wandering when you got to Fargo?" Was Sunny the reason?

"After five years of nothing but leads that turned into dead ends, yeah, I gave up." His gaze took on that faraway look of someone remembering their past. Or maybe regretting a choice they made. "I liked Fargo. Very friendly people there. I worked as a cook at a diner for a year."

"That's where you learned to cook and bake."

A fond smile warmed his face. "An older couple owned the place. She had health problems that got steadily worse over that year, and they decided it was time to retire. Their house sold quickly, so they shut down the diner, moved to Arizona, and let the realtors deal with the diner's sale. I needed a paycheck and heard the Swensons were looking for help on their farm."

"And that's where you met Sunny."

"We met soon after I got hired but didn't start seeing each other for about a year." Almost sheepishly, he added, "I'd been

warned to stay away from her. That was one of Ty's big rules
—stay away from his daughter. I guess there had been workers
in the past who got a little handsy."

"And you decided to ignore the warning?"

He gave an unapologetic shrug. "We really liked each
other, and because of Ty's rule, we didn't *date* in the normal
sense. It's a small town, so going anywhere together in public
without him finding out would have been impossible."

"In other words, you snuck around."

His brow wrinkled in a scowl. "For lack of a better term,
yes. We found places on the farm or in the countryside where
we could be together."

I winced at that.

"It wasn't about sex, Jayne." He tilted his head side-to-
side. "Yeah, okay, there was some of that, but mostly we talked
and went for walks at night. We played cards and took turns
reading to each other from books and then discussed what we
read. After all those years on the road with my life constantly
changing, I felt unfocused and like I was a failure. Sunny gave
me something to focus on."

His look of longing—For that time? For her?—was like a
stab to my heart. "Did you want to be with her? As in, get
married?"

The seconds that passed before he answered felt like an
hour. "I don't know. Honestly, I didn't think that was in my
future. But after eight months of dating, or whatever you
want to call it, I figured it was time for me to stop
wandering."

"How old were you then?"

Like I often did when trying to remember something, he
stared up into the trees. They were waving about as though
trying to get our attention but not making any sound. None
that I could hear, at least. I *really* needed to stop at Unity and
find out what was wrong with my ears.

"I was twenty-five," he recalled, "when I started working

for the Swensons. Twenty-six when Sunny and I started hanging out."

The boat wasn't big enough to pace around, but if he could have, that's surely what he would have been doing. Sometimes when he had something on his mind, like he did on Thursday and yesterday, he would leave the house and walk up the driveway or into the woods or even clear over to the village for a coffee or ice cream. I knew he might try to take off for a walk when I opened this topic, which was partly why I decided to hold him captive on the boat. Also, there was little chance of us being interrupted out here. Instead of pacing, he made a quarter turn, so I could only see his profile. Little of this was easy for me to hear, but it was worse for him to talk about, so I did my best to tamp down Jayne the Jealous Girlfriend and be Jayne the Understanding Girlfriend.

"Then one day," he continued, "with no warning whatsoever, Sunny told me she couldn't see me anymore. At the time, I guessed one of the other farmhands had seen us together and threatened to tell Ty." Tripp rubbed his hands over his face as though wiping away the memory. "I went to one of the local bars that night, had way too much to drink, and then a couple more when I saw Sunny there. She wouldn't even look at me. By the end of the night, she was talking to Colton."

Ouch. "Did you know him then?"

"Everyone knew Colton. Spoiled rich boy who tried to buy friends by racking up huge bar tabs and poker losses."

Meeka had paddled over to check on us, then turned and swam away again when she heard the venom in his voice.

"I beat him a good dozen times. At poker." An uncharacteristic smirk settled on his face as he added, "I only physically beat him once."

"You beat him up?" I couldn't imagine Tripp even making a fist in anger, let alone hitting someone. "Is that the incident you were talking to him about on the sundeck?"

He nodded but said no more about it. "I liked Sunny a lot but wouldn't say I was in love with her. It was more that being with her made me feel like my life was finally settling in to something normal. I spiraled after she broke up with me. Spent my days on the farm and my nights spending my money on beer and poker. And I dated a lot of women."

Seriously? Who was this person he was talking about?

"It all came to a head one night when Colton and Sunny showed up at the bar. He was acting like he was king of the world with her on his arm, except he was being an even bigger jerk than he was during their argument on the sundeck Thursday night. He said something rude about her, loudly, and then taunted me to do something about it. Since I'd already had too much to drink, I took the bait and hit him. I ended up in the drunk tank for the night. The cop who brought me in said he despised Colton as much as I did so wouldn't press charges that time, but he warned me not to do it again. Ty heard about it, though." Tripp rolled his eyes. "Everyone in town heard about it. Ty pulled me aside the next day. He thanked me for the hard work, handed me a big bonus check for defending his daughter's honor, then said he wouldn't be needing my help anymore. Said the farm held its employees to a high standard but because he liked me, he ignored my bad behavior and hoped I'd straighten out." Tripp gave a little laugh. "Bad behavior. Sounded like something my uncle would have said. At the time, Ty never mentioned me and Sunny hanging out, but when we talked yesterday, he said he knew from the start."

"You hung out for eight months so were still twenty-six when you stopped seeing each other, and you were twenty-eight when we met. What happened during year twenty-seven? Did you leave town?"

"I didn't have much of a choice. Everyone had a reason for not hiring me despite the *Help Wanted* signs in their windows. I was a troublemaker. A hot head. I drank too much.

Got branded a womanizer . . . After hearing enough of those comments, I decided it was time to revive my 'wayward ways,' as my aunt called it. I bounced around the Dakotas and Minnesota doing whatever odd job I could pick up. One guy hired me onto his construction crew building a house. What my uncle hadn't taught me, this guy did. It was good, hard work and helped me get my head on straight again. When we finished the house, he didn't have any other jobs lined up but did have some leads. He wanted me to give it a couple weeks to see if something came up, but I told him it was time for me to go. He asked where I was headed, and I said I didn't have a clue. I'd just wander until I found the next thing.

"We were in a restaurant at the time, and an old guy from town was in the booth behind me and heard what I'd said. He turned around, clapped me on the shoulder, and said, 'That's no way to live.' I told him it had worked out well enough for me." Tripp smiled and shook his head. "I'll never forget his next words. 'Well enough isn't good enough, son.' Then he told me about this little village he'd heard about in the Northwoods of Wisconsin. He didn't know exactly where it was but had a general idea. I figured it was as good a direction to head in as any, so I packed up my stuff, hooked the pop-up onto the back of the truck, and drove east. How I ended up here, I have no idea."

"Yes, you do."

"Now, sure. The woo-woo of Whispering Pines summoned me."

We sat for a few quiet minutes, both of us processing all that he'd said. Then I opened what I hoped was an easier topic.

"Looked like you and Ty were having a pretty intense conversation yesterday."

Tripp's head bobbed up and down. "Cleared the air and cleared up some questions. One of his favorite sayings is 'a man owns up to his mistakes.'"

I chuckled softly. "I heard him say that."

"He said he needed to own up to one of his and told me he regretted letting me go. Also, he should have let me and Sunny date because I was a good guy and she'd been happy, but his pig-headedness got in the way of sense."

"What did you say to that?" I held my breath, waiting for the answer.

For the first time in many minutes, Tripp turned his head to look directly at me. "I told him I have no regrets. My life turned out exactly as it was meant to and that it's a damn good one."

Tears prickled my eyes, but I willed them to dry up. There was still one more big thing for us to talk about. "I saw you and Sunny on the patio earlier. What were you talking about?"

"Same as with Ty, we cleared up some things. Turned out Nell was the one who had seen us together. The girls were six, four, and two at that time, and Nell was completely overwhelmed. She told Sunny she wanted a better life for her. That she should open the hair and nail salon she always talked about and not get tied down to a husband and kids."

"Looking out for her baby sister." I smiled, imagining myself doing the same for Rosalyn.

"She meant well," Tripp agreed. "Sunny said when she talked to Colton at the bar that night after breaking up with me, she was trying to save my job by making me want to stay away from her. If not for one stupid decision after another, I might still be working there."

I could identify only too well with that. Time for the big question. "Is Clyde your son?"

This time, he turned his whole body toward me and took my hands in his. "I asked her that. No. Colton is his daddy."

My head dropped forward as I pulled his hands to my heart and let tears of relief fall. "That couldn't have been easy to ask."

"It wasn't, but we needed to know."

We needed to. He couldn't have said anything better at that moment.

Out of nowhere, one of the freaky wind gusts that happen here sometimes blew across the pond and spun the boat. It also blew the treetops, making them look like they were high-fiving each other. Best of all, I heard them! Nothing was wrong with my ears. I was simply too wrapped up in believing all the lies in my head to hear the truth.

"Thank you for telling me all that."

Tripp wiped the tears off my face. "Sorry for making you wait so long. I never expected to see that group again and had to sort through all the memories."

"I understand. And I love you." I grinned and echoed his words from earlier. "Don't doubt that."

Meeka wanted back in the boat then, so Tripp grabbed the handle on the back of her vest and hauled her in after giving her a good shake, water flying everywhere. "Any idea how long we've been out here? Should we head back?"

"Just another couple of minutes."

We sat side by side, held hands, and stared up at the puffy white clouds floating past.

Chapter Twenty-One

IT WAS ALMOST THREE O'CLOCK BY THE TIME WE GOT BACK TO
Pine Time. Sunny, Nell, and their parents were sitting on the
back patio. Bruce watched the kids as they ran around the
yard. Victoria and Harlan were still at the hospital as were Tex
and Arizona. I suspected Boone and Dinah were in the
village.

Unsure what to do for them, Tripp, Rosalyn, and I
assembled trays of cheese, meats, crackers, fruits, and
vegetables. Food generally helped with any situation. We
brought the trays along with a variety of beverages out to
them and had just set everything on a skirted folding table
when Sunny's phone rang.

"Oh, God," she breathed, staring at the screen. "It's
Harlan."

She stepped inside while the rest of us stayed outside to
give her privacy. When she came back out a few minutes later,
she was pale and a little unsteady. "Colton died ten minutes
ago."

She wasn't crying, however. If not for the shellshocked
look of disbelief on her face, the suspicious side of me would
think she didn't seem surprised by this news. Like maybe she'd

done something to her husband while alone in the hospital with him earlier.

There is absolutely no evidence to support that, Deputy Jayne hissed in my head. *The man had a severe head injury and never regained consciousness.*

True.

How about figuring out who actually killed him?

I gave Sunny a few minutes to recover from the news. Despite her plan to divorce him, her mind had to be spinning with what exactly this meant for her now. I approached her as she filled a plate with food and a glass with white wine.

"My timing may not be the best," I began, "but can I talk to you?"

"Okay if I bring this with me?" She held up the full plate and glass of Chardonnay. "I should probably eat something."

"Of course." I took the plate from her so she wouldn't have to manage both. "Let's go back to the office."

She followed me through the great room and down the hall. I told her to take a seat and set the plate on the desk in front of her.

After she had a few bites and a fortifying gulp of wine, she asked, "What did you want to talk about?"

I started by telling her about Gus.

"Really? Gus did that?"

"I've got evidence." I brought up the security video at the point where Gus approached Colton and spun the laptop so she could see the monitor.

She leaned closer to the screen. "That definitely looks like Gus."

I hit play and she grimaced as she watched Gus fling Colton's legs over the railing and let him drop.

"Are you surprised Gus would do such a thing?"

She thought while chewing a cracker with cheese. "I want to say no. The Gus I've known for years is a sweet, gentle man, but he's had a bit of a crush on me. There were a couple other women in town, too, but I've been his focus lately." She seemed embarrassed by that.

"Maybe because he knew you needed protecting."

Her eyes went wide at the suggestion. "You may be right. I've seen him shift into macho man mode when someone he cared about, woman or man, needed help. You said you took him to the station. Can I see him?"

I shook my head. "The county deputy will have picked him up by now."

"But Gus didn't kill Colton? The hit to his head did that, right?"

"I don't know those details or what the final charges will be, but Gus was involved." I backed up the video to the first attacker. "Do you have any idea who that is?"

She studied the man on the video closely, grew very quiet, and asked me twice to back it up and play it again. After the third viewing, she deflated and her voice broke as she said, "That's Bruce."

He was one of the two we'd narrowed it down to, but it still shocked me when she said his name.

"You're sure?"

"Positive."

"Did you have any knowledge Bruce was planning this?"

"None whatsoever," she answered immediately.

Other than when she saw Harlan's name come up on her phone, the only time Sunny showed even a little emotion was when her voice shook while saying Bruce's name. Was she telling me the truth? I thought again about the comment she made right after Colton was taken to Unity. That her girlfriends swore to keep her secret. In my experience, friends revealed all sorts of things to each other. Especially if there was, say, a bottle of wine involved. Was she really innocent of any involvement in her husband's death? Had she planned this weekend to get the undeniable truth about her husband's feelings for her out in the open? Had this been a setup all along?

"I'll need you to stop in at the station to fill out and sign a document restating what you just told me."

"No problem."

When she got up to leave the room, I cleared my throat. "On a personal note, I'm sorry for everything you've been through."

"Me too." She gave me a half smile. "I assume Tripp told you about us. Meaning me and my family."

And his relationship with her. "He did."

"*I'm* sorry you were confused and upset for the last couple of days. For what it's worth, that man is completely in love with you. When we talked earlier, we spent a few minutes clearing up old business, then he spent three times that long talking about you, your home, and this amazing place you live in. You're truly blessed. Both of you."

"We are." Why did I feel like I was being played now? "Thank you, Sunny."

I followed her out to the patio, then asked Bruce to come with me. As soon as he stepped into the great room, I pulled out a pair of zip-tie cuffs. "Bruce Lockwood, I'm arresting you for the murder of Colton Alexander."

As Martin had earlier with Gus, I read Bruce his rights as we made our way to my car. The family appeared around the corner, Mamie and Ty demanding to know what was going on.

Nell, notably, remained stoic. Was she in shock? Was she thinking that she was finally free of the "absolute girly dishrag of a husband" she'd tied herself to years ago? Had she and Sunny been in cahoots with each other from the start to free themselves from their miserable relationships? Two men, Bruce and Gus, willing to do anything for the women they loved. Or were they weak and had been manipulated by those women? Would I ever know?

Bruce remained silent on the way to the station, but when I brought him to the interview room and turned on my voice recorder, the first thing he said was, "Nell didn't know."

"Really?" I replied. "Because she didn't look at all surprised to see me hauling you away."

He stared at his hands cuffed to the metal loop on the table. "After all the fighting Thursday night, we went out to the dock. She told me that something needed to be done about Colton."

"What did she mean by that?" I asked while Martin went to a corner opposite Bruce and leaned against the wall with his arms crossed.

"Nell blamed all the family's problems on Colton. She says we got along perfectly before he came around."

That didn't quite jibe with Tripp's statement about Nell not wanting Sunny to end up trapped in a marriage with kids. "Did you agree with that feeling?"

"I didn't disagree with it."

"What did she ask you to do?"

He tilted his head as though trying to understand the question then said, "Nothing. She didn't ask me to do anything in particular, just said we needed to do something about him. I've been married to her long enough to know she meant *I* needed to do something."

"She left the details of that instruction up to you?"

"Yes."

Was there a crime I could charge her with? Possibly. It would be really hard to prove, however, because lovesick Bruce would insist she hadn't been involved in any way.

"You could have gone to the police and reported Colton for domestic violence. You could have confronted him man to man. There are any number of things you could have done, but you chose to wallop him with a horseshoe."

He sank back in his chair. "How—"

"Security video."

I waited nearly three full minutes for him to respond. Finally, he said, "It would be easiest if I confessed."

"Since you're not likely to get out of it, yes, it would be. I have one other question, though. Did you ask Gus to drop Colton's unconscious body into the lake?"

"Gus did that? No. No one, not Nell or Sunny or anyone knew what I'd done. If Gus did that, he was acting on his own."

Which would fit with the number of times I'd seen him spying on the family since they got here. I got a form and a pen, and placed them on the table in front of Bruce. "Please write your confession."

He held up the single sheet of paper questioningly.

"You can write on the back too," I told him. "If you need another sheet, let me know."

While he did that and I waited for Deputy Adkins to return to the station for the second time today, this time to take Bruce to the county jail, I started writing my report to close out my side of this crime. The lawyers would have a lot to sort through with this one.

After Bruce was finished, Martin locked him in a cell and sat by my desk to read his statement. "He states that he 'hit Colton with a horseshoe that was in my truck,' and then he 'threw it back in the truck' after leaving Colton on the sundeck."

I called across the building, "Bruce? Do I have your consent to search your truck for that horseshoe?"

"Yeah, fine." He sounded much more subdued than earlier. Reality must be hitting him.

"I'll have him sign a consent form," I told Martin, "and grab it when I get home."

Martin nodded and said of the paper in his hand, "This lines up with Gus's statement. He said he overheard the argument between Colton and Sunny and decided to hang out by the boathouse in case she needed help. He said it was dark, so didn't see who it was, but he saw a man go up the stairs, heard him get into a fight with Colton, and then heard a loud noise like something falling."

"Colton falling unconscious to the deck most likely," I guessed.

"Most likely. He waited to see if the man would return. When he didn't, Gus went up, saw Colton lying there, and you know the rest. When I asked him why he dropped Colton over the edge, he said it felt like the right thing to do."

Heightened emotions made people do unimaginable things. "The family probably has questions. I should go home and field what I can." I stood, walked toward the door, then turned back. "Is it just me or does something feel off about this one?"

"It's not you," Martin replied, "but I often feel like things are off when it comes to a crime like this. Probably because there are so many questions we never get the answers to."

Meeka and I left through the station's back door, and as I opened the car hatch, a group of crows called out from the branch of a nearby pine. The same three, I presumed, that had been following me for the last couple days were perched there.

"Now what?" I asked with a sigh. "Why are you stalking me?"

One swooped down, and I prepared to duck out of the way of a falling pinecone. Instead, it dropped something shiny on the ground in front of me.

"My ring?" I held the silver band in the palm of my hand.

In unison, they let out a single *caw*.

Had they stolen it? Not likely. That would mean one of them had gotten into our apartment, and there's no way that could have happened. I probably dropped it while helping Reeva bring the food to the basement, then one picked it up and kept it. And returned it because I gave them bread?

"Thank you," I said while slipping it onto my finger.

The trio flew away, the only sound the flapping of their wings.

Accepting my bread offerings didn't mean the crows had left the village. If anything, there seemed to be more of them in the treetops. One issue at a time. I needed to talk to the Swensons first. And the Alexanders if they'd come back from the hospital. Despite how awful Victoria had reportedly been to Sunny, my heart hurt for the woman. She loved her son so much.

Deputy Evan Adkins arrived just as I got in my car. I waited for him to take custody of Bruce, then he followed me home to collect the remaining piece of evidence. We found the horseshoe in the back of Bruce's truck right where he said it would be. I bagged it, labeled it, and Evan took it with him to the county jail.

The Swensons had moved from the patio to the great room. Mamie sat between her daughters on one of the sofas. Ty positioned his wheelchair near them, and Rosalyn was watching the kids in the backyard. The Alexanders had returned, too, but they were in their rooms. Tripp went upstairs to get them, so I'd only have to give the details once.

When they were all seated, I stood where I could see everyone. "First, I'm so sorry about what's happened. I gathered you here because I thought you might have questions."

"What's going to happen to Bruce?" Nell asked immediately.

"I don't know exactly what he'll be charged with. The lawyers will handle that. Some of it will depend on what the cause of death is determined to be."

Victoria inhaled a gasp at those words. "I want to see this video you have."

"No, ma'am," I answered gently but firmly. "I only let Sunny see it hoping she could identify the person who struck

Colton. There's no reason for you to see it, but rest assured I have no doubt that we have the right men in custody."

"Is there anything we need to do?" Harlan asked.

"Not tonight," I said. "Someone from the hospital and the county will get in touch with Sunny and Nell, respectively."

"I want them to call me as well," Victoria demanded.

"I have to say no again, ma'am. The wives are the next of kin. I'm sure Sunny will work with you on the next steps."

Victoria mumbled something about not wanting to speak to her.

"You'll have to at some point, Victoria," Sunny stated. "Colton is gone, and you can continue to hate me if you want, but Clyde is still here. He adores you, and I want him to have a good relationship with his grandparents, but I won't stand for you badmouthing me to my son."

"I think," Ty interrupted, "this is a conversation we can have once we're home. We're all overwhelmed right now." To the Alexanders in general, he said, "We're going to the village to get a bite to eat. You're all welcome to come with us."

"No," Victoria stated bluntly. "I don't want to stay in this godforsaken place a minute longer than necessary. We've already started packing our things. We're leaving tonight. You will be hearing from me, Sunny."

I couldn't tell if that was a threat or a promise to cooperate.

The Alexanders scattered. Sunny, Nell, and Mamie went outside to get the kids. I crossed the room to Tripp, who had stood off to the side and listened to everything.

"Good job." He placed a kiss on my temple. "Just enough to satisfy them for now."

Ty rolled his wheelchair over to us. "Despite the awful stuff, a lot of good came out of these last three days."

"Sunny will be okay," Tripp assured him.

"I have no doubt about that. She's a bit in shock right now, and despite her feelings regarding Colton, she will grieve.

She's talked with us a few times about the salon she always wanted to open. That's likely the direction she'll go."

"Already looking to the future," I commented. What an awful stew of emotions she had to be going through. Hopefully guilt over offing her husband wasn't one of them.

Ty nodded, both pride and heartbreak for his daughters etched on his face. "Like I said, we're going to get some dinner, call it a night, and then head out early in the morning. Don't worry about breakfast."

"I can put together something for you to take on the road," Tripp offered.

Ty swatted a hand at him. "You've dealt with us enough. If you're up, coffee will be fine. Otherwise, we'll stop somewhere." He held out his hand to me. "If this had to happen, I'm grateful we had someone so capable to deal with the fallout."

"Thank you, Mr. Swenson," I said, shaking his big rough hand.

He placed his free hand on top of mine and gave it a pat. "You've got yourself a fine man here, you know."

I smiled at Tripp, and a thrill rushed through me when our eyes met. "I do know that."

"And you, my boy." He gave Tripp a fond smile and extended his hand to him. "Don't know if we'll ever cross paths again, but it was good to close loops. I'm happier than I can say that your life has finally settled in."

"It was good to see and talk with you, too, sir." When Tripp grasped his hand for a shake, Ty pulled him in for an emotional slap-on-the-back hug as well.

The back door opened, and the four kids came bursting in. Having no understanding of what had happened, they raced happily upstairs to get ready for dinner. Mamie and her daughters filed through next, followed by Rosalyn who joined Tripp and me.

"Speaking of dinner," Tripp said, "It's only four thirty, but I'm starving."

"Me too," I agreed. "That's because we didn't have lunch."

"How about burgers?" he asked us both.

"I could eat a burger," I answered. "A double with cheese and bacon. And tater tots if we have any. And a beer."

"I'll go gather the ingredients."

"Don't worry about me," Rosalyn called after him. "I'm going to see Marty for a little while before meeting my crew to disassemble The Event That Never Really Happened."

I looked into the backyard at the hay bale seating and sunflower-covered arch. Then toward the front yard. "We're all set up for a party."

"We are," Rosalyn answered. "All Sunny wants is the stuff she came with. The rest is ours, I guess. You want to throw a party?"

"Maybe." I laughed at her ready-to-pivot expression. "I've got an idea. Go see your guy. I'll tell you about it later."

I helped Tripp carry everything up to the roof. Then I sat back with a beer in hand and my dog at my side and watched while Tripp scattered frozen tater tots in a pan that he set on the grill. He gave Janus a pat to stop her snaking around his legs and then got the burger meat ready. Ty was spot on; I had a very fine man.

With the first bite of the perfectly prepared, juicy burger, my eyes rolled back in my head. "If it wouldn't slowly kill me, this is what I would eat every day."

"We're young," Tripp replied. "We've got time to reverse the damage. Right?"

"I'm not sure it works that way. I'll ask Jola next time I see her, though."

After another few bites, Tripp said, "We have the day off tomorrow. What should we do?"

"First, we sleep in."

"Agreed," he said with a nod.

"Then, we should get married."

He froze with a tater tot halfway to his mouth. "We . . . what?"

I went to his side and took his hands in mine. "Marry me, Tripper Bennett. Or handfast me. We need a license to get married, and that will take a few days to get. We can make it legal later." I motioned toward the backyard and then the front. "Everything's all set up, and we may not get this opportunity again until winter. Then we'd have to do all that planning and reset up what's already set up . . . Now, we could just make a few calls and—"

He shot out of his chair and gave me a kiss that made my knees go weak.

"Does that mean yes?" I asked, breathless.

"Didn't think I had to say it. Of course I'll marry you. Or handfast you or whatever else I have to do to make sure I can spend every day of the rest of my life with you at my side."

Shivers of happiness spread all over my body. "Good answer."

A gust of wind blew across the rooftop, and the trees celebrated loudly. All was right in my world again.

Chapter Twenty-Two

Rosalyn couldn't decide which of us to hug, so she started with me, then Tripp, then both of us at the same time. Then happy tears started to flow.

"This is so perfect." She blotted her eyes with the sleeve of her T-shirt. "Oh my gosh, I've got a lot to do. Do me a favor, brother-in-law to be, and make a big pot of coffee. This is going to be a long night. I've got phone calls to make and—"

"Hang on." I literally held her by the arm with both hands to keep her from running off. "We need to tell a few people first. Then you can have at it."

"Can I start planning tweaks?" She gestured toward the setups in our front and back yards. "Not sure sunflowers are your thing."

"Sure. Plan your tweaks."

She gave a happy squeak and clapped her hands. "Don't worry about anything. I've got this."

The first thing we did was video call my parents.

"Where are you?" I couldn't tell from the scene behind them. They were outside and the sky was dark, so nowhere in this country. Probably not even this side of the globe. The buildings behind them appeared to be stone or stucco, with small balconies on the upper floors, some overflowing with plants.

"Granada, Spain," Mom announced. "It's simply lovely."

"We just had tapas," Dad added, "and were about to head to bed. It's almost midnight here. To what do we owe the pleasure of your call?"

They looked happier and healthier than I'd seen them in years. Decades even. Retirement and travel agreed with them.

"We have an announcement," I began.

"Jayne asked me to marry her," Tripp blurted, "and we're doing it tomorrow."

"You're what?" Mom exclaimed.

"There was supposed to be a wedding," I began and gave them a shortened version of Rosalyn's first event, less the murder part. "Since it didn't happen, and we're all set up . . . not that *that's* a reason to get married . . ."

"But you two getting married at some point was a given," Dad supplied. "Congratulations to you both."

"We're going to set up a live feed," Tripp said. "We'll email you the link."

"Fabulous!" Mom dabbed a napkin beneath her eyes. "Being there in person would be best, but this will work fine."

We chatted for another couple of minutes and promised to schedule a time to have a longer chat so we could catch up. Then we had the same basic conversation with Tripp's Aunt Addie and Uncle Jim. They also promised to watch and wanted to plan a visit soon.

That made Tripp happy. "Tell us when, and we'll hold a room for you."

"I imagine you're booked solid," Uncle Jim replied. "Tell us when you've got something available, and we'll make that work."

Another retired couple with time on their hands. How nice.

We debated about hiking up to Blind Willie's cabin, but it

was a long way, and we had other people to contact. So we video called him next, which took two attempts.

"What's so urgent?" he barked in greeting. "I was on my way to take a bath."

Willie bathed in the creek in the summer and fired up his solar-powered water heater when it got too cold outside. This also explained why he wasn't wearing a shirt.

"Can you still perform weddings?" I asked.

"Sure can. I'm legal and everything."

"Then the timing of your bath is perfect," I said, "because we need you to perform a wedding tomorrow."

"Tomorrow? Who's getting married?"

"We are," Tripp announced.

Except for his eyes darting between us, Willie froze. "You're—" His voice broke, and tears flooded the big old softie's eyes. "Married. Well, that's fine. That's just fine. Lucy would be tickled. And you want me to officiate?"

My voice caught as I answered, "It would mean the world to me, Willie."

"Do you have a license?"

I shook my head. "No—"

"Won't be official without a license."

"We understand that," Tripp said, "but for a bunch of reasons, tomorrow is the best time to have the ceremony." He explained the situation.

"Taking advantage of an opportunity. I like that." Willie scratched his bearded chin and pondered our dilemma. "You know how folks around here feel about handfasting."

"We thought about that too," I replied. "Handfasting doesn't require a license, right?"

"It doesn't, but it's also not legally binding. It would be a good reason to throw a party, though. File the paperwork for the license on Monday. You should have it by the end of the week, and we can make you two legal then."

"You'll still come tomorrow, won't you?" I asked.

He looked straight at me through the camera. "I wouldn't miss it. Besides, if I didn't, Lucy would come back and haunt me. What time should I be there?"

"Rosalyn is handling everything. I expect she'll be activating the call tree."

"Don't got a phone," Willie reminded me.

"I'll tell her to video call you. Or you can check with the Barlows. They'll know."

"Rosalyn's going to have a lot to do. I'll ask Briar or Morgan." He paused, then cleared his throat. "Some things in this world don't make any sense, and some make quite a lot. This is the best decision I've heard since you decided to move here, Miss Jayne. And I'm pure touched that you asked me to be part of it."

"It wouldn't be right without you, Willie. We'll see you tomorrow."

I signed off, and Tripp asked, "Suppose he's wearing any clothes at all?"

"My bet is no. I was praying the whole time he wouldn't stand up."

Our next announcement, face to face this time, was a no-brainer.

"This is wonderful news," Briar declared. "Not sure I can make it tomorrow though . . ."

"Hush, Mama." Morgan wrapped me in a hug. "Of course we'll be there. What's your plan? Do you need help with anything?"

I unwrapped from her. "I'm not allowed to do anything, but as we speak Rosalyn is making tweaks to the front and back yards."

"I'll call her right away and see what we can do," Morgan promised.

I lowered my voice. "How is River doing? Do you think he'll come?"

River appeared from around the corner with Juniper in his

arms. "Of course I will attend, Proprietress." He kissed my cheek and shook Tripp's hand. "Your concern for my well-being is appreciated, but I vow to set my problems aside and be fully present for your day."

Briar gave his shoulder a good-boy pat. "Tell us, how did this come about? Where were you when he proposed?"

I shook my head. "Never thought of you as being old-school, Briar. *I* proposed to him during dinner on the roof." Then I looked up at Tripp. "When something is this right, there's no need to overthink it."

Morgan took my left hand. "Your ring. Where did you find it?"

I gazed at it and twisted it around my finger. "Believe it or not, a crow returned it to me. Looks like Lily Grace was right about leaving them gifts."

River grumbled something incoherent about the birds.

"Just in time to move them to your right hands," Morgan added, "and replace them with—"

"I'm happy with this one," I interrupted her as Tripp said basically the same thing. I added, "I've never cared for diamonds or flashy things."

She let my hand go and stepped away, but the look on her face told me she was planning something.

Tripp turned me toward the door. "Much as we'd love to stay and chat, we've got another stop to make."

Outside, I whistled for Meeka, and she squeezed through the hedge. On the other side, Pitch crowed goodbye.

We hopped into Tripp's truck and followed the creek for maybe thirty seconds to Reeva's house. We found her, Jozef, and Ruby sitting by her firepit with a bottle of wine.

"Hey, you two," Reeva greeted. "What a nice surprise. Join us?" She pointed at the bottle.

"Sure," Tripp agreed, "because we've got something to toast."

"Don't say a word." Ruby jumped to her feet. "I'll be right back with glasses."

There was a fourth glass on the table between them, but not a fourth person. Ruby's mystery beau? Did he duck for cover when he saw the truck? Was he inside the cottage, waiting until it was safe to come out? Why was this such a big secret and when would we finally learn his identity?

Ruby returned with not only glasses, but another bottle of Cabernet. And no beau. Curiosity was killing me.

Reeva poured for us and topped off their drinks. "What are we toasting?"

They reacted with as much joy as everyone else had.

"How exciting," Ruby said. "I'm thrilled to toast that."

"Grand news," Jozef declared. "We'll need to throw a bachelor party."

"Well, it'll have to be when I'm not a bachelor anymore," Tripp said. "The wedding is tomorrow, and we wanted to know if you'll perform a handfasting for us, Reeva."

She placed a hand on Tripp's cheek. "I'd be honored."

We explained the reason for the rush while drinking the wine and discussing colors for the handfasting ribbons with Ruby. Like Morgan had, Reeva said she'd contact Rosalyn to find out what they could do to help.

Later, at home on the roof, Tripp texted with someone while I tried to identify constellations. *Tried* being the operative word.

"The light from your phone is messing with my darkness," I scolded him.

"Sorry." He dimmed the screen's light.

"Who are you chatting with anyway?"

He pulled his phone away from me when I tried to take a peek. "Nothing you need to worry about."

About an hour later, Rosalyn's head popped up through the hatch in the floor. "Time for you to get off the roof."

"Why?" I was getting very drowsy and contemplating sleeping right there, but we followed her directive.

"You have two choices," she announced after we'd descended the ladder. "You can stay together in your apartment for the night, or you can honor the long-standing tradition of not seeing each other on the day of the wedding until you meet at the altar."

"It's not technically a wedding," I said.

"And it's almost midnight anyway," Tripp noted.

"Alrighty, then." She grabbed a big roll of craft paper that she'd left by the stairs. "You are officially forbidden from leaving this apartment. No coming downstairs for anything. I'll take Meeka with me and let her outside to do her business." She bent to ruffle the pup's ears. "No going back up to the roof. We are going to be busy setting up and don't want you to see or hear anything."

"Who is *we*?"

"Me and some people," Rosalyn replied dismissively while taping long strips of the brown paper over our windows. "Don't worry about it. Not your concern."

Tripp pulled me to him and, in a sultry voice, said, "Guess we'll have to do something else, then."

I wrapped my arms around him and purred, "Works for me."

"Wait until I'm gone, please," Rosalyn sang out. "Oh, Tripp, something came for you. It's on the coffee table."

Still in his arms, I leaned back and looked up at him. "Secret delivery?"

Without replying, he grabbed the lunch-sack-size paper bag from the table and took it into the bathroom, the only room with a door in our loft apartment. A few minutes later, he came out and set the bag by the stairs. "Roz, will you take this back with you? I'll tell you when I want it."

"Um, sure. What is it?"

"A surprise. Don't look, okay?"

"Fair is fair." After putting the last piece of tape on the paper, she announced, "Okay, I'm done. Have fun doing whatever it is you crazy kids are going to do, and I'll see you in the morning. Don't come downstairs until I say, and no peeking."

"We won't peek." I threw my arms around her. "And for whatever you and some people are doing, thank you."

Chapter Twenty-Three

MEEKA MUST HAVE DECIDED TO HAVE A SLEEPOVER WITH Auntie Roz because we didn't see her again until morning. We slept in, wrapped up in each other, until eight o'clock. The last time we slept that long was when a February snowstorm trapped us in the house for two days. We would have kept sleeping, but a knock on the door woke us.

"Are you decent?" Rosalyn's voice called up from the second floor.

"Hang on," I answered and found my pajamas in a tangle on the floor. Tripp pulled on his boxers. "Ready?"

"Let the festivities begin," he replied while slipping a T-shirt over his head.

Rosalyn appeared with a tray of food. "Reeva made breakfast for you." She set the tray in our sitting area and then went to the kitchenette to make coffee.

"Is this how our guests feel?" Tripp asked me.

"Probably, except we make them go all the way downstairs to eat." I groaned as though that were such an inconvenience.

"It's dark in here." Rosalyn set two full mugs next to the tray. "Guess completely covering the windows was overkill."

"Did you sleep at all?" I asked her.

"Yes, we took shifts." She pulled the paper from the top half of each window. "Enjoy your breakfast and then get ready to go on a hike."

When we finished eating the lovely spread of poached eggs, fresh fruit, thinly sliced meats and cheeses, and mini pastries, we dressed in hiking clothes and met Rosalyn in the foyer where she blindfolded us and led us to the driveway.

"Definite overkill," Tripp muttered good-naturedly as she handed us off to Rourke, who was waiting to drive us to the trailhead of our choice.

"I told you," Rosalyn chirped, chipper as ever, "I don't want you to see anything."

"You realize how high our expectations are now, don't you?" I teased her.

"Meeka can go with you." Then she said, presumably to the Westie, but I didn't know for sure since I was blindfolded, "If you get dirty, you'll have to take a bath when you get back. Fair warning."

Meeka whined in reply.

It was a perfectly uneventful walk through the woods. The air blew warm but not hot, the pines smelled amazing, Meeka managed to not get covered in twigs and dirt, and while the group of three crows followed us, they didn't drop even a single pinecone. When we got home again, we were led, blindfolded, inside where the front curtains were all closed, preventing us from seeing the reception tent. There were no curtains at the back of the house, because why would we ever want to block the lake view? Instead, Rosalyn hung a tarp across the patio so we couldn't see into the backyard.

"Go upstairs and relax," she instructed. "Lunch is waiting for you. Shower and come back down at one o'clock. Tripp, you will meet River, Martin, and Jozef in the Grand Suite where you'll get dressed."

"What am I supposed to wear?" he asked, gesturing at his hiking clothes.

"Jozef brought something for you."

"It's not a tux, is it?" He tugged unhappily at an imaginary collar.

"It's not a tux," Rosalyn promised. Then she told me, "You come to my room. The ceremony will begin at three o'clock. Guests will start arriving at two thirty."

Shortly before one, as we prepared to go to our assigned staging areas, I took Tripp's hand in mine. "The second-best decision I ever made was asking you to help me with this house. I never expected that would lead to all this, but bravo to the Universe for bringing us together."

He lifted my hand to his lips and pressed a kiss on it. "What was your first-best decision?"

"Today."

I left him at the Grand Suite and found my sister, Morgan, and Briar in Roz's room.

"You three look amazing," I praised. Rosalyn wore a short light-blue sundress with spaghetti straps, a tied back, and ruffled skirt. Briar looked summery in a black shift dress covered in pale-lavender flowers. And Morgan had swapped her usual black for a deep-purple and floral maxi dress with a high halter neckline. Then I saw a stunning white lace dress hanging on the closet door. "Is that for me?"

"Figured it could be your something borrowed," Rosalyn said. "I bought it a while ago but haven't worn it, so there's no juju attached. Try it on."

The dress would have overwhelmed my slender sister but fit me like it was made to be mine. It hit just above my knee, which was perfect because I wouldn't have to wrestle with a long skirt all afternoon. There was a simple spaghetti-strap V-neck underdress that could be worn on its own, and a lace overdress that elevated it to casual-bride status. Bell sleeves fluttered to mid-forearm, the neckline plunged to a band of lace that encircled me just below my breasts, and the A-line skirt draped beautifully with gentle gathers.

When I stepped out of the bathroom, Briar got teary as Morgan sighed happily. Rosalyn gasped, clapped her hands, and gushed, "Oh, Jayne."

"It's just right." It really was. Comfortable and feminine without being too girly.

"These are the only white shoes I have." Roz held up a pair of four-inch platform sandals that I'd surely twist an ankle wearing.

I tried them on, walked five steps, and decided, "You know what? I think I'll go barefoot."

She laughed but then realized I was serious.

"Okay, but you have to let me give you a pedicure, then."

I took the dress off again, and for the next hour, they pampered me. Rosalyn gave me a pedicure, buffed my fingernails, and styled my hair. Morgan, promising a light hand, did my makeup. Briar, who preferred a natural look like I did, supervised to make sure I didn't end up overdone. When they were finished, I put the dress on again.

"Something new and blue." Morgan took a necklace from her pocket, a silver medallion with a blue stone at the center. It nestled below the V of the neckline right at my breastbone. "The silver, of course, is associated with the moon and stars. Lapis Lazuli will strengthen the bond you and Tripp have already forged as you follow the next path of your lives together."

Rosalyn dabbed her eyes as the emotion of the day hit her. "You still need something old."

"I have that," I told them and pointed to the clothes I'd worn down from the apartment. "In the pocket of my shorts."

Briar went to them and gasped when she saw what I had in there. She lay the dangly earrings on the palm of her hand so we could all see them. Each earring was a nautilus shell. Tiny blue crystal slivers formed the chambers of the shells while a pure-white pearl dotted their centers.

"These were Lucy's," Briar explained. "She bought them

while traveling . . . somewhere with Keven because they were the exact color of her lake."

"I found them when I was cleaning out her room." My voice quivered, and my heart clenched at the memory of going through all of her things. "I couldn't possibly keep everything, so I chose a few pieces of clothing, and when I saw those, I had to have them."

"She'd be honored that you're wearing them today." Briar gently attached them to my ears and declared me ready. "Oh, one more thing."

She went to a corner and then stepped closer to me, something hidden behind her back. "I made you a bouquet." She produced an arrangement of woodland greenery. "Pine sprigs because we all know what these trees mean to you. Oak leaves for luck. Cedar for protection. Rosemary for love and lust. Pinecones are the trees flower. I thought about adding a splash of color with—"

"No." Tears stung my eyes. "It's perfect just like this. Thank you, Briar."

With my bouquet in hand, I looked in the mirror and smiled at the radiant Jayne looking back. For so many reasons, I'd never felt more beautiful or blessed. Ready to walk down the aisle to the man of my dreams, I started worrying about other things.

"The live stream—"

"Is all set," Rosalyn promised. "Emery hooked everything up. And yes, we tested it with Mom and Dad and Tripp's aunt and uncle."

Every minor detail I asked about, Rosalyn had already taken care of.

"You really are good at this." Then, out of nowhere, a thought struck me, and I blurted, "Willie! Is he here yet?"

"I'll go find him." Before doing so, Briar stopped in front of me. She touched her fingertips to my face, brushed a lock of hair behind my ear, and touched the earring there. "So many emotions today."

I clasped her hand in mine. "I've made so many friends here, but I never expected to find a mother figure. If I haven't said it enough, thank you for the love and guidance when I needed it most."

She took my hand and pressed it over her heart. "I've got plenty of room in there for more children. You are a beautiful bride, my dear. And if you're wondering, Lucy is here, and she is so very proud."

I nearly started crying then, and Rosalyn pushed us apart. "You need to stop, or we're going to have to redo your makeup."

While I waited in the great room for Willie, Rosalyn finally let me see what was behind the tarp. She signaled for Schmitty and Elsa to pull it aside, and my jaw dropped. The only thing remaining of what had been there yesterday was the pine log arch. The hay bales had been taken away and replaced with pine log benches and stumps.

"Are those from the Meditation Circle?"

"Yep," Roz replied, "we borrowed them."

The hundreds of sunflowers were gone, and in their place was a thick garland made of the same sprigs, leaves, and pinecone clusters Briar put in my bouquet. On either side of the arch, there were also a few streamers in pine green, lake blue, and pale dove gray—the colors we told Ruby she could use for the ribbon. And that was it. The view of the lake, the clear blue sky, and the glorious woods surrounding us provided all the additional decoration we needed.

Willie came in through the back door then, took one look at me, and cleared his throat. "What a sight you are, Miss Jayne."

"Be quick," Rosalyn said. "Tripp will be coming down soon, and you need to be out of sight."

"I only need two minutes." But I pulled Willie into the

Lakeside suite to be safe. Same as I didn't want Tripp to see me until I stepped outside, I didn't want to see him either.

Ten minutes later, Rosalyn came to get me with a knowing smile on her face. She must have asked Willie what I talked to him about. "Perfect addition that I *didn't* think of. Are you ready?"

"I am." I held my sister close and thought of how our relationship was non-existent until Whispering Pines brought us back together. This village, both the place and the people, gave me the life I never knew I wanted. "Thank you for all that you did."

She pressed her cheek to mine and made kissy sounds. "You would do the same for me."

"I would, just not as well."

She led me to the patio. "He's ready when you are."

I was ready. No doubt, no hesitation. Easiest decision ever. The tarp across the patio had been replaced with gauzy curtains which were currently pulled shut, obscuring the audience's view of me. Willie was there waiting for me. What I hadn't expected was for him to be holding a cell phone.

"What's that for?" I asked, thinking maybe he was going to record our walk.

He turned the phone toward me, and I saw my dad's face on the screen. "Willie told me you asked him to stand in for me and walk you down the aisle. He figured we could both do it." Then he gasped. "My God, look at you."

Mom's face appeared next to his. "Sorry, I can't wait another second." Willie stood back and gave them a head-to-toe look at me. "Oh, Jayne. You're perfect."

"Thanks, Mom. Let's do this." I stood on my tiptoes and kissed Willie's cheek. "Great idea."

Again, he cleared his throat. "Let's go fast your hands."

Chapter Twenty-Four

Tripp looked as casually dressy as I did in tan pants and a white linen shirt with a small cluster of pine, cedar, and rosemary on an oak leaf pinned over his heart. Meeka and Janus stood at his side and were also dressed for the occasion with braids of blue, green, and gray ribbons around their necks. Meeka looked up at me, head tilted in confusion. It was probably the dress and makeup.

"Blessed be, everyone." Reeva, dressed in a deep-green robe, stood beneath the arch. "Family and friends, we have gathered beneath the sun, a symbol of energy and strength, during the moon's new phase, a time of beginnings, to celebrate Jayne and Tripp's love for each other. A few minutes ago, I cast a circle around their home and us. I ask you all to envision that circle and see it filling with peace and love for Jayne and Tripp."

Meeka let out a little *ruff*.

Reeva laughed. "And Meeka, of course."

Over the next minute of silence, the air around us seemed to almost pulse and envelop us with the blessings and love everyone was sending our way. I looked around at the gathering villagers and realized there weren't anywhere near enough seats. Our backyard overflowed with the people who had become not just neighbors but friends.

Reeva held out her hand to Tripp. "The rings, please."

Tripp slid the silver band off my left hand, took his off, too, but instead of handing them to Reeva, he slid them into his left pants pocket. From his right, he pulled two others.

He answered my questioning look with a wink that sent a shiver through me. What had he done?

As I remembered her doing when she performed Morgan and River's handfasting, Reeva held the rings in her left palm and cupped her right hand over them. "I ask the guardians of the earth to bless this union with a solid foundation. Guardians of the air, surround this couple every day with clarity and a renewed understanding of each other. May the guardians of fire bless them with light, passion, and a warm loving home. Guardians of water, bless them with excitement, adventure, and the ability to move through their lives along the path of least resistance. And I ask the spirit to bless this union, keep Jayne and Tripp connected, and remain with them on their journey together.

"There is nothing stronger than true love. *True* love grows in both the light and the dark. It's a blessing that stays with you for all your days. May the infinite circle seen in these rings echo your commitment to one another. May the Goddess bless this union as Jayne and Tripp come together as a single being."

As she spoke, Tripp and I stared at each other, and I swear I felt our souls merge a little closer. Almost as though her words had woven a spell that was already coming true.

Reeva then motioned to a small pine table off to the side that I hadn't even noticed until this moment. Two misty-gray taper candles were burning there. A blue and green pillar candle stood between them.

"Using the tapers," she instructed, "light the pillar together."

We held the two flames at the pillar's wick until we were certain it had lit. Then we blew out the tapers' flames and stood before Reeva again.

"May the infinite light of the Goddess shine upon this couple. May the four directions and five elements bless Tripp and Jayne's union now and throughout their life together." Reeva held up the smaller ring. "Tripp, please take this ring and give it to Jayne. Do you promise to always show Jayne honor and fidelity, to share in her laughter and joy, to support and stand by her in times of happiness and struggle, to dream and hope with her, and to spend each day loving her more than the day before?"

Tripp slid the most unique ring I'd ever seen onto my finger, his eyes never leaving mine. "It is an honor and my pleasure to make that promise."

Reeva gave me the larger band of silver and gold with three colored stones. As with everything else surrounding us today, I knew there had to be a meaning behind these rings.

"Jayne, please present Tripp with this ring. Do you promise to always show him honor and fidelity, to share in his laughter and joy, to support and stand by him in times of happiness and struggle, to dream and hope with him, and to spend each day loving him more than the day before?"

"Every day for the rest of my life and beyond, I do."

"With these promises made before this gathering of loved ones and myself, I ask that you now join hands."

Reeva positioned my left hand on top of Tripp's, palms together, and then held up a braided rope for us all to see.

"The traditional handfasting colors are white for purity, red for passion, and blue for fidelity. Jayne and Tripp's ceremony colors are blue, green, and gray, so this braid also includes green for growth and gray for stability." Reeva wrapped the cord loosely around our hands and wrists and tied a knot. "Tripp and Jayne, this cord symbolizes your life, your love, and the unbreakable connection the two of you have found with one another. The ties of this handfasting are not only formed by this braid or the knot joining the ends, these ties that bind are also formed by your souls, your hearts, and the promises you have made to each other." She glanced between us and gave Tripp a grin. "You may kiss your bride."

"Hang on." Willie joined us at the arch. "Jayne and Tripp also intend to have a legal ceremony. Since you're all here, figured you might want a peek at what that will look like." He cleared his throat. "Tripp, do you take Jayne to be your wife?"

"I sure do."

"Jayne, do you take Tripp to be your husband?"

"Absolutely."

He turned to the crowd. "That's pretty much how it will go. We'll make it official when the license gets here. For now, yeah, go ahead and kiss your bride."

The crowd laughed and then cheered as Tripp clutched our still-tied hands to his chest and gave me a kiss that made me think we were the only two people in the world, let alone our backyard.

When we parted, Reeva address the crowd. "I ask you all to once again send loving energy toward Jayne and Tripp. When I reopen the circle, imagine that energy flowing through our village and out into the world."

She placed her palms together in front of her heart, closed her eyes, and then after a short pause, pushed her hands away from her with her palms facing outward. Like before, I was certain I felt a ripple swirl around us. Reeva smiled and then pressed her palms together again. "So mote it be."

Chapter Twenty-Five

"How did you do all this in one night?" I asked Rosalyn.

My almost-husband and I stood on the front porch of the house with her and stared in amazement at the front yard. Not only had she transformed the reception tent from something that resembled a barn into a woodland wonderland, she had turned the yard into a massive dining room.

"First," she began, "we used the call tree to find out who could attend. Which turned out to be pretty much everyone. Only those who were ill, taking care of someone who was ill, or tending to something they couldn't walk away from couldn't come. Emery sent the live stream link to those folks so they could watch."

She explained that the shop owners told their customers the shops were closing at two o'clock so they should get their shopping done quickly. Skål closed but Triple G and The Inn stayed open since there were still tourists in town who needed to eat, but they ran with minimal staff and only offered limited menus. The carnies canceled tonight's performance in the big tent so they could attend. To the delight of the villagers who didn't see the shows very often, they graciously did a bit of their sideshow acts at the far end of the front yard. The reception tent obviously wouldn't provide enough seating for this many people, but it was perfect for the buffet.

"Based on the call tree counts, Reeva and Jozef decided how much more food we'd need. Then they, his staff at Skål, and the kitchen witches got busy in Skål's kitchen, which was why they closed for the day. The garden witches showed up with their cars full of greenery. Craft witches met Ruby at The Twisty Skein to make the handfasting ribbons and guest gifts."

She pointed out a rack of witch bells—three-inch grapevine wreaths decorated with ribbons, bells, and beads that guests could take home and hang on their front doors to keep negativity out. On a table beneath the wreaths were dozens and dozens of the cutest little witch brooms I'd ever seen made out of twigs and rosemary sprigs and held together with twine.

"Since there's no chance of rain, we figured more tents weren't needed. Instead, Mr. Powell showed up with a truck full of tables and chairs, and had his team set them up. And I have to say, it's awesome how this village is always ready for a dinner party. People showed up with tablecloths, dishes, flatware, and beverage containers of all varieties."

That was why none of the tables matched and also what made them absolutely perfect.

"Wait until you see the cake," Rosalyn teased.

"I don't want to wait." Tripp took my hand and pulled me into the tent. The cake, like everything else for this event, was just right.

"For the record, I didn't design it." Rosalyn reached her hand out to Martin as he came over to us. "And Honey didn't just recycle Sunny's cake. She made a fresh one."

It was a simple, multi-tiered tower of beauty. The chocolate and vanilla marble was filled with chocolate cookie crumbles and cream between some of the layers, and fresh strawberries and cream between the others. It was coated with white frosting and sat on a thick piece of pine engraved with a heart that had *Jayne & Tripp*, and today's date inside it. The cake was further decorated with sprigs of pine, rosemary, cedar, a few oak leaves, pinecones, and a grapevine twining up the layers.

Honey appeared next to us. "What do you think?"

"I think," I began, "you all know us way better than we ever guessed. It's simple and beautiful. I love it. Honestly."

"I do too," Tripp said and kissed her cheek in thanks.

As a crew of kitchen witches, directed by Reeva and Jozef, put the final touches on the buffet, Tripp and I made our way around the yard. We thanked everyone for coming and received hug after hug. I smiled so much my face hurt. Clover Flowers had chosen photography for her high school summer project. She followed us all around and snapped pictures of pretty much everything. I couldn't wait to see them.

As we made our way back to our table, we passed one where Jola, Lily Grace, Oren, Emery, Keiko, Violet, and Telly sat. Lily Grace got to her feet, wrapped me in a hug, and murmured in my ear, "This is what I saw. You wearing a white dress and glowing with happiness. Congratulations."

I held tight to the young woman I'd formed a bond with on my third day in the village. She was so important to me. "I love you, LG."

"Right back at you . . . Mrs. Bennett?"

I shook my head. "I'm happy to take Tripp as my husband, but I'm keeping my name."

"Good for you."

Finally, we sat to eat with Morgan, River, Rosalyn, Martin, Briar, and Willie. Two video screens were also set up so Mom, Dad, Aunt Addie, and Uncle Jim could take part in the reception too. There was so much food and all of it was so good, I couldn't choose a favorite. After we cut the cake and settled back at the table with big slices in front of us, I asked Tripp to explain the rings.

"The bands of gold and titanium," he began, "are for the sun, moon, and stars. They're twisted together to represent our handfasting ribbon. Because you don't care for shiny and flashy, the metal and stones embedded in the bands were left unpolished." He pointed out a pink stone. "Rose quartz strengthens love. Green garnet is for harmony and is a nod to our beloved pine trees. Blue topaz is for communication and the lake." He looked across the table at Morgan. "Did I get all that right?"

"You did," she praised.

"Wait," I said, "is that what all the texting was about last night?"

They answered, "Yes," in unison.

I looked from the ring on my hand to Morgan. "You made these? Last night?"

"I've had the bands for six months," she explained. "I thought of you two the moment I saw them but knew if you didn't want them, I could sell them to someone else."

"How long were you going to hang on to them?" I asked.

"Until you finally agreed to make things official. I suggested leaving the stones raw. Tripp said there needed to be blue and green, so I presented a few options including the rose quartz. He made the final decision on everything."

A collaboration. Like everything else about this day.

None of the Barlow-Carr clan wanted to miss a minute of the night, so they set up the play pen, lid in place, in the sitting room where the twins could sleep and easily be checked on. The festivities started to wind down around ten and most everyone left by midnight.

River asked a group of us—me, Tripp, Rosalyn, Martin, Morgan, Briar, Reeva, Jozef, Willie, and Josephine—to stay.

"Effie and Cybil could have joined us as well," he began mysteriously, "but they have returned home already.

"Briar, Willie, Effie, and Cybil," I noted, my instincts tingling. "The remaining Originals. What's going on, River?"

"My apologies for doing this now, but those of you who need to understand are already gathered."

"Those of us who need to understand what?" Martin asked. His instincts were clearly also activated.

"About the crows." River then recited a poem that had to be the chant Morgan said he'd been muttering for the past few days.

One Crow for sorrow,
Two Crows for mirth;
Three for a wedding,
Four for a birth;
Five for silver,
Six for gold,
Seven a secret that shan't be told.
Eight for a wish,
Nine for a kiss,
Ten a surprise not to be missed,
Eleven for health,
Twelve for wealth,
Thirteen beware it's the devil herself.

Three for a wedding. Well, that explained the trio that had been following me around town. And the devil was a woman? I immediately thought of Flavia. By the look on Reeva's face, so did she.

Goosebumps had risen all over my body, and my voice came out as little more than a whisper when I asked, "River, who is the devil?"

As if on cue, a crow swooped down and landed in the middle of the table we had gathered around and began picking at leftover bits of food. Meeka started barking. Janus hissed. A few seconds later, the striking woman in black I'd seen around the village appeared, and the animals calmed.

"Sorry," Tripp told her, "we're closed for a private event."

"She brought the crows," River intoned.

"No," she replied, "they came before me. You know how I like to make an entrance, darling."

Darling? Who was this woman?

I looked from River to Morgan, wanting to see her response to this stranger. She sat with her hands folded and a neutral expression on her face. When she saw me looking at her, she raised her chin almost regally and pinched her eyebrows together ever so slightly. Whatever was going on here, it wasn't good. Not at all.

"River," Briar stated tightly, "why don't you tell everyone who she is?"

From her tone, Briar already knew, and she also was not happy.

River cleared his throat. "This is Raven Carr . . ."

Carr? A sister?

". . . my wife."

I nearly fell out of my chair. "You mean ex-wife."

"Oh, no," Raven answered. Those two words were loaded with confidence. And a warning? "River and I are still very much married."

We all turned to look at him.

"Raven and I married ten years ago," River explained.

"Which means you're an adulterer," Raven spat, her calm and cool composure cracking.

"I thought you were dead," River insisted. It was like the rest of us disappeared and they were the only two present. "You vanished without a trace. We searched for you for six years. After eight years, the court declared you legally deceased."

River was usually unflappable, so to hear the pleading

tone in his voice and see the shadow of panic on his face made my heart race.

"Although clearly I'm not dead." Raven's words were coated with icy venom. "You're telling me that with all your billions you couldn't find me? You mustn't have looked very hard."

"Six years," River repeated. "I hired the best investigators in the world. Why did you never contact me? One word in a voicemail or text, and I would have redoubled the effort. The team had no idea where to look or even start looking."

Raven gave him a closed-lip smile that was as chilly as her words. "We'll talk later, darling, but understand one thing: this can be easy or this can be hard. Easy means you honor the contract."

Without another word or giving River even a moment to respond, she spun on her heel and left, disappearing into the night like a shadow.

Josephine spoke up then. "What does that mean? What contract is she talking about?"

River sank back into his chair. "Our prenuptial agreement. As I told you and Jayne yesterday, I need you two to step up and handle the business and the village. This is why. Things are going to get messy. Raven will want half."

I froze. "Half of . . ."

"Everything," River said as though in shock. "Including, if I'm not mistaken, the village."

At that revelation, we were all left dumbfounded. Except for Briar, who was still spitting mad.

She turned to face her daughter. "I told you and told you, summon them and send them on their way. Now look at the mess you've created because you wanted to break with tradition."

"Not now, Mama," Morgan pleaded with as much poise as she could muster. Which wasn't much. She looked about to crumble.

"What should we tell people about the crows?" Martin asked. He was a good sheriff and had the potential to be a great one. Right now, however, he looked completely out of his depth.

My people were falling apart, so I needed to get myself fully together. I stood and wandered around the tables in my front yard that had been cleared of food and dishes but wouldn't be taken down until morning.

"What are you thinking, missy?" Willie walked next to me.

I gave a little semi-hysterical chuckle. "Right now, I'm thinking about having to manage the village on my own while also helping my friends. You know, I was happy when River took charge and only relied on me to gather information. Now the big decisions are up to me. What if I mess up?"

Maybe I needed to do another moon spell.

"Remember the conversation we had about queen bees?" he asked.

The apparent shift of topic seemed so out of left field I stopped walking. Then I realized it was on point, and my shoulders dropped from their high and tight position. "You told me that when the queen dies, the hive will sometimes groom one of the others to become the new queen."

"And?"

"You felt the village had been grooming me to take over for my grandmother during my first year here."

"And what did we say about Lucy?"

I suddenly felt exhausted from the highs and lows of the last few days.

"We said," Willie answered for me, "that Lucy saw something in you. Which was why she left that note in the box of Samhain tablecloths thanking you for taking over."

"She trusted me." A tiny spark of energy flared.

"That says a lot, Miss Jayne. She didn't trust many people. Not unconditionally, at least. During that conversation, we also talked about you not taking on everything yourself. You have an almost husband who will do anything for you. Same with that sister of yours. Your friends will also be there if you ask, and you saw firsthand today what this village is capable of when a call goes out." He put his arms around me and pulled me close. "You, my dear, will do fine and be fine."

I sank into the comfort of his hug for another few moments. "Thanks, Willie."

We went back to the table where Martin was still looking unsure.

With all the confidence of my grandmother, I told him, "Lily Grace's idea to offer gifts to the crows seems to be working. We'll just tell everyone that this is a characteristic of the birds and that to keep them happy, leave them some food."

"What do we say," he pressed, "if they ask why there are so many of them?"

My mind spun like a Roulette wheel before landing on, "Why are any of us here? Tell them the birds must have been summoned."

More likely, they were somehow sent by a supremely unhappy woman to cause chaos before she could get here and cause some of her own.

"My eternal thanks, Manageress," River said while Morgan and Briar went to get the twins.

"Of course. Tell me one thing. Did the Ladies Barlow know about Raven?"

He released an exhausted sigh. "After the crows arrived and appeared fixated on Blackbird Cottage, I suspected what was going on. I contacted one of the private investigators who had searched for Raven and asked him to look into her whereabouts again. All he could tell me was that she resurfaced last year. I have no idea what happened to her or where she was all that time. As for Morgan's knowledge of her, yes, she knew I was previously married well before we handfasted. Because I honestly believed Raven to be deceased, I told Lady Briar about her as well but have never spoken in depth about her or the circumstances surrounding her death. Since I had no idea what had happened to her, I had no details to give. I told them yesterday that she had returned."

From the dead?

She's not a vampire or a zombie, Logical Jayne scolded.

I knew that. I was suddenly *really* tired, though. "This had to be quite a shock for you."

"It was and is."

"Give Morgan and Briar time to adjust."

"I shall. It's a fortunate thing that I have bedrooms at my disposal at Blackbird Cottage. I suspect I may need one for a night or two."

"In the meantime, you may want to have your legal team go through every aspect of that prenup."

I can't imagine what it would mean for a stranger who knew nothing about us to own half of Whispering Pines. It was bad enough when River bought it and most of the villagers already knew him.

"I will be making phone calls to them first thing in the morning."

Tripp and I said goodnight to the rest of the group, thanking them wholeheartedly for all they had done for us. Martin was the last one in line.

"Thanks for having my back earlier," he said quietly.

"Your thanks isn't necessary. We're a team. We always have each other's backs."

He nodded. "And the team can do without you tomorrow. Take the day off."

I saluted him. "Don't have to tell me twice."

⁂

Tripp and I lay in bed until the early hours of the morning, wide awake yet exhausted from the ceremony, the party afterward, and the shocking news about River.

"I knew he had a secret," Tripp said while we held our left hands side by side to admire our new rings.

"I did, too, but never guessed it would be a wife. You didn't know, did you? I mean, did he say anything about her when we were over there the other night?"

"Not a word. I'm as shocked as you are."

"It's crazy how fast life can change course."

"No kidding. Last week, everything was normal, then the North Dakotans showed up and—"

I placed a finger over his mouth. "I'm sorry about what happened to Colton, but I'm not sorry that Sunny came here. It gave you the opportunity to close that part of your life." After my first year here, I knew firsthand how important it was to slay any lingering personal dragons in order to truly move forward. "And if the village hadn't summoned them, we would not be handfasted right now and soon to be married."

He kissed my finger. "The woo-woo is strong with you lately. First a moon spell and now the village summoning people from my past."

"It already brought people from mine here. Why shouldn't people from yours show up too? And River's."

"And everyone else? Wonder who's next?"

I closed my eyes, and our breathing began to sync. Then I jolted awake again. "I mean, she was declared dead. That should dissolve their marriage *and* the prenup, so I'm not going to get too worked up about her getting half of the village yet."

"Glad you're not worked up."

"Okay, I admit I'm a little worried about her causing chaos. We've got enough of that around here."

"There is something to be happy about."

"You mean other than us being handfasted?"

"Yes, it's good that River and Morgan are handfasted instead of legally married, or he could be charged as being a polygamist."

"But like I said, she was declared dead, so their marriage should have been nullified. He didn't do anything wrong. I hope." I turned my head to look at Tripp. "Do you have any secrets I should know about?"

"I told you my biggest one in the boat yesterday. We covered pretty much everything else while sitting on the sundeck or the roof these last two years. You know everything worth knowing about me."

"We really have started down a fresh path, then. Wonder where it will lead us?"

"You know what? I'm really content where I am right now."

"Here? In bed?"

"Well, I'm always content in bed. Especially when you're in it with me." He hooked his arm around my waist and pulled me spoon-style against him. He ran his hand down my side and over my hip as he said, "I mean, life is going to do what it's going to do. As much as possible, I want to live in the present and not worry about what tomorrow or the next day will bring. I spent five frantic years searching for my mom, chasing one dead-end lead after another, and ended up nowhere."

"Correction, you ended up here."

"Very true." He kissed my neck. "What I want to do now is spend at least five years being a boring married man who runs The Best B&B in Wisconsin with his amazing, beautiful wife."

I smiled and settled in against him. "I can't think of anything better."

Well, I *could* think of Whispering Pines as a place where secrets didn't keep oozing up through the cracks. That would be nice. Briar and Reeva had me convinced that The Well blessing was slow but working, and then the crows arrived. Then Raven. I knew better than to ask, but what was coming next?

It didn't matter. I was almost married to the best man in the world. We lived in a place where everyone dropped everything at a moment's notice to celebrate a joyous occasion with their fellow villagers or come to their aid if necessary. What a magical place this was. My almost-husband was exactly right; we needed to live in the present and deal with the next problem when it came.

Then again, the next problem was already here, and I had a feeling Raven Carr wasn't going away anytime soon.

About the Author

Mystery and fantasy author Shawn McGuire loves creating characters and places her fans want to return to again and again. She started writing after seeing the first Star Wars movie (that's episode IV) as a kid. She couldn't wait for the next installment to come out so wrote her own. Sadly, those notebooks are long lost, but her desire to tell a tale is as strong now as it was then. She lives in Wisconsin near the beautiful Mississippi River and when not writing or reading, she might be baking, crafting, going for a long walk, or nibbling really dark chocolate.